PEAK OIL

DAVID J. FREILICH

For my amazing and indulgent wife, Heidi

and my wonderful sons, Adam, Andy and Austin

plus my noble parents, Max and Anita

and the ever-inspiring employees of AB Volvo

"Peak Oil is the point of maximum oil output, resulting in chaos, to say nothing of war, starvation, economic recession and possibly even the extinction of homo sapiens."

(As reported in The Wall Street Journal)

CH. 1

By mid-September, only a scattering of yachts remained moored in the marina on Marstrand, a seasonal island resort positioned on the coast to the north of Gothenburg, Sweden.

As the early autumn sun began to set, an eerie calm settled over the island.

Inside his obscure laboratory on Marstrand, Axel Carlsson's hands trembled slightly as he tightly closed a lid on a stainless-steel canister filled with a pungent-smelling fluid. Then he removed a silver foil pouch from a cryo-fridge, whose chill lingered on his fingers as he placed both items in a backpack and zipped it shut. With his staff off for the weekend, Axel found solace in the solitude of the lab. Gazing toward the building's exit, the weight of his mission pressed on him. Tonight, could change everything.

Much like Newport, Rhode Island, Marstrand has long served as a bastion for the elite of Sweden who keep exclusive summer homes there and in the surrounding archipelago. Most of the dwellings on the island rock get passed down through the generations, and during summer season, a genteel, if not clubby air, prevails.

A hulking seventeenth century fortress sits on the crest of Marstrand, keeping watch over the island village and the expansive sea to the west. Now desolate, the stronghold had outlived its historic role of repelling marauding Norwegians and Danes, who left the dominating citadel largely unmolested.

A few private business concerns and non-profits also kept a reticent existence on the island. Axel headed one of them, the Svenska Biomarina Forskningsinstitutet, or the SBF, and he served as its sole registered representative. Axel had spent the summers of his youth on the island, exploring every inch of the ancient fortress and its surrounds. In time, he inherited the family compound and decided there was no better place from which to operate the SBF as a private foundation and lab.

Swedish children learn to sail and navigate at a young age. Beginning when he was just six years old, Axel's parents enrolled him in sailing lessons which lasted throughout the summer. As he eventually gained experience handling ever larger vessels, sailing took him to more exotic destinations like the Galapagos Islands and the Great Barrier Reef. Through long-distance sailing, Axel developed his deep love for the ocean and the diversity of life he observed both above and below its surface. More than any other coveted location on earth, the ocean was blessed for its spirituality and isolation. Through heart-pounding sea crossings, Axel felt his connection to the world around him come alive.

Already as an adolescent, Carlsson determined that he would dedicate his life to protecting the marine environment that he so loved. After finishing high school with his idealism intact, he attended Chalmers University and graduated with a degree in bioengineering. From there he earned a master's from Stockholm University's prestigious School of Business. To gain the financial freedom he needed to pursue his lifelong ambition, Carlsson realized he needed to devise a way to tap into the charitable impulses of Swedish industry, which had long supported environmental causes.

Just prior to graduating from business school, Axel founded the SBF and used its core mission of "Research and protection of the marine environment" to begin soliciting contributions from well-meaning corporate donors. After just one year of aggressive fundraising, sufficient funds had poured into the Foundation to allow him to commence operations. Utilizing the IKEA business model and his connections within Sweden's close-knit business network, the ambitious Axel knew he could outsource just about any type of work or service he would require. He planned to keep the Foundation's staff to a trusted few, to ensure maximum privacy and control.

That was ten years earlier.

It was Sunday evening, and Marstrand's village lay still beneath a star-filled sky. Axel had spent the weekend in the SBF's lab in solitary preparation. Midnight approached, and with it a last trip to the loo, where he splashed some water on his face and quietly examined himself in the mirror. His sandy hair was meticulously trimmed flat and was starting to show some signs of silvering around his temples. Years of exposure to the sun had added a ruddy tinge to what used to be a fair complexion, and his close-set eyes and angled, thin brows portrayed a look of confident determination, which indeed was embedded in his DNA. Daily workout routines had saved his body's frame from going slack from days on end of bending over a microscope. Despite approaching midlife in years, he retained the youthful look that he used to attract classmates and donors alike to the causes he championed. A swipe of lip balm came next, after which he donned a slicker hanging by the door. Prepared to depart, he gingerly lifted the backpack from the top of a lab table and exited the Foundation. From the front entryway, he gazed up at the twinkling heavens while adjusting the backpack on his shoulders.

As he stepped out into the night, a chilly sea breeze bit at his face. Now, the fortress loomed in the moonlight, a silent witness to his clandestine preparations. The sight steeled him with resolve. Axel began to tread softly toward the quay where his skiff bobbed alongside the dock, taking care to avoid tripping on the slick and uneven cobblestones that studded Marstrand's cozy pathways.

The foul-smelling fluid inside the stainless-steel canister was a sample of North Sea Brent crude, one of many stored in the SBF's laboratory. Axel paused before boarding his small craft and knelt on the dock. He couldn't shake the feeling that someone was watching, a shadow moving just beyond the edge of his vision. He smoothly slung off the backpack and reached into it for the canister of oil and the small, silver pouch. He unscrewed the canister's lid and set it carefully on the dock as the moon glinted on the surface of the black liquid. At last, he pulled apart the silver pouch's zip top and carefully squeezed each last drop of its thawing contents into the canister.

The fuse that would change the world was thus lit.

CH. 2

Although the U.S. Embassy was tucked away in a leafy section of urban Stockholm, Foggy Bottom had teamed with the Department of Commerce to operate a central Nordic consulate in Sweden's industrial Port of Gothenburg.

Daniel Lake found himself spending most of his time at the Gothenburg office as its commercial attaché. The southern tip of Sweden, with its dense concentration of manufacturing firms, kept the trade office busy with visas, shipping clearances and other routine documentary services. Beneath the surface, agents lurked in the shadows, gathering intel amidst the routine bureaucratic processes.

With degrees in law and international relations, Lake was amply prepared for his career in facilitating international trade. Putting deals together, lining up the financing with state agencies and sorting through the local customs, tax and myriad other issues energized him. He was also no stranger to tradecraft.

But being an envoy had taken a toll on him. His high school sweetheart, who had followed him across three continents, had left a note on the kitchen table one day in Nairobi, stating that the life of a diplomat's wife was not meant for her. He found the note late in the evening, after another long day at the embassy, and read it with a sinking heart. He had seen it coming—her increasing detachment, the way she avoided talking about the future. Yet, it still hit him hard. Nairobi had been the final straw, a place too far from home, too fatiguing, and ultimately, too foreign for her to bear. Now, in his late thirties, Daniel had nothing left but his career. The ambitions he once shared with her had become his alone.

Daniel reckoned the job in Gothenburg would be his last overseas assignment. It was time for him to return to Washington and hunt for a post there. His reputation as a deft problem solver and intel officer would help his prospects. He had great people skills and easily forged close ties with his foreign counterparts. Like all career diplomats, he had paid his dues in places like Haiti and Kenya. With luck, he might eventually return to the field as an ambassador, an appointment he longed to receive.

Gothenburg, with its provincial charm and easy access to Europe's great cities, had been a welcome respite. And it was easy for him to shuttle between Gothenburg and the embassy in Stockholm for monthly status meetings on one of the comfortable trains that traveled between the two cities every hour.

But as Daniel settled into his business class seat on the train ride home from Stockholm on a Friday afternoon, he found himself restless, yearning for something he couldn't quite name. Across from him, a woman caught his eye—willowy, with alabaster skin and blue-grey eyes that seemed to see right through him. Her waves of golden hair had a nice bounce and fell over her shoulders, while the rectangular reading glasses she wore complimented her sophisticated look. It occurred to him that this classic Swedish beauty could have easily sat as a studio model for

Anders Zorn, Sweden's equivalent of the virtuoso painter John Singer Sargent. When she smiled at him, a small, knowing smile, it left him wondering what she saw in him.

His confident chin and dimpled return smile did not go unappreciated. Karin liked the casual way he had loosened the knot of his striped silk tie from his button-down shirt and was amused by the preppy way he wore no socks with his dress shoes. A thick head of wavy brown hair, combed to the side, complimented his chestnut-colored eyes. She surmised he was about her age and checked to see if he was wearing a ring on his hand, noticing there was none. *And where did he get that tan?*

But on this afternoon, like most others, Daniel did not especially desire to engage in idle chit-chat with who he surmised would be one more overly discerning and independent Swedish member of the opposite sex. From his experience with women so far in Sweden, it was hardly worth the brain damage. In fact, since starting his job a year earlier, there really was little time for dating, and he had been politely rebuffed by the few prospects he encountered. So, when he pulled out the *Wall Street European Edition*, Karin surprised him by inquiring if she could read the first section after he was through with it. It was her cheery eye contact that signaled a more than passing interest in him. Daniel remained off-hand, at first.

After perusing the Journal's Opinion pages, she folded the section up and handed it back to Daniel.

"I'm Karin Lofgren," she said. "Thank you for sharing the Journal. It's not very well distributed, and I always enjoy reading the editorials."

"So do I, they're well-written," he replied. "Usually right to the point, aren't they? I'm Daniel, nice to meet you."

"You as well." A shift then, by Karin, into a more relaxed position in her seat while Daniel stowed some files he was perusing into his briefcase.

As the train rumbled through the countryside of farms, craggy hillsides and lake lands, she told him she was a junior partner at the Gothenburg branch of Persson & Frandberg, an accounting firm with an international practice. She specialized in such dry but strategically key areas as withholding taxes, transfer pricing and licensing—essential competencies for trade-hungry Nordic conglomerates. Like Daniel, Karin frequently made the commute to Stockholm for client meetings, and today she was returning home from one of them. Daniel's interest piqued, appreciating that her work overlapped with his in some ways.

By the time they rolled into the station in the shadow of Lilla Bommen's "Lipstick" building, Karin was easy-going and talkative, happy to use the English she had polished to perfection as a teen *au pair* during two summers in Texas. As they walked together from the train station, each realized they did not want their chance encounter to end too abruptly. Daniel offered to walk Karin back to her apartment, and she accepted. Surprised with his desire to see her again, Daniel politely handed Karin his card as they stood outside her entryway in one of the orangey-yellow brick apartment buildings that lined Gothenburg's central avenues. Meanwhile, a lady strolling with her long-haired dachshund walked by, and he instinctively bent low to pet the dog as it busily sniffed him. Karin looked on, admiring Daniel's athletic physique before stooping down to scratch the inquisitive dog as well. As they caressed the dog's neck, their fingertips touched briefly, providing them with a pleasing sensation, and in that moment, they felt a connection as they looked into each other's eyes.

She stood up and tucked his card in her jacket pocket while he held the door. As she entered her apartment, she glanced back to give him a farewell waive, hoping he'd fulfill his promise to call her. Daniel waived back and watched her graceful form as it disappeared into the lobby before he turned in the direction of his apartment. That touch, he wondered, a spark that perhaps portended more?

CH. 3.

Just off Tverskaya Street, in a nondescript office building over-looking the walled entrance of the Kremlin, Gnady Pankov lifted a cerulean, guilloche enamel Fabergé egg from its carved amber stand. The cool weight of the glittering orb rested in his palm, where he caressed it in a rare moment of tranquility in his otherwise chaotic life. As he depressed a tiny, filigreed cap at its bottom axis, the oval sprang open, revealing a pearl-surrounded pond whose surface was made of rock crystal. Hidden inside the imperial egg's lower half was a revolving cylinder that produced sounds by using tiny pins to pluck the tuned teeth of a steel comb. Instantly, the delicate mechanism began to sweetly play "Dances of the Swans" from Tchaikovsky's *Swan Lake*, as four tiny swans attached to gold posts circled around the pond's perimeter.

Pankov allowed himself to smile a brief smile. This exquisite bauble had been a calculated acquisition, bought during the market crash of 2008. The famous MS Rau antiques firm of New Orleans brokered the sale on behalf of the seller, a desperate Wall Street hedge fund owner who had no idea how much value the egg would recover. Pankov, however, had known. An earlier 2004 Forbes extraordinary sale of Fabergé eggs had shattered auction records, and he had been certain that the prices for such imperial items would soar again. Now, his magnificent theatrical wonder could fetch three times what he paid, though he had no intention of selling. Indeed, there were plenty of Russian moguls in search of such exotic toys. He'd never consider parting with it, as there was no greater mark of success than installing such a sublime treasure in one's office to impress visitors. It was more than just a trophy—it was a testament to his cunning.

But the elegance of the Fabergé egg stood in stark contrast to the brutal world Pankov truly inhabited. Trading securities was his lifeblood, not the delicate artistry that adorned his office. His firm, GP Pankovneft, specialized in crude oil options and futures contracts, a business that had grown from nothing in the early '90s to an energy powerhouse. The firm grew from its infancy as Russian power companies and energy users sought out a stable and reliable source of energy to help them operate. No longer would they need to rely on coal railed in from Poland, when abundant oil lay beneath the petroleum-rich taiga of Siberia, under the Urals and elsewhere within the Federation's borders. His firm saw an opportunity in supplying the fast-growing economies of the former Soviet satellites since they had scant domestic oil supplies of their own. The downside risk was limited, and his firm prospered beyond his wildest dreams.

Yet, despite his success, Pankov felt a cold dread creeping into his thoughts. The firm had prospered, but at a cost. Four years earlier, powerful neo-apparatchiks of the State aligned with the *Solntsevskaya Bratva*, the Russian mafia, had forced Pankov to accept a hefty sum for a majority stake in his firm. The global footprint of his firm's dealings unfortunately aligned well with the gangsters' international ambitions. They threatened his life and simply muscled in, and so he took their money reluctantly; what choice did he have? As silent partners, they demanded a high return on their investment, and thus far he had managed to meet their expectations, playing a ruthless game of balancing the demands of the mob with the volatile market he navigated daily.

Now, that game was reaching its end. The oil market had turned against him. His once sure-fire bets on rising prices had soured, leaving him exposed to catastrophic losses. In recent weeks Pankov had become desperate for the price of oil to rise, having placed a series of huge bets on continued, dramatic appreciation in the price of oil. But the upward price momentum he had come to rely on simply evaporated. Emboldened by steadily rising prices that appeared to have no end in sight, Pankov had thrown the dice once too often. To his great chagrin, Chinese demand had slowed, and expected supply disruptions in Syria, Yemen and Azerbaijan had not materialized. Plus, now the damned Americans were releasing oil from their strategic reserves and fracking untold tanks of liquefied natural gas from the Permian basin and Andarko shale fields. Unthinkable even a few years earlier, America had become an exporter of the stuff, having become energy independent. Renewable energy was denting demand for carbon-based energy. And finally, embargoed Iranian oil was being sold through third parties at more than double the level of a year earlier. The Paris-based International Energy Agency estimated that European stocks were at their highest level in 6 years. Consequently, with too much supply in the market, his firm's huge position of leveraged option contracts, bought as a sure bet ten months earlier, was set to expire out-of-the-money, or worthless, in less than a month, wiping out all Pankovneft's equity.

Pankov realized he was at the helm of a jarring Enronesque debacle, although this time it involved private capital. Recapitalization *might* be possible, but he would never be allowed to remain with the firm. Another option was bankruptcy, a difficult if not treacherous wick to light under the mercurial rules of Russian law. His shadow board, populated with some of Russia's most ruthless crime bosses, would remove his raven-haired head if he attempted that route. They would never countenance being exposed to such humiliation or the intrusive course of the Federation's insolvency process. Either way, Gnady faced either the disgrace of being removed from the company he founded or death by gory execution, and to him, the latter was more appealing.

Fear affects the mind, body and emotions of most traders. However, Pankov was largely immune from such reactions, possessing steely nerves and a cool disposition that helped him keep his fear at bay. Gnady managed the emotions confined within him as an edge in dealing with such threats. He knew the stakes. He possessed a Rasputin-like ability to cast spells on his adversaries when he needed to control them.

He was also resourceful and cagey. He had contrived a powerful hedge for the day his luck would run dry, when his bets on the direction of crude prices would become ruinous. If — and only if — all went as planned, a devilishly clever fix would soon be in for the looming catastrophic losses his firm was now facing.

Gnady carefully placed his cherished Fabergé egg back on its stand, its delicate beauty a stark reminder of the precariousness of his situation. He stroked his handsome cleft chin and then adjusted the knot of his Loro Piana tie while contemplating the game he was playing. The stakes were *his life*, and he knew that the clock was ticking.

CH. 4

The sea whispered its secrets as Carlsson clambered into the skiff and untied its rope tether. He cast one last glance at the fortress, its ramparts bathed in cold moonlight, bracing him for what lay ahead. Axel's mission had always been clear: to protect the marine environment he loved. But tonight, the lines between right and wrong, safety and danger, seemed as blurred as the horizon where the sky met the sea.

With the push of a button, the biodiesel Volvo Penta duo-prop engine growled to life in the stillness of the night. A few moments later, the boat propelled out of Marstrand's small marina and cut through the jet-black seawater, leaving a churning wake behind. Axel squinted into the darkness ahead, noting the glassy smoothness of the sea and the gentle push of a headwind.

He steered south, hugging the coast and maneuvering past the smoothly worn skerries and islets that dotted the shoreline like ancient sentinels. An hour later he emerged near the Arendal business park, where he heard the cue of the nearby wind farm's steady "whoosh, whoosh" of turbine blades fracturing the silence from on high in their towers. After a few more minutes of cruising, he turned in and landed the small craft alongside the granite-strewn promontory next to Goteborg Energi.

Here, the thick forest of tall pines and scrub trees provided the cover he needed. He dropped anchor, tethering the boat to a sturdy pine, and slung his rucksack over his shoulder. He set off along the gravelly waterline and trekked a few hundred meters until he turned into the woods. He trudged on until he reached the start of a clearing and crouched low in the shadows to watch and listen for several minutes. The late evening mist swirled around him, casting the world in shades of grey, like an old film reel.

Axel listened intently, his senses on high alert. Only a slight breeze, sighing through the needles of the tall pines, could be heard. Satisfied with the calm, he left the protective cover of the woods and approached an old, misshapen chain link fence that had only one row of lazily strung barbed wire along the top. No surveillance cameras, he noted with satisfaction; in any event, his charcoal-colored sweat suit would render his movements nearly invisible in the darkness. In a swift, fluid movement, Axel scaled the fence and landed inside the industrial complex that housed the crude oil storage tank farm and refinery complex adjacent to the Port of Gothenburg.

The last of the midnight sun had long faded. Before him lay a crepuscular, *en grisaille* landscape dotted with huge steel storage drums that shimmered silvery white in the ambient moonlight, like swollen marshmallows over a campfire. In a few moments he reached the nearest oil storage tank and sprinted up the winding stairwell that hugged its gleaming walls. Upon reaching the top platform, he set the backpack down and surveyed the landscape, exalting in the seminal moment that had been preceded by years of painstaking effort.

There's no stopping us now, he thought, holding fast to his convictions.

Axel stood on the tank's rooftop and scanned the slightly convex surface for the lidded air vent which he spotted and stepped lightly toward. The hinged lid was held in place with a stainless-steel cotter pin that he eased out with a pair of needle-nosed pliers that he took from his backpack. The lid squeaked open, and he poured the canister's viscous concentration down the hatch and into the darkness below, taking care to avoid spilling any fluid on the edges of the opening. Then he swung the lid back into place, reinserted the pin and groped into his backpack for a radio transmitter. He flicked a switch on the side of the transmitter and signaled that the insertion was accomplished.

Gnady, sipping a Bloody Mary and scrolling through his morning emails at an ormolu-mounted *bureau plat* in his bedroom, was the recipient of the encrypted message heralding the beginning of something irreversible. When he heard the faint beeping tone emit from the receiver resting on a nearby coffee table, he closed his smooth eyelids and held his almost empty tumbler aloft, while murmuring a quick supplication to the Holy Mother for the exercise in personal salvation that had just begun.

Axel descended from the storage tank quickly, retracing his steps with practiced ease. Before slipping back into the forest, he glanced at the dew-covered turf, noting the trail of bent blades his sneakers had left behind. *No matter,* he thought. By morning, the dew would have evaporated, and the grass would stand tall once more, hiding any trace of his presence.

The skiff bobbed gently in the water, its engine purring as Axel guided it back through the archipelago. The sky had started lighting up by the time he reached the marina on Marstrand. The sleepy island was still cloaked in tranquility as dawn finally appeared. Axel cut the engine and secured the boat to its berth, his movements slow now, the adrenaline fading. As he trudged up the slope to the unassuming building that housed his Foundation, fatigue washed over him. Another brief stop in the loo, and in a sparsely furnished room that served as his office and bedroom, he collapsed on a daybed, sleep claiming him almost instantly.

CH. 5

A few blocks from Karin's apartment, Daniel caught one of Gothenburg's slim blue and white electric trams. The soft hum of the tram soothed him as it glided steadily through the city streets, finally stopping across from the Elite Park Avenue Hotel. The square that housed Gothenburg's art museum and symphony hall complex was steps away. A two-story, verdigris statue of Poseidon holding a triton aloft adorned its center. The figure's muscular legs and sensual hips were reminiscent of the *contrapposto* pose of Michelangelo's David which graced the domed central chamber of Florence's *Gallerie dell' Accademia*. Daniel paused to admire it, his thoughts momentarily drifting to his time in Florence years ago, a different life altogether.

His apartment house was just a short walk away, nestled in an enviable part of the city brimming with shops, bookstores, and cafés. The public library nearby was more than just a place to borrow books—it was a hub where meetings could be arranged discreetly, and intel dropped, undetected, among the stacks. Daniel had come to appreciate the orderliness of Swedish life. The cycling lanes that crisscrossed the city kept him fit, but it was the order and quiet efficiency of it all that truly appealed to him.

He checked his mailbox in the apartment building's foyer, sifting through the usual accumulation of *Goteborgs Posten* newspapers. Only today's edition caught his eye; the rest he tossed without a second thought. As he climbed the stairs to his third-floor apartment, he felt a pleasant comfort in the routine. Inside, the motion-activated lights flickered on, casting a soft glow over the sparsely furnished space. It was minimalist, almost spartan, yet it suited him perfectly. After retrieving a cold Pripps from the fridge, Daniel sank into his well-worn armchair and took a long, satisfying swig. "Ahhh, no place like home," he murmured, though his voice lacked the conviction it once had. The fridge, as usual, was nearly empty. A jar of JIF, some water crackers, a tin of sardines, and a bag of soggy grapes were all that remained. Daniel sighed. "This won't do," he muttered to himself, finishing the beer in a few quick gulps before heading out the door again with the morning's newspaper tucked under his arm.

A few blocks away, the *Haga* district beckoned with its eclectic mix of used clothing stores, low-end art galleries, and quirky cafés. It was a bohemian section of town that didn't quite fit in with the rest of the city's polished veneer, and perhaps that's why Daniel liked it. The scent of freshly brewed coffee and baked goods filled the air as he strolled through the narrow streets, his footsteps echoing off the cobblestones.

Within *Haga*, Daniel often frequented Smakling, a restaurant favored by the local university students. Its signature dish was a large plate filled with savory meatballs complemented with tart *gurken* salad, tangy lingonberries and a huge snowdrift of mashed potatoes floating in a lake of creamy *brun* gravy. Klaus, the gregarious, muscle-bound waiter, hailed Daniel with a grin from his post at the bar.

"My usual table, Klaus," Daniel said as Klaus nodded and disappeared into the kitchen.

A minute later, Klaus reappeared and made his way over to Daniel. "Is this what you call 'comfort food' in the States?" he asked, thumping a plate of meatballs on the table with a flourish in front of Daniel.

"That's right, and apart from our classic Thanksgiving dinner with all the trimmings, we can't top this dish," Daniel offered amiably. He'd become friends with Klaus from frequent meals at Smakling.

"And you certainly can't top our coffee," Klaus continued. "Do you know what American coffee and having sex in a canoe have in common?" he taunted with a wry grin.

Daniel raised an eyebrow, unable to suppress a smile. "I can't imagine. What?"

"They're both fucking close to water!" Klaus roared, his laughter filling the air before he moved on to the next table.

As Daniel began to eat, he unfolded the newspaper, his eyes scanning the business pages with aide from a flickering table candle. The headlines were predictable— earnings season would soon begin, and there was a lot of speculation about a possible negative impact on results due to the strength of the Krona. That, along with the touchy global economy, which was weakened by impending downgrades of sovereign debt, had begun to put pressure on share prices on the OMX, the Nordic stock exchange. As robust as Sweden's economy was, it was utterly dependent on export sales. Like their Viking forebears, the Swedes relied heavily on foreign trade to keep their larders filled at home.

A short article above the crease on page two of the *Posten* caught his attention: *'Brun Sauce' at Oil Refinery Investigated.* Something odd was brewing at the Port of Gothenburg's oil storage facility and refinery, he read. The irony wasn't lost on him as he glanced at the pool of burnt-caramel colored gravy puddled on his plate. He chuckled softly, but a nagging thought lingered. There was something unsettling about the article, something that made him pause. Shaking off the feeling, Daniel scooped up the last of the savory meatballs, swirling it in the sauce before popping it into his mouth.

Still, the unease lingered, like a faint shadow at the edge of his mind.

CH. 6

Within the shelter of Tor Harbor, the deep-water Port of Gothenburg serves as a full-service facility for ships carrying all classes of cargo. The port also serves as a regional hub for crude and refined oil products. Large-scale oil transport and storage had begun in earnest in the harbor as early as the 1930's.

The supertanker *Smolensk II* was moored alongside a pumping station located on the harbor's outer boundary, having entered the port with the aid of GPS satellite navigation. Her flag was registered with the Russian Federation. It had taken nearly a week for the *Smolensk II* to complete her charter — highly profitable to the tanker's owners — embarking from the Port of Murmansk with two other stops *en route* to Gothenburg. The ship, nearly a quarter mile long, was lashed to the wharf and sat indifferent to the waves that lapped at her starboard without consequence. Her cavernous hold was roughly the equivalent of what a major cathedral could contain within its walls, or enough energy to satisfy the needs of a decent- sized city for a year. The tanker's double inner hull was divided into compartments for the crude which was loaded and emptied by pumps. Huge pipes ran down the length of her deck to direct the oil as it sloshed from one tank compartment to the next and finally onshore.

Midshipman Dima Mostov, wiry, hollow-eyed and stubble-chinned, drew a fresh pack of Marlboros from his coat pocket as he paced back and forth on deck. He'd picked up the smokes the day before while on shore leave. Smoking was prohibited on board the ship, but such rules were routinely ignored by the crew. He lit one and enjoyed his first draw as he examined the ragged nails on his finger-bitten hands, a habit he had found impossible to break. Then he carefully blew the match out and crushed it underfoot as an extra precaution.

In his youth, Dima had been a petty drug seller, peddling mostly hash and other opiates smuggled from Afghanistan by returning conscripts from the conflict. A kilo of opium successfully smuggled home was the soldier's equivalent of winning the lottery. Being a small-time trafficker exposed him to lower level *brodyagas* who in turn were connected to mafia captains higher up the chain. They discreetly accepted assignments for cash, no questions asked.

Dima had always been a survivor, a trait that had served him well in the harsh streets of Moscow where he'd first learned to navigate the underworld. Yet, even now, years after leaving that life behind, the ghosts of his past lingered in his thoughts. The merchant marine had given him an escape, a semblance of legitimacy, but as he paced the deck of the *Smolensk II,* he couldn't shake the feeling that he was still running— from what he wasn't sure.

One evening back in the day, after selling a vial of the tarlike opiate *khanka* to an undercover officer, he was arrested. Because he was connected to the *sytema,* some strings were pulled on his behalf, and he was given the choice of either joining the merchant marine or being imprisoned in a dank and dangerous Siberian jail where men without the right connections were sent. It really was no choice at all for Mostov, who took the first and only option. After serving four years on a State-owned oil supply ship that plied the frigid Barents Sea, his dues were paid, though he was hardly reformed, and he was released.

The skills Dima gained on board the supply ship qualified him as a low-level midshipman with the Vostok Transea shipping line, and when his servitude ended, he decided his days of peddling drugs on the street were over. His links to Moscow's powerful underworld syndicate remained, however, and now he discreetly offered his services as a freelancer, smuggling high-value contraband between Russia and the various ports of call visited by the *Smolensk II*. Such work was easy, for the most part, and entailed little risk but plenty of reward.

Strolling through Gothenburg while on shore leave seemed like paradise to Dima after spending nearly two weeks in the cramped, rank quarters he occupied aboard the ship. The flaky, dilled cod and buttered potatoes, the milk chocolate and the other delicacies he sampled while exploring Gothenburg's *Centrum* topped anything he had eaten for weeks. On the other hand, to his mind the stunning and saucy beauties of the Motherland were preferable to the often-antiseptic Swedish women who stiffly paraded Gothenburg's streets. Women in Russia were bred to be admired and to please the opposite sex.

In the same pocket as his smokes was a wireless receiver removed from a shopping bag that Axel had discreetly passed to Dima when they met for lunch earlier that day in the crowded Fish Church Market and Restaurant. The receiver was like the one Pankov had used. Earlier in the day, Axel waited in one of the lengthy lines of the market lunch counters for Dima to appear. Dima was recognized as soon as he entered the market, his clothes wrinkled, hair greased back and dark tattoos visible above his shirt collar, extending to his wrists. His attire, skin and furtive eyes made him easy to spot. At their table, Axel explained to Dima that later in the evening, at 22:00, he needed to pour the liquid from the shopping bag's thermos into the oil stored in the ship's belly, before the crude was pumped out to the Port's storage cavern the next morning. After reviewing the assignment, the two sat down to eat.

As far as assignments went, this one couldn't be easier, Dima thought as he gulped his lunch silently next to the serious, if not self-important Swede. There was something about the Swede that unnerved him, a clinical detachment that made Dima wonder if Axel saw him as anything more than a disposable pawn. But he was in too deep now; backing out wasn't an option. After lunch ended, Dima left the building and made his way back to the ship. Carlsson drove back to Marstrand.

The twilight of evening came swiftly, with Dima resting in his cabin aboard the ship, enjoying a beer and munching on some pretzels he brought on board from a convenience store near Gothenburg's Opera House. Reclining in his bunk, he nervously examined the receiver for the umpteenth time. It was a simple device, with just one "on" button and an LED light. At 19:50, he rolled out of bed and ascended four levels to the aft deck of the ship. He positioned himself between two large pipes where he could see if any unwelcome crewmates might approach. The deck was clear. He turned the device on and cradled it in the palm of his hand as he waited in the damp, chilly sea breeze. Forty kilometers up the coast, at the SBF's office on Marstrand, Carlsson typed a code into a wall safe and pulled a transmitter from the spare cavity when the safe's doors sprung open.

Earlier that day, a contact of Axel's who consulted for the lab at the oil tank facility confirmed the existence of an investigation into the mysterious slurry discovered in one of the large oil storage tanks at the Port. Axel learned that spectrum analysis and titration were nearing completion, with no explanation confirmed yet for the contamination. The Gothenburg police also had paid a visit to the facility and took samples from the tank as part of a cautious, dual investigation. Simpering to himself, Axel could have saved them all a lot of time and effort. And they'd soon have another bite at the apple, if all went as planned.

At precisely 20:00, the light on Dima's receiver emitted a faint green glow, the signal from Axel to begin his operation. Dima swiftly returned the device to his pocket. He planned to ditch it while on shore the next morning, on his last day of leave before the empty tanker embarked for its home port of Murmansk.

Dima ducked into the aft stairwell and found his way back to his berth. From his locker he removed the small thermos that Axel had also passed to him in the shopping bag earlier that day. He tucked it inside his jacket and headed to the main pump room, centered mid-ship. Inside, he spun the gate valve wheel closed, thereby depressurizing the steel exit pipe of the tanker's central hold. Next, he opened an inspection hatch in a baffle next to the hydraulic pump and held the thermos up in a moment of fascination before unscrewing the lid and letting the thermos's syrupy concentration flow down the small opening.

As Dima poured the thick liquid into the throat of the hatch, a bead of sweat trickled down his brow. The hum of the ship's machinery felt more ominous than usual, as if the vessel itself was aware of the treachery unfolding within its steel belly. He knew that this was more than just another job; the weight of its consequences pressed on him like a vice. If this operation went south, he sensed that it wouldn't just be his life at risk, but the delicate balance of global power.

After closing the hatch, he re-opened the valve, and an instant "swoosh" swept the smelly solution back into the middle hold of the ship whose reservoir of crude was set for delivery the next day. After wiping away any fingerprints and residue of the liquid with a rag, he hurriedly made his way back to his cabin and signaled to Axel that the insertion was accomplished.

The next morning, the tanker's load of contaminated oil would be pumped through the ship's bulkheads and into the largest storage depot in northern Europe.

The *Smolensk II* was an iron cage on the open sea, a vessel bound by purpose and direction, much like Dima himself. But as he looked out at the vast expanse of water stretching endlessly towards the horizon, he felt a pang of something he couldn't quite name— longing about what might have been, perhaps, or the bitter taste of dreams deferred.

Axel placed the transmitter back in the floor safe but first changed its frequency and transmitted one more untraceable signal to a receiver that Gnady anxiously cradled in Moscow. Axel's signal, coming on the heels of the one he sent just a few days earlier, confirmed that Phase 2 of their operation had begun.

CH. 7

Late the next morning, police Captain Gunnar Bodin thumbed through a report that lay on his desk. Its envelope had been dropped off that morning from the lab at Gothenburg's central crime investigation unit where Gunnar was stationed. His eyes were narrow and alert as he perused the table of contents and flipped to the executive summary.

Gunnar had seen his fair share of strange cases in his twenty years on the force, but this one was different. As he skimmed the report, his mind wandered to the countless nights spent chasing down leads, the long hours that had cost him more than one relationship. This time, though, the stakes felt even higher. There was something unsettling about the way the oil had been transformed, something that gnawed at the edges of his usually stoic demeanor.

With a raised eyebrow, he read, in part:

> "Laboratory analysis of the Urals oil split samples
> evidences a breakdown of the oil into a neutral pH
> composition of primarily H_2O, CO_2, some sulfur and
> miniscule amounts of trace metals, suspended with a
> high concentration of (non-viable) single-cell, amoe-

ba-like bacteria. The crude oil has been chemically
transformed and is neither hazardous nor flammable.
It emits no volatile gasses. Genetic analysis of the organisms has not been performed and is recommended
for identification of the species involved........"

"It's worthless as shit!" he breathed to himself. As Gunnar read the
lab report, a cold chill ran down his spine. There was something
about this case that didn't add up, something that gnawed at the
edges of his usually clear-cut worldview. He couldn't shake the
feeling that they were only scratching the surface, that this was
just the beginning of something far more sinister.

Gunnar's cubicle was a cramped, cluttered space, a far cry from
the sleek, modern look of the rest of the building. The walls were
lined with old case files, the edges yellowing from age, and his
desk was a chaotic mix of paperwork, coffee cups, and a half-eaten
sandwich from the day before. Over the years, his bosses pleaded
with him to maintain a clean desk, but Gunnar's routine reply
was, "You can have a clean desk, or you can have productivity."
He invariably wore them down. Gunnar could hear the familiar
hum of activity around him, the low murmurs of his colleagues
as they went about their tasks, but it suddenly all felt distant, as if
this case had placed a barrier between him and the world.

As he shut the binder and made his way to Deputy Chief Eva
Dahlquist's office, he couldn't help but notice the quiet tension
in the air, the way the usual banter between colleagues had been
replaced with hushed whispers. Something about this case had
everyone on edge, and Gunnar could feel it in his bones. He
knocked on Eva's door, the sound echoing in the silent hallway,

and waited for her sharp "Enter" before pushing it open.

Eva was short and squat, with pointy eyeglasses, a high-pitched voice and a pleasant demeanor. Thick makeup did its best to mask the wrinkles that had encroached on the corners of her eyes and mouth from a habit of heavy smoking. A little old-fashioned, prone to wearing fashion jewelry pins on matronly dresses she'd preserved for years on end with an ample reliance on mothballs and dry-cleaning. In another year she could take early retirement, and she planned to do just that so she could spend more time perfecting her Spanish and relaxing at the small condo she bought with a girlfriend on the Costa del Sol.

"Have you seen the lab report on the oil contamination at the refinery?" Gunnar asked as he stepped into Eva's office, his voice tight with barely contained tension.

Eva looked up from her desk, her gaze sharp behind those pointed glasses. "Not yet," she replied, her tone guarded. "What does it say?"

Gunnar hesitated for a moment, choosing his words carefully. 'It's…astonishing, really. The entire storage tank 71 is filled with jellified crap—neutralized oil and high concentrations of dead bacteria are in both samples, and there's no way those bacteria could ever be present in such quantities. It's like nothing I've ever seen before. Almost like someone's playing God."

Eva leaned back in her chair, her expression unreadable but her thoughts miles ahead; Spain would have to wait if her beloved Port had been struck by malevolent offenders.

Just when I thought I'd seen everything.

"Might it involve industrial sabotage?" she finally asked, though her tone suggested she wasn't entirely convinced. She reflected, "From what I learned when I first got the call from the Port, their routine is to identify the origin of the crude and take samples of it before it's pumped into each of the storage tanks. Based on prior samples, everything was fine with tank 71 and the initial delivery of the crude. What happened afterward is a mystery; why was only tank 71 affected?"

"We're dealing with something big here, Eva,' Gunnar said, his voice low. 'This isn't just about a contaminated tank. There's more to this; I can feel it."

"Perhaps, but let's not jump to conclusions. It looks as if this *could* involve industrial sabotage. Let's get a team together, Gunnar. Include a biologist; maybe add someone from Chalmers University in life sciences, or with a microbial background. Wouldn't hurt the professors to get their hands dirty a bit, would it? You take the lead and get right on it. We'll have a lot of people clamoring soon for details about this fine kettle of fish. And the press is already speculating. An investigation was briefly mentioned in yesterday's *Post*; it won't be long before someone leaks the analysis made over at the refinery lab. The cost of the contaminated oil is one thing, but learning how the contamination happened is quite another. We need answers, fast."

Captain Bodin was Eva's likely successor, and they worked well together. He'd been in the department for nearly twenty years and was skilled in managing investigations of all types. He nodded in agreement and retraced his steps along the short hallway leading from Eva's office to the large open room where his indistinguishable cubicle sat amidst twelve others, in a sea of blond wood and blue carpet tiles, a testament to Swedish egalitarianism.

After a couple of calls, he selected the core of his team. The first was Anna Peng, a young and inquisitive behavioral expert. She had moved from China to attend Gothenburg University, where she graduated with a degree in criminology. Her opinions and tenacity were highly valued after only a few years in the force. In her spare time, she enjoyed playing classical music on the piano and teaching Chinese language lessons. The second was Stig Renell, a salty, straight-talking investigator who was not above bending a few rules to pry facts from reluctant witnesses. Stig was tenacious and street smart, able to read a room as well as a crime scene. A pointy chin and piercing brown eyes seemed to emphasize his determination. Other resources within the department would be added as needed.

Bodin asked the team to meet in their conference room in thirty minutes, the time it would take to have copies made of the lab report, to print up schematics of the oil tank and refinery complex and to order some fresh pots of coffee, shrimp sandwiches and a tray of *kanelbulle*, the ubiquitous, cardamom-laced cinnamon buns Swedes loved to eat at any hour of the day or night, but especially with coffee while on afternoon coffee breaks.

He surmised a long evening was in front of them.

CH. 8

"OK everyone, let's review the facts we have collected so far," Bodin began.

As the team settled into their seats around the conference table, Bodin took a moment to observe them. Anna was already flipping through her notes, her brows furrowed in concentration, while Stig leaned back in his chair, arms crossed, his usual skeptical expression firmly in place. The room smelled of fresh coffee and cinnamon buns, a sharp contrast to the grim task ahead. Bodin cleared his throat, drawing their attention.

"Alright, let's get down to business," Bodin said, leaning forward with a sense of urgency. "Two days ago, the refinery's security office called with a unique situation—something that doesn't fit the usual patterns. They requested our assistance, and frankly, they're rattled." He glanced around the table, gauging the team's reactions. Anna's pen hovered over her notepad, her eyes wide with curiosity, while Stig let out a low whistle, his expression hardening. "What exactly are we dealing with here, Gunnar?" Stig asked, his voice a mix of concern and intrigue.

"That's what we're here to find out," Bodin replied, his tone leaving no room for doubt. "It turns out that one of the tanks that stores crude there was totally contaminated and its contents rendered worthless. Of course, there is a civil loss to consider, but the root cause of the spoliation was unknown by the refinery staff and therefore it could constitute a criminal offense. They properly reported it as a case of possible criminal misconduct," he continued, "and so I asked our lab techs to take their own samples from the tank right away. That was yesterday."

"If you turn to the lab report, p. 3, you'll see that the crude has been basically turned into harmless effluent, presumably by the dead bugs or bacteria that render the oil into a slimy mess. That's quite a feat, and if it weren't so serious, it would be a God-awful joke. The refinery made an analysis of the oil and it's much the same as ours. In addition, our lab recommends DNA analysis to identify the bug species. This morning, I asked them to arrange for one with an outside genetics firm. We should get the results in about a week. In the meanwhile, there are a lot of potential motives and leads to develop in this case," Bodin continued. "A disgruntled employee or lone wolf? Perhaps a little subtle pressure from the Union? Industrial sabotage?"

He paused, letting the weight of his words sink in. "Or something we haven't even considered yet. We're dealing with forces that may be far more nefarious than we've encountered before. We need to be prepared for anything." The room fell silent, the tension palpable as each team member considered the implications.

"What about the Greens?" Anna offered, her voice cutting through the tension. The environmental activists had been vocal in their opposition to the refinery, and it wasn't beyond them to take drastic measures.

Stig chimed in, his tone skeptical. "Could be they're working with someone else, someone who prefers to stay in the shadows. Or maybe it's a splinter group, acting on their own." The room buzzed with speculation, each theory more unsettling than the last.

"A possibility", Gunnar concurred, "please follow up on it and speak with Human Resources at the facility to review all employee terminations and resignations in the past year. Also, anything they might have heard about union discontent. Anna, the Greens have been pushing for alternative energy sources and certainly have the wherewithal to instigate a fiasco such as this. You have a good point. But so far no one has taken any credit for it, and the Greens usually take credit for their operations quickly and very publicly."

Renell spoke next. "Let's also consider where the oil in tank 71 originated from," he said. "Do we know that yet? The lab report says that crude has a unique signature of origin based on its chemical composition. Most likely the oil was delivered from the Middle East, Norway or Russia, meaning there could be some dubious connections, depending on the origin. So, we need to speak with the companies that produced and sold the oil and the owner of the ship that delivered it. Perhaps they've seen something like this before, strange as it is."

"More good points. We don't know the precise origin of the oil yet, Stig," Gunnar answered, "but we can ask the refinery to tell us more on that; they are eager to cooperate."

Stig spoke again as he stroked a roughly clipped beard that traced the outline of his jaw and melted into his neck. "Or," he theorized, "perhaps there was something foreign in the tank before the crude was pumped in. A bad batch of cleanser or a fungus, perhaps some other substance that affected the oil after it entered the tank. I can poke around and see who has access to the tanks between resupply and what the protocols are for that," he offered, using his gumshoe instincts. "I'll also pay a call on the tank field security office and review the refinery's security procedures."

"Very well," Bodin responded. He continued, "I think we have some follow-up to do. Let's meet again on Thursday at 14:00. Anna, would you please get in touch with Chalmers University to see if one of its biologists can join us on Thursday to tell us more about the significance of the bacteria being present? Maybe Chalmers can also perform some further experimentation on the bacteria, identify its origins, and augment the report provided by our crime lab."

The formal part of the meeting adjourned, but the team lingered on to finish their coffee and chat further about the unfolding oil tank investigation at the Port. When they were done, the office had closed and the hallways were darkened, but Bodin poked his head into Dalquist's office to give her a summary of how the meeting went, in case she was still there. He found her at her desk, and she looked up at him expectantly.

Eva listened intently and after a moment of silence said, "Gunnar, I'm getting a little old for all of this." She lit up a cigarette, blew out a smoke ring and leaned back into her chair to reflect a bit.

"Tell me about it, Eva."

"You know, I remember way back. When I was young, the air was clean, and sex was dirty. Just look at how things have switched around since then," she said with a sigh.

CH. 9

Gothenburg's Tor Harbor not only serves as a terminal for vessels delivering crude to Scandinavia, but it also maintains a huge underground cavern for interim oil storage and subsequent transshipment to markets outside of Sweden, including Asia and the U.S. The underground cavern, carved out of ancient rock, was a marvel of modern engineering. Recently refurbished and equipped with cutting-edge automation, it stood as a testament to human ingenuity—yet, beneath its sleek exterior, there was a sense of something almost primal, as if the earth itself was holding its breath.

The cavern was seen as more environmentally safe than having ships lightering with oil out at sea. It served as one of the main reasons why nearly 25 million tons of oil passed through the harbor every year.

The harbor's two oil quays were in frequent use. Ships like the *Smolensk II* could berth there and pump their contents to any of several terminals that accepted raw crude, fuel oils or middle distillates.

Two days after the *Smolensk II* had once again put out to sea, a profound stench began accelerating through the series of air vents that were part of the cavern's vapor treatment system, designed to capture and treat any fumes emanating from the Port's oil facility The foul odor was uncontainable by late evening.

At about the same time, air quality meters in the cavern's control room began to display low levels of nonvolatile biogenic compounds rising from the cavern. Sensors detected a mix of carbon monoxide but also some sulfur and other vapors. Sensors also registered increasing air pressure, triggering the alarm in the lightly manned control room.

The skeleton crew on site alerted the head of engineering, Magnus Persson, who was enjoying dinner in his overalls at home when he received the call. Magnus immediately drove to the facility, a tight grip on the steering wheel, his mind racing. He'd overseen the cavern's refurbishment personally, signing off on every system, every protocol. It was supposed to be foolproof, a fortress of safety in a hazardous industry. But now, as the foul odor grew stronger the closer he got to the facility, doubt began to creep in. What had they missed? He arrived on the scene in his electric car thirty minutes later and was greeted at the front gate by an old friend, Ole Ericson, the storage facility's chief of security, who lived in a company-provided, tiny Victorian house on the site.

"Tell me what's happening," Magnus spoke with a puzzled look.

"Well, we are not sure other than the obvious odor," Ole said. "We have some read-outs that are abnormal too, that have me concerned. We need you to look at the controls to see if you can make sense of any of it. I'll have to write an official report for the safety committee and will need your help with the technical details. Let's go down to the control room now," Ole motioned to follow him.

The two entered the storage compound through a security gate which was buzzed open by an obliging guard who first entered their names in the visitor's log. They walked into the modern, one-story edifice and headed for the elevator doors behind the receptionist's desk.

As they descended in the elevator, Magnus couldn't shake the feeling that time was running out. According to text messages he received, the pressure readings were climbing steadily, and the air quality was deteriorating by the minute. If they didn't find the source of the problem soon, the entire facility could be at risk. And with so much oil stored in the cavern, any mishap could spell disaster—not just for the harbor, but for the entire region.

Three floors below, the doors opened to an ultramodern, expansive control room with an open floor plan and group seating at long desks, banks of equipment and an adjacent laboratory. On the far wall of the chamber was a long bank of ceiling to floor windows that enabled viewers to peer down into the huge cavern, much like an observation deck.

The control room was a stark contrast to the dark, foreboding cavern below. Bright fluorescent lights illuminated the space, casting harsh shadows on the rows of monitors and control panels that lined the walls. The hum of machinery filled the air, a constant reminder of the complex systems at work. But tonight, there was an undercurrent of tension that permeated the room—every beep from the consoles, every flicker of the screens seemed amplified, as if the machines themselves were anxious.

The two stepped into the familiar setting and were greeted by Stefan Wahlin, the deputy chief of operations who was waiting anxiously for them.

CH. 10

Karin searched her pocketbook in vain for Daniel's business card, frustration bubbling up as she rifled through old receipts and stray pens.

Can't believe I've misplaced it! How typical of me, she thought, her heart sinking slightly. It wasn't just the card she was missing—it was the ease with which they'd connected on that train ride and then outside her apartment building. She shook off the feeling, determined not to let a small setback ruin what could be an important moment.

Undeterred, she googled the US Consulate in Gothenburg and dialed its general number.

The operator transferred the call to Daniel's assistant, a civil service veteran who in a professional yet sympathetic voice intoned, "Hello, this is Heather Woodland, Mr. Lake's assistant. How may I help you?"

"Hi Ms. Woodland, my name is Karin Lofgren," Karin began. "I met Mr. Lake two Fridays ago on the train ride from Stockholm. I'm embarrassed to say I've misplaced his card which had his cell phone. By any chance is he available?" she asked sincerely.

Heather hesitated for a moment, considering whether she should inform the caller that her boss was in a meeting, or to place her on hold while she told Daniel about the caller. Daniel, sipping coffee nearby, looked at her quizzically. Heather decided to go with her customarily good instincts on this one.

On the other end of the line, Karin breathed a quiet sigh of relief. She wasn't in the habit of calling practical strangers, especially not ones she felt a personal connection with—but something about Daniel had made her bold enough to try. As she waited, her mind raced through potential scenarios. What if he didn't remember her? What if he was too busy? The thought made her stomach tighten, but she forced herself to breathe deeply. It's just a phone call, she reminded herself, but it could be something more.

"Would you please hold a moment, Mr. Lake should be with you shortly," she said with authority. Heather pressed the hold button and told Daniel the name of the caller. His face lit up.

Heather handed Daniel the phone and took it off hold. After a moment, Daniel greeted his caller.

"Hi Karin, what a nice surprise!" Daniel's voice was warm and his tone immediately placing her at ease. "How are you?" he asked, genuinely curious.

"I'm fine, thanks," she replied, feeling a bit of the tension slip away. "Sorry to track you down like this, but I fear I misplaced your card with the cell phone number. I hope it's alright," she offered, trusting she didn't sound too forward.

"Of course," Daniel said, his smile almost audible over the phone. "I'm glad you did."

She paused, then said, "Well, my firm is having its annual client appreciation dinner next Saturday, and we're renting out the Wasa Museum as the venue. I know this is last minute......." Karin continued with optimism in her voice. "But I'm tired of attending these events by myself, and was wondering if....."

Daniel commiserated, having attended countless official functions as a solo. Without so much as a second thought, he mercifully interceded. "You know, I'll be in Stockholm on Friday again, and I would actually *love* to stay over and join you. The Wasa Museum is one of my favorites, and come to think of it, I could even do a little networking with your guests, take their pulse on the business climate, if you wouldn't mind. Nothing official, mind you," he said with a laugh.

"Oh, that would be really great," Karin rejoined. "The firm is putting us up at the Grand Hotel on Friday and Saturday, shall I get you a room there, too?"

"That would be nice, but I can stay at the Embassy, we've got some quarters that are usually available over the weekends. I'll speak with our staff and reserve one of the rooms. If you are free, why don't we also have dinner Friday evening, and pick up where we left off?" he offered.

"Wonderful, Daniel." *Damn he's sweet.*

"Great", have you been to Mårten Danzig's restaurant?

"Yes, I adore the menu there, and the ambience."

"Ok, it's set then. I'll reserve a table and meet you in the lobby of the Grand at 20:00. We can walk to the restaurant from there. I'm looking forward to seeing you again."

Pleased with the call and her decision to invite him, she closed with a simple "Thanks, Daniel, me too."

As he replaced the phone and looked up, Heather's face held an approving smile. "Looks like you've got a busy weekend ahead," she said, her tone light but knowing.

Daniel nodded, already thinking ahead to Friday. *This could be interesting,* he mused, his mind drifting back to that train ride and the intriguing woman who had just invited him into her world. Whatever happened next, he knew one thing for sure—he was looking forward to it.

CH. 11

Pankov was working in his fourth-floor office, standing beside one of the darkened windows and looking down at the street activity in front of his office building, a line of three dark SUVs parked below, when the buzzer on his intercom sounded. The luxury and privacy of his office soothed him, the dim light within casting long shadows that matched the secrets he kept. But today, that silence was broken by the persistent intercom buzz from his secretary, pulling him back into reality he couldn't escape. As he turned away from the window, a bitter taste welled up in his throat.

The suits in the SUVs were now at the gates. The visit by Sergei Mikhailov, the head auditor of the Moscow branch of the Federation's National Settlement Depository (NSD), was unannounced, but not altogether unexpected by Gnady. This is how they all arrived, Pankov understood, in a familiar game of cat and mouse. His fingers drummed a steady rhythm on the edge of his desk as he puckered his mouth and shook his head from side to side, waiting for the inevitable knock. Each finger-beat echoed the ticking clock on the wall, a countdown to the confrontation he knew was coming. Such visits only appeared to be casual, offhand; they were calculated, however, each one a move in a high-stakes game where one misstep could mean ruin.

Mikhailov presented Pankov with a card identifying him as the chief of the NSD's fraud division. The NSD dealt with the debt and equity securities of Russian issuers, providing a range of accounting and storage services to market participants. But it also routinely monitored derivatives, federal bonds and other transactions such as the option contracts traded by private equity firms and investment banks, and it had full autonomy to investigate transactions that fell under its jurisdiction. The NSD held close links to the Moscow Exchange and the Central Bank of Russia which relied on the NSD as a settlement center. It also closely cooperated with the Federal Security Service of the Russian Federation, or FSB, which was akin to the USA's Federal Bureau of Investigation.

Apart from his official duties, the calling card Sergei presented also bestowed him with a literal license to steal. One word from Sergei, and an individual or company could be found guilty without so much as a trial, such was his power. Over the years, Sergei learned how to sew his needle with discretion.

The last thing I need, Gnady thought, is this turdy durak nosing around at this critical point in time.

Gnady sighed, the sound barely audible above the hum of the air conditioner. He could see it coming, the inevitable tango these encounters always followed. His office, a sanctuary of quiet luxury, now felt suffocating under Sergei's gaze. The rich mahogany of his desk, the deep, plush Aubusson carpet, the priceless artwork on the walls— all of it seemed to shrink in the presence of this odious functionary. But Gnady was no stranger to this game. He'd played it before, with men just as repulsive, and he knew exactly how to play his hand. He would simply ask Pankovneft's law firm in Cyprus to open yet another trust account for the blackmailer or one of his greasy family members. It was an open secret that Russian officials, seeking to secure a comfortable lifestyle for themselves, held more untraceable accounts in Cyprus with wealth management firms than practically any other segment of foreign account holders.

Mikhailov, smarmy and overweight by about twenty kilos, had pushed past Pankov's shocked secretary and into Gnady's plush office. He took a generous look around at the luxurious décor before speaking. He had an oversized head with bushy, black eyebrows to match. Before he spoke, he pursed his fat lips.

"Ah, Gnady, you're looking well," Sergei cooed, his pudgy hands spreading wide as if in an embrace. But his eyes, cold and calculating, betrayed the warm tone of his voice. They were the eyes of a predator sizing up its prey. "What a fine place you have. Life must be treating you well, no?"

"State your business, Inspector," Gnady replied in a deep and steely tone, "I have no time for your pleasantries or overstated concerns for my health." It was essential to come off as the alpha male when beginning negotiations.

With a feigned look of hurt, Sergei pouted, "Gnady, there is no reason to be harsh. We have some minor questions about the trading activity we have noticed at Pankovneft and are simply coming to you for advice. Surely you will not deprive my superiors of your wisdom in these matters?" Sergei tendered. "They hold you in such high esteem."

Gnady intoned dryly, "Of course. What exactly do you wish to know?"

But Sergei was totally absorbed with the aura of the Fabergé egg and walked over to it. Without a word, he lifted it from its stand and held it aloft.

Sergei let out a chuckle of joy as he cradled the Fabergé egg, his fat fingers caressing its delicate surface. Gnady watched, his jaw clenched, every muscle in his body tensed with barely controlled fury. The audacity of this man, to touch something so precious, something that symbolized all the power and wealth Gnady had accumulated. But he forced himself to remain calm, knowing that anger was a luxury he couldn't afford right now. Sergei would pay for this— he would pay dearly— but not yet. Gnady needed to buy time, to play along until he could strike.

"Such a beautiful piece, timeless. I would do *anything* to own a treasure such as this. You are a lucky man, indeed." Sergei carefully reset the imperial egg on its holder.

He turned to Gnady and watched him studiously. "Futures contracts, like eggs meant for czars, are full of riddles", Sergei proceeded. "Option contracts have winners and losers. Sometimes the buyers are also sellers looking to hedge their positions. They are frequently unregistered, but everyone knows who the large players are. Such dichotomies," Sergei waxed philosophically.

"All of what you say is well understood by your superiors, whoever they may be. So, what is your point?" a now irritated Gnady flashed.

"Very well, then," answered Sergei in a low tone. "Over the past year or so, in my modest position overseeing the audit activity at the futures exchange, I have noticed that an unusually large volume of crude futures contracts has been bought not only here in Russia, but simultaneously on several other major bourses. Coincidentally, the Chicago Mercantile Exchange and the German DAX, among others, have contacted my office to see why so much forward interest exists, and what we might know about the imbalance. Your firm is one of the Federation's premier players in this market, no? And much of the premium money appears to have flowed out of your firm. So, dear Gnady, what is it that you know, that I should know?"

Gnady sighed. So predictable, he thought. Shaking his head, he said "Sergei, there is nothing I am personally aware of, it's business as usual here. We buy and sell positions to ensure the free flow of oil to Mother Russia and the Federation members. Most honorable. Nothing more, nothing less. Now, if I were to hear something, you have my word that you will be the first to know. In fact, due to the large volume of crude option contracts that you cited, it has become quite costly to purchase oil at a reasonable cost. We not only buy options, but we buy shiploads of crude as well for spot delivery. My firm needs new, steady suppliers just at this moment. Sergei, you are well connected, are you not? Surely you have some excellent ties with producers in Latin America or Southeast Asia. Guyana, perhaps? Or, maybe an acquaintance in Nigeria? I would be happy to reward you handsomely for facilitating introductions to them. Names and numbers are all that is required. Would this interest you?"

"Indeed, it would", Sergei replied with a wry grin. "I welcome such a partnership with you in the interest of aiding the Federation."

"Excellent, I'll set up an account in Cyprus in whatever beneficiary name you provide, of course, to keep our arrangement confidential. It could be a Cyprus company you set up, or maybe a family member….".

"By all means. Please use my daughter's name, Viktoria, if you would. And now, a glass of your fine vodka, dear Gnady, to cement our arrangement?"

Gnady recoiled at yet another affront and found it hard to keep his temper. Drinks with this crooked imbecile?

Sergei walked over to an exotically decorated Bugatti drinks cabinet and opened its doors. He spied on a prize decanter and poured two generous sized shots, pursing his fat lips together a few times in anticipation. As Sergei clinked his glass against Gnady's with a steely *Na zdorovje,* Gnady took consolation in the thought that he had just bought perhaps three or four more months of silence from this presumptuous jerk. Well before then, an absolute fortune would be in hand, and he could afford to *triple* the lucre of all such shits on his payroll.

However, for his brazen lack of grace, Gnady intended to make Sergei pay dearly in due course. This wasn't over— not by a long shot. Gnady detested everything this coarse and insufferable man represented. Sergei's unexplained disappearance would send a clear message to other would-be extorters who thought they could pry into Gnady's affairs. After Pankovneft's intrusion by the unpleasant hacks from the Russian mob, enough was enough, already. But for now, he would play the game, knowing that every move he made brought him closer to the day when Sergei, and others like him, would be nothing more than a footnote in his rise to power.

CH. 12

The security chief at the Port of Gothenburg's storage facility and refinery complex welcomed his old friend Stig at the front door of the prefab trailer home that served as his office. The trailer, though unassuming from the outside, perched sturdily on a foundation of cinder blocks, its weathered exterior standing in stark contrast to the high-tech facility it oversaw. Inside, the air was thick with the scent of strong coffee and the faint, lingering odor of oil—a reminder of the facility's constant activity. The narrow central hall led to small, cramped rooms, their sterile fluorescent lights casting harsh shadows on the walls, giving the place an almost clinical feel.

Stig helped himself to a cup of coffee and added two heaping spoons of sugar to it. After tossing the wooden stir, he turned and peered at the stack of boxes which sat on the oval conference table in front of him and felt a familiar sense of anticipation.

"As you can see, we've taken the liberty of assembling a few things before you came over," the security chief said.

The files in the boxes represented pieces of the puzzle, and Stig had always been good at seeing the bigger picture. He glanced at the security chief, who was watching him with a mix of curiosity and concern. "Thanks for getting these together," Stig said, his voice steady.

"We've gathered the following items for the last two years," he began. "The names of oil vendors having access to the tanks are here, plus their contract files. The boxes are alphabetical, there are six of them in total. Mostly chronological delivery information once you get inside each company file. Next, you'll find a log with names of ships and references to their manifests. These ten boxes contain summaries of lab analysis of the deliveries, but if you wish to inspect a complete report of each sample analysis the lab performed, I will have to get those from off-site storage for you. Lastly, I've brought along the original security log which my office maintains. Hardly any outsiders ever visit the tanks, as we use our own employees for weekly inspections. I've reviewed the log myself, and in the last month there were no unusual entries as far as I am concerned, but naturally you will want to confirm that yourself. You can make copies of anything you wish, but if you don't mind, we would like to keep the originals here under lock and key while our internal investigation continues," he noted.

Stig nodded in appreciation. "Before I dig in, I'd like to visit the tank field including tank 71, see what it looks like. Could you take me there?"

"Of course," replied the security chief. "We can go by bike. That's the quickest way." He paused for a moment, glancing at Stig with a hint of unease. "It's been quiet out there since the contamination was discovered, but something about this doesn't feel right. I'm glad you're here to take a look."

The two left the office and the security chief led them to a nearby bike shed. They followed along a macadam path adjacent to the security fence until they peddled to tank 71. Stig gazed upward.

"Who has been here since the contamination of the tank was discovered?" he inquired.

"Well, me of course. Two analysts from our lab and one from yours. It's isolated here. We've left it unguarded. Oh, also Detective Larsson who initially responded to my call. I think that's all."

"Alright, has anyone noticed anything unusual; something broken, out of place?"

"No," the security chief replied, "All seems in order."

"Then why this particular tank?" Stig mused aloud, his eyes narrowing as he surveyed the grounds in front of him. "What strikes me is its location. It's pretty far away from the office complex, and out of sight. If someone wanted to tamper with a tank, it was likely to be this one. Not visible from the road and is about as close to the water as any of them. And that perimeter fence, it's begging for trouble. For years now we have been warning the refinery that this entire complex is vulnerable to sabotage or attack. The tanks and the entire refinery complex are sitting ducks as far as that goes. It's clear to me that if anyone *was* to target one of the tanks, these are the ones they would most likely choose. He felt a chill run down his spine as he spoke, the implications of his words sinking in. "Easy in, easy out," Stig concluded, "no likelihood of being surprised or discovered. Whoever did this understood exactly what they were doing."

"I can agree if you believe there was an attack involving a saboteur or some other type of mischief maker," said the security chief with doubt in his voice. "But the more likely scenario has to do with those bugs that we found in the samples. We'll know more as soon as the DNA test results are in," he added with confidence.

Meanwhile, Stig walked over to the fence and knelt in a crouching position, until he was able to eyeball the ground from a low angle. "Look here," Stig said, motioning to the ground. He crouched down, his fingers tracing the faint depressions and skid marks in the gravel. The security chief joined him, his breath catching as he saw the evidence of recent activity. "These weren't made by accident," Stig murmured, his voice tense. "Someone's been here recently, and they didn't want to be seen. We need to check the other side of the fence—if there are fresh footprints, we might be dealing with more than just contamination. This could be the work of a saboteur."

The security chief's heart raced as he followed Stig, the reality of the situation sinking in. They were on the brink of uncovering something much more dangerous than he'd anticipated.

CH. 13

For years, the mysterious metabolism of micro-organisms such as *A. Borkumensis* had baffled scientists. The way these bacteria devoured hydrocarbons was a puzzle that remained unsolved—until the genome project helped to unlock the secrets hidden within their DNA. With the ability to decode the oil-eating genes and understand the inner workings of these cells, a new frontier of bioengineering was suddenly within reach. But this breakthrough wasn't just about scientific curiosity; it was a race against time, with enormous stakes. If Carlsson could harness this power, he understood the SBF would not only revolutionize oil spill clean-up technology but also potentially hold the key to forcibly ending the world's dependency on fossil fuels.

Carlsson's goal for the SBF was to decode the secrets of the bacteria and be the first developer of a genetically modified version with an enhanced ability to literally eat oil and multiply at a speed not seen before. He toyed with the thought of obtaining patent protection for his creation, as such protection for living organisms was now available in the developed markets. A designer bug able to clean up spills would have a high valuation and years of exclusive protection. Deploying such microbes at oil spill sites would largely supplant traditional cleanup techniques, especially ones made ineffective in the northernmost oil fields located in the Barents Sea and Alaskan North Slope, where the wintry climate inhibited spill recovery.

Successful exploitation of such organisms would enable his Foundation to greatly expand the number of its projects, the scope of its research and its advocacy for a cleaner, more sustainable environment.

It was Pankov's failsafe proposal and funding of clinical milestones that actually got the ball rolling. After the project began, Axel divided the SBF's research work into three experiment workstreams to ultimately propagate the organisms with a turbo-charged appetite for eating carbon molecules. One team, comprised of biologists and geo-chemists, studied the ocean floor habitat where the bacteria lived to learn which enhancements to their environment would help them thrive. This work was outsourced to a Danish oceanographic firm. It turned out that ordinary seawater having a pH level of around 8 was all the bacteria needed, apart from a food source. A second team of bio-engineering scientists and pharmacologists worked on altering the microbe's ability to metabolize oil. This team, working in donated lab space from a nearby pharmaceutical manufacturer, concentrated its focus on the enzymes the bugs created to break down and digest complex hydrocarbon molecules. The last team was led personally by Axel at the SBF lab at Marstrand, where he used data developed from the first two teams to experiment in genetically altering the more resilient specimens that they isolated from ocean water samples and then grew in petri dishes. By experimenting with genetic combinations, Axel finally produced a strain of *Oceanospirillum* that voraciously consumed oil and required only the smallest amounts of oxygen, opportunely generated as a byproduct of the digestion process. The only thing that could stop his creation's hyperbolic growth was running out of a liquid hydrocarbon food supply. Best of all, by manipulating the microbe's reproductive process, the bacteria underwent binary fission every six minutes. Designing cells that divided more rapidly became increasingly difficult, as they needed time to consume a great deal of food, rearrange their molecules — including DNA and proteins — and finally split into two cells. He considered his lab creation to be finally optimized after rounds of experimentation, when he proved that exponential pullulating made the designer species capable of overwhelming and neutralizing a hypothetical, large spill in a matter of days.

As Axel's experiments progressed, a chilling realization began to take shape in his mind. His creation, while designed to devour oil quickly, had the potential to do much more. It could not only neutralize oil stored in tanks but also consume entire underground fields of oil. The implications were staggering. What had started as a hail Mary insurance policy to help Pankov hedge his option contract bets was now a force that could cripple the global economy. Axel knew he had created something powerful—perhaps too powerful. But with that power came the possibility of radical change, and he wasn't sure if he could—or should—keep it contained.

Over the years, Axel's commitment to environmental causes had evolved from concern to obsession. The more he learned about the devastating impact of fossil fuels, including microplastics, the more he felt driven to act. It wasn't just about cleaning up spills anymore; it was about stopping the damage at the source. Each new study, each grim report on climate change and its effects on marine life, fueled a fire of retribution within him. Axel's frustration grew to the point where he could no longer stand by and watch as politicians debated and delayed as the planet suffered. His work at the SBF had become more than a job—it was a *mission*, and his genetically modified bacteria were the weapon he needed to make a difference. He had become particularly intolerant of the world's unsustainable thirst for fossil fuels and its slow pace in converting to greener energy alternatives. He was alarmed by the effect of carbon-based energy and greenhouse gases on climate change and its devastation to marine life. And he anguished over the ocean's corrosive warming of the barrier reefs, expansive ribbons of which were already bleached out and crumbling.

With his genetically modified *Oceanospirillum* bacteria, Axel comprehended that he possessed a more powerful weapon in the fight against global warming than whatever measures an army of dithering, carbon tax-obsessed politicians might dream up.

Pankov, with his deep pockets and shadowy influence, continued to fund the SBF's operations, seemingly oblivious to the Pandora's box Axel had opened. But Axel knew the time had come when he would force the world's leaders to confront the consequences of their inaction, and his bacteria would be the catalyst for revolutionary change.

He drafted up an anonymous Manifesto, which he planned to share with Pankov, meant to force the G7 nations to decrease their use of carbon, or the bacteria would be unleashed upon the world, causing a panic over the global supply of oil. In one move, Axel would satisfy Gnady's need to suddenly increase the price of oil and achieve his own lifelong goal of ending world's addiction to fossil fuels. He realized the SBF would have to sacrifice commercially exploiting the bacteria, since he could not afford to have them traced back to him after the harm he caused at the port's oil storage facility. There would be no golden annuity of royalty streams from licensing the patent. But that was a sacrifice he was willing to make. His interest in forcing environmental change *now* was aligned with Gnady's need for a skin-saving spike in the price of crude.

Yet, in the back of his mind, a nagging fear lingered. What if the timing of releasing the bacteria on the world came too soon? What if, in their rush to end the world's dependency on oil, they unleashed something far more destructive? Axel pushed the thought aside, but it refused to be silenced. He had created a weapon, and weapons had a way of turning on their creators.

As Axel stood in his lab, gazing at the petri dishes where his creation thrived, he couldn't escape the gravity of what he had done. This wasn't just a scientific achievement, it was a turning point, one that could lead to either salvation or catastrophe. If he played his cards right, the threat of his new life-form could offer an elegant solution to the world's addiction to oil. But what if it spiraled out of control? What if the bacteria escaped the confines of oil storage tanks, spreading unchecked and wiping out oil reserves across the globe? Oppenheimer himself had faced similar unknowns when he unleashed the powerful chain reaction of the atomic bomb. Axel's mind raced ahead with the possibilities, each more terrifying than the last. He was holding the future in his hands, and the weight of that responsibility was almost too much to bear.

CH. 14

Nodding toward the cavern below, Magnus spoke to the deputy chief of operations, a young engineer who enjoyed working the evening shift. "Stefan, I need a summary of the readings, and I need it fast," he said, his voice edged with the tension of the escalating crisis.

"Of course," Stefan replied, his eyes flicking nervously over the fresh notes on his clipboard. The control room was bathed in the harsh glare of fluorescent lights, the air thick with the acrid scent of oil combined with and the faint but unmistakable stench of something far more dangerous. "So far, the air pressure in there is at .83 bars, and it's rising steadily," he continued, his voice low. The steady hum of machinery around them seemed to pulse in time with the growing tension, each beat a reminder of the pressure building below.

"As you know, there should be very little pressure. The vent system is more than adequate to control it for now. But the whole facility and everyone in it will be at risk if the pressure rises further and the fumes begin to permeate into the office complex. The vents have leaky joints, they're decades old and take only so much pressure anyways. Noxious fumes are spewing through them as we speak, contaminating the air we breathe. You can already smell them. We can keep pumping fresh air down here as long as the pressure holds steady, but that won't be long, judging from the steady rate of acceleration. We're basically sitting in the middle of a balloon that's being blown up. From a safety standpoint, my best guess is that we will need to evacuate the control room in the next few hours. Of course, we can prolong the evacuation and keep working down here to monitor the situation with the help of oxygen compression suits and tanks. But if it turns out the air is flammable as I suspect, we will be forced to leave. My crew is readying the suits, just in case."

"Is there anything else we need to know?" Magnus asked, his voice tense. He could feel the weight of the situation pressing down on him, every second ticking by like a countdown to disaster. "Have you collected samples of the oil and air yet? We need answers, and we need them now."

"I called in a lab tech to collect both, and he is working on it now. He noticed immediately, though, that the oil had clearly changed, its color and the viscosity were not right. We have excellent techniques for oil analysis and should know more from the sample in about an hour. The air sample will take a little more time," Stefan conceded, a knot of anxiety tightening in his chest.

Ole spoke next. "Alright, given the fact that the oil is somehow changing, I need to alert the State Office of National Security. The oil stored down there must be worth billions of Kronor. The owners, private and publicly held companies, won't be pleased with what's apparently happening. Not to mention the safety risk to our personnel and our likely need to evacuate. We're sitting on a powder keg, and if we don't act quickly, the fallout could be catastrophic. This looks to me like a repeat of the situation last week at the storage tank farm, but on a much more massive scale. I sit on the Port's safety committee, and its security chief briefed us on their situation which is still under police investigation. One entire tank of crude somehow spoiled and turned into useless slime. No one knows how or when it happened, but we just might be witnessing the same process here and now. It's up in the air whether this is a possible crime or natural occurrence, but either way, we have a rare opportunity here to monitor the oil's transformation in real time. That's something which is over my head. The right resources will be needed," he reflected out loud.

"We need to develop a plan— fast," Ole said, the urgency in his voice unmistakable. "There's a lot to manage, and we can't afford to make any mistakes. Every decision we make now could be the difference between containment and catastrophe. For now, let's get everyone out of here. I think I've heard enough, and there's no point in risking life any longer. We can monitor the situation from a safer distance, but no one needs to stay here and breathe in this shitty air."

Stefan and Magnus nodded in agreement, their expressions grim. As the three men made their way out of the facility, the tension among them was palpable, each one silently contemplating the disaster unfolding on his watch. But as they stepped outside, the disgusting stench of the fumes lingered in the air, a reminder that the danger was far from over. They knew that whatever was happening in the cavern below was only the beginning—and the real test was yet to come.

CH. 15.

It was a blustery Friday afternoon later that week when Daniel was given the key to the Stockholm Embassy's guest suite which he reserved for the weekend. His favorite room was available, a sanctuary of neo-classical elegance that never failed to soothe his senses. The parquet oak floors gleamed in the soft afternoon light, each step producing a gentle creak that added to the chamber's old-world charm. Ceiling-length damask curtains framed the windows, their rich burgundy fabric lending warmth to the room, while the garden views outside provided a tranquil retreat from the bustling metropolis. A small floral arrangement graced the marble-topped coffee table, filling the air with the aroma of roses and peonies. Here, in this cosseted refuge, the pressures of his work seemed distant, at least for the moment.

At the Grand Hotel closer to town, Karin checked in and took the brass-accented elevator to the fifth floor, her heart beating a little faster with each passing floor. The soft chime of the elevator bell brought her back to the moment as the doors slid open. She stepped into her room, taking in the serene color palette and the elegant Gustavian furnishings. The quiet luxury of the space was calming, yet she couldn't shake the anticipation building within her. Each moment was a step closer to the unknown, and the possibilities it held.

A bottle of sparkling mineral water and a welcome note left by her firm rested on the desk opposite the bed. She glanced into the bathroom, where the walls and floor were covered in old grey and white veined marble. After unpacking her suitcase, Karin showered, enjoying the luxury of towels heated beside the shower door. Then she slipped into a chic Max Mara cocktail dress and took a case from her luggage containing a strand of smoky grey pearls with matching earrings she had bought in a Beijing jewelry market some years before. After fastening the necklace, she looked in the mirror, her lips slightly parted, deciding whether to apply lipstick or simply some gloss, and settled on the latter in the end. Then she sat down to apply some blush and brush her hair.

Daniel unpacked and hung up his clothes to loosen their wrinkles a bit. After showering, he shaved and dressed in the mirror. He chose an open-collared white shirt, a blue hounds-tooth Italian sport coat with a pocket square, and grey wool trousers.

Each contemplated their evening together, their thoughts a mixture of excitement and curiosity. Karin couldn't help but wonder what the night might bring, feeling a flutter of nervousness she hadn't experienced in years. It wasn't quite a date, but it felt like one—a chance to reconnect, to see where their paths might lead. Daniel, too, found himself smiling at the thought of their dinner, the easy conversation on the train still fresh in his mind. He was intrigued by her—her intelligence, her grace, and the way she seemed to carry a world of stories behind her eyes. As they prepared for the evening, both couldn't help but wonder if this meeting might be the start of something more.

With some time to spare before dinner, Daniel sank into one of the two *bergères* flanking the pedestal table in front of the window that overlooked the garden. In the diffused light he began reading the *Dagens Industrie*. On the first page ran a feature story concerning the enquiry over the unfolding events at Gothenburg's oil storage cavern in Tor Harbor. Word of the massive contamination had leaked out to the ever-watchful Swedish press, which was playing the story up sensationally. Indeed, scientific teams from the U.S., Russia, and an assortment of oil company giants had been dispatched to survey the loss and provide help in whichever way they could. The article recounted the evacuation that was hastily ordered after a putrid stench enveloped the area but then abruptly dissipated after a day. The nearby Akusborg suspension bridge had to be closed over concerns for safety, and since it spanned the Gota River and linked Hisingen Island to the city, traffic was snarled around town for two days. Quoting from anonymous government sources, reporters linked the cavern and tank farm losses together and confirmed that the oil in each facility was deemed a total loss. They openly called into question the Port's security and future viability as a strategic oil depot and refinery, with its proximity to the City of Gothenburg. There was speculation on where new shipments of oil to Scandinavia might be diverted until a new, more secure facility could be built. Dutch and Danish firms were said to be interested. The implications for the city were profound. A related article mentioned the opening of a criminal investigation, and yet another article reported on the weeklong string of trading sessions in which the price of crude oil futures had snapped higher with each passing trading session. Journalists from Reuters, AP and assorted international press had descended upon Gothenburg to report on the science teams' progress and see what they might uncover in this breaking story.

Daniel closed the paper and sat quietly for a few moments, the weight of the news settling over him. The chaos in Gothenburg was certain to consume his next few weeks, with the consulate likely becoming a hub of activity. He knew that the stakes were high, not just for the Swedish government, but for the international community as well. He expected to meet with city and national officials to offer the full support of his office and the assistance of specialized U.S. agencies such as the EPA, the CDC and others. He felt badly for the Swedish government which faced a looming public relations disaster if it couldn't get to the bottom of the situation quickly, and he vowed to do whatever he could to help with the situation. Yet, even as his mind raced with the tasks ahead, his thoughts kept drifting back to the evening with Karin. There was a strange comfort in knowing that amid the turmoil, there was something personal, something human, to look forward to. It wasn't just another social obligation; it was a chance to escape, if only for a few hours, into a world where things were simpler, where a conversation over dinner could bring a sense of normalcy.

There was also something about the unfolding events that felt like calm before the storm— not just in his work, but in his life. And as he prepared to meet Karin, he couldn't shake the feeling that the night would bring more than just dinner; it might bring a turning point, in ways he hadn't yet imagined.

CH. 16

The pavement glistened from the overnight rain as Gunnar approached the stairs to the crime unit where he and his team worked. Thick, huge clouds billowed overhead in the early dawn. He reached into the pocket of his raincoat to fish out a security pass and then let himself in the door. The officer stationed in the lobby grunted as Gunnar passed him by. It was only 07:00, and Gunnar had come in early to prepare with his team for an 08:30 meeting that Deputy Chief Dahlqvist had texted them to attend.

Gunnar and his team were seated at the conference table and chatting when Dahlqvist entered the conference room accompanied by Anna and Professor Mats Gisslen. Anna had introduced Gisslen to her boss a few minutes earlier. Stig, a keen observer, eyeballed the Professor, thinking he very much looked the part, not unlike Indiana Jones, with rounded wire spectacles, disheveled hair and a solid knit tie underneath a wool cardigan with worn elbow patches. He was also a handsome man, with intelligent eyes, an average build and a strong chin. Entering the room last was Thor Bjornsson, an intelligence officer with the State Office of National Security, based in Stockholm. Stig perceived the officer too had the requisite official air about him, all business, with brown hair clipped short, a smooth complexion and ripped build. Everyone stood up during their introductions, exchanged cards and then helped themselves to coffee.

Dahlquist began. "Professor Gisslen has joined us today to help us understand more about the organism that overwhelmed the oil tank at the refinery. He was also fortunate enough to have spent some hours on site at Tor Harbor, monitoring the spread of the contamination. The Professor has been retained by the State Office of National Security. Officer Bjornsson is also here to be updated on our investigation. He will serve as the central contact between the City of Gothenburg's police department, Port Security and the National Security office. His main contact in our office will be Gunnar. Our offices are now in full cooperation with each other."

"Thank you for inviting me," the Professor began. "As Deputy Chief Dahlqvist just said, I've been asked by the government to lead the technical aspects of this investigation. My goal is to identify the organism responsible for spoiling the oil and advise on how to contain it. I have priority access to all of Chalmers University's resources as well as the Swedish health, oceanographic, mycological and epidemiological services, among others.

"What we discuss here is classified under the State Secret laws. I have been authorized to brief you on what we know about the organism so far and to answer any questions that you have. We believe it is important for you to understand what it is we are dealing with, to help you determine how to provide security for the Port's oil services infrastructure, since it has been targeted twice thus far. My team will also be working with police in other potential target areas of Sweden to make sure they are brought up to speed and understand the risks and challenges. Any questions so far?" There were none.

"The process of identifying a microbe is straight forward enough. Chalmers has a class-A lab service which routinely examines microbes referred by the State's Health Services Department to us. This most often happens when they need to pinpoint contamination in various production environments, from plant and animal processing facilities to restaurants. We use DNA sequencing and microscopic analysis, and this gives us a quick and accurate result. Unfortunately, when we checked our first samples, we were not able to match them with any known species of bacteria, fungus or other organism in our database. This initially led us to believe that our little friend came from outside of Scandinavia, as they frequently do. The Port of Gothenburg receives a huge variety of imports from all over the world, so finding a DNA match to local organisms is not a sure thing. So, we compared its DNA samples to those at GenBank, an international DNA sequence database that pretty much covers everything from standard flu viruses to the black plague, at the low end of the phylogenic tree. Much to our mutual surprise, they could not validate a match either. So, we believe we have a newly discovered and unclassified life form that occurs naturally, has mutated, or was created in a lab. For several reasons I do not need to bore you with, we believe it is the latter. There are some telltale markers that have us greatly concerned.

"When I arrived at the oil cavern complex in Tor Harbor, I only had a few hours to work before we received the evacuation order. Within the oil samples I took, luckily there were some live micro-organisms, and we have been keeping them well-nourished in Chalmers' lab. They are amazingly active and efficient, metabolically speaking. To thrive, they simply require an organic environment having a lengthy hydrocarbon backbone, as the organism is a chemoorganotroph. Its DNA resembles that of a strain of bacteria we have seen primarily living near the ocean floor. That's as close as we have come to classifying this microbe. And we do not yet know how it changes the oil. Ingestion is likely but other processes or methods could be at work. So, more analysis is needed to understand how oil gets broken down by the organism. We also plan to run a series of antimicrobial testing to determine the best ways to disinfect these little bastards. That will take some more experimentation, so we have frozen several samples for future study."

"Thank you for this introduction, Professor. "Are there any questions?" Anna surveyed the room. There still were none, but Stig finally spoke up after Gunnar nodded his approval.

"When I visited the refinery last week, I noticed some scuff marks in the gravel on either side of the perimeter fencing. It was clear to me the markings were human footprints, recently made. Someone obviously climbed over the fence, very near tank 71. So, we believe industrial sabotage is a possible motive, but we are also considering other motives and investigating them as well. We also plan to learn more about crew members taking shore leave from vessels that recently berthed at piers next to the harbor's oil storage cavern. We hope to have some profiles developed soon."

"Very good, please press on and keep me updated," Bjornsson said. "I would also appreciate it if you could send me a summary of the protective resources you have at your disposal to add to a comprehensive, nation-wide security plan we are developing. It's vitally important that business continues as usual for the Port and beyond, with no further incidents."

Intelligence Officer Bjornsson was pleased when he heard Gunnar tell him that an enhanced security plan was already being prepared and that a crisis committee staffed with Port personnel had already held its initial meeting. He would review them with

State security specialists and see what additional resources could be provided. Gunnar offered to share minutes from each meeting with Bjornsson.

Bjornsson then said, "To facilitate regular comms, we are scheduling Zoom meetings twice per week, and I would like this team to join them. My assistant will email the invitations to you with a secure link."

The meeting ended with Deputy Chief Dahlqvist thanking Professor Gisslen and Officer Bjornsson and assuring them that she and her team looked forward to cooperating with them and solving the mystery that had gripped the region.

CH. 17

After the meeting, Anna informed her colleagues that she planned to spend the afternoon visiting the Port's Registry Office, which maintained the list of vessels calling on Gothenburg's terminal facilities. Commercial ships entering the Port were obliged to register with the Office, whose staff in turn assisted in referring local suppliers for restocking a ship's canteen, making repairs and so forth. For convenience, the Registry was also authorized to issue day passes to crew members on behalf of the Immigration Office. Anna wanted to develop profiles of people who might have played a role in the sabotage which both Stig and Gunnar suspected.

Anna called the Port Registry for an appointment and asked for a list of all the vessels that had entered the Port during the previous two weeks. The manager of the department was all too willing to comply with the Inspector's request. He estimated there were upwards of two hundred ships with international crews who could have been given entry visas during the period in question.

Arriving on time, Anna was escorted from the lobby to an antechamber that looked as if it had not been touched in a hundred years. Even the air seemed a bit stale as it hovered above the burnished, wide-plank floorboards.

Something about these old mariners, she thought. *They love to preserve their past.*

The amber-hued, quarter-sawn oak walls were adorned with half-hull models of brigs, clippers and tugs from the nineteenth century. She walked over to them and marveled at their detailed construction. Also gracing the walls were double rows of sailor-made ship portraits framed under glass and made from polychrome wool, known simply as "woolies." Anna paused before an especially beautiful example to admire a composition that featured a large bark on rough seas, surmounted with three crowns that were flanked on either side by a blue and yellow ribbon flag that traced a large arabesque against a blazing sky. Sextants and various other nautical instruments also adorned the room's walls, conjuring the Port's rich seafaring heritage.

Before long, a staffer carrying a box of folders arrived.

"Do you have an ID?" he inquired.

"Yes, this is my security photo and here is my badge," which he dutifully examined.

Satisfied, he escorted Anna to a space that was used as the captain's guest lounge. It faced the wide river just below. A bank of windows allowed an even stream of light into the room from the clouded sky to the north.

Turning to business, the staffer said, "You can work over there and are free to use our amenities." He motioned toward a cut-glass tray of assorted tea cookies and an old electric kettle poised next to it.

"And the lady's room is down that hall," he said, pointing to Anna's left. Then he placed the box on a worktable, and Anna thanked him before settling into one of the room's overstuffed leather sofas.

"Feel free to stay here as long as you like. Our office remains open 24/7. I'll be upstairs, just call on the intercom if you need anything. I'm at extension seventeen." And with that he departed.

Anna took the top folder from the box and began to read it in the tranquil room. Inside each folder was a hefty spreadsheet with chronological details of ship entries from the last two weeks. Fresh printouts contained details on each ship such as its name, type, owner, manager, home port, flag, tonnage, length of draft, deadweight, custom's declaration sheet, a manifest of crew names and contact information. It was thus easy for her to start narrowing her search, as she went through the folders.

First, she placed a checkmark next to the names of ships that anchored at the two quays that took delivery of oil bound for the huge storage cavern. There was no other way for a crewmember from other ships to gain access to this area of the Port. It took about four hours to complete her review, and just a mere eight ships received checkmarks next to their names. For the most part, all the other ships carried dry goods, and consequently they docked at the numerous terminals and wharves closer to the city, a good distance from the underground oil storage cavern, refinery and tank farm.

From her list of eight ships, she next crossed out all local shipping lines, most of which shuttled predictably back and forth from the Port to the Nordic Sea, transporting oil pumped directly from the ocean floor off the Norwegian coast. Not much of a security risk there, she reasoned. That left only four tankers to prioritize in her review, including one of Panamanian registry that delivered oil from Venezuela, two Russian transporters that emptied loads from the depot at Murmansk and one Israeli vessel drawing a load due to disruptions in the Egyptian supply lines near Gaza.

During the rest of the day, Anna concentrated on the crews from these ships. She called the Consulate Offices representing each tanker and requested dossiers on each crew member, including any prior criminal convictions. The list was surprisingly small, confirmed by the staffer who told Anna that such ships were highly automated and needed only a few sailors to handle the work.

It wasn't until before lunchtime the next day that a list of suspects with the right profiles emerged from the emails Anna received, a total of three sailors, two of which received day passes during their stay in Gothenburg. All the Israelis were squeaky-clean; most had high security clearances from their former service in the Israeli navy. The one Panamanian suspect had not taken shore leave according to the Registry's file. So, that left the two crewmembers on board the Russian liner *Smolensk II* who were candidates for questioning. Each had spent time in the Port. Pleased with the research, Anna left the Registry Office and drove back to the office where she went straight to Stig's cubicle to share her findings.

Stig opened Anna's two files on the Russians and began to thumb through their contents.

"There's not a lot to go on," Anna cautioned. "The first sailor, Luk'yan Sakolsky, was age twenty-six and served three years' jail time at prison 44, one of a few hundred such places spread out across Siberia. He was sent there for aggravated assault after a drunken spree. He was denied early parole, based on his poor attitude while serving time. Sakolsky spent just one day in Gothenburg according to his electronic visa records. The second sailor, Dima Mostov, is aged thirty-eight and has a record as a drug dealer in Moscow and Murmansk. He spent three days on shore leave in Gothenburg."

There were fingerprint records and photographs of each seaman plus a copy of their passports.

Stig pointed to the Mostov file. "Well, either one could be involved, but this fellow spent the most time on the streets in Gothenburg. He's older and a petty crook too, unlike the other one who seems to be a simple alcoholic thug, from a third-tier city. My money is on Mostov. This guy's been around, nothing would be beneath him."

Anna nodded her head in agreement. And each recognized how difficult it would be to question a sailor whose ship had already been put out to sea.

CH. 18

The *Smolensk II* had made good time out on the open sea to the west of Norway, but now she was encountering large surges that pushed and pulled the hollow tanker as she steamed southeast on the last leg of her return voyage. Instinctively, the captain steered the vessel closer to the coast, where shallower waters would offer some protection from the large, frigid rollers bearing down from the arctic as the ship made her final approach to her home port of Murmansk.

In the darkness of his cabin, Dima Mostov heard a sharp "snap", followed by a high-pitched screech, and he rolled with satisfaction from his bunk, steadying himself on the glossily painted floor as he stood up. In pitch black, he deftly switched on the lamplight riveted above his locker door and peered across the room to the prize that waited: a dark grey rat whose twist-ed neck was caught in the trap's burgundy-stained teeth. The vermin's glassy eyes bulged, and its hind legs and tail twitched sporadically. Dima crouched down to pick up the trusty steel trap. He lifted the hinged bar to release the ensnared rodent and dropped it with a thud into a waiting garbage pail. Then he re-baited the trap with a thin slice of cured sausage and placed it back on the floor. He poured himself a shot of vodka, straight up, from the bottle he kept in a dresser drawer and toasted his dead adversary.

Filthy bastards, I'll get each and every one of you.

Once again lying in his bunk and gazing up at the crusty rivets in the low ceiling above, he began imagining what he might do with the large sum of rubles he'd collect for the quick side job he performed while docked at Gothenburg's oil terminal. It was three days since the ship's departure from the port, and he was looking forward to calling on Nadia, a charming prostitute he frequently patronized, as she understood his curious desires. He would bring her a bottle from the two cases of high-quality Swedish vodka he bought on one of his shore excursions. Together, they would share a night or two of debauchery in celebration of his homecoming. The rest of the vodka, cigarette cartons and *snus* he purchased would be bartered back in Murmansk for other favors in the weeks ahead. There was no lack of demand for quality items among the weak, the bold, the rich and the poor.

This had been a very profitable trip, he thought contentedly.

Nadia was a sympathetic listener as well, so he had confided in her about being approached by none other than one of Pankovneft's security officers. The officer engaged him to meet with that weedy, arrogant Swede in Gothenburg and follow the instructions he would be given. The connection between Pankovneft and the oil his ship just delivered seemed innocuous enough, and he paid little attention to it.

This was an easy assignment, and it had worked out fine, he told himself and began to wonder what new business he could drum up. Before drifting off to sleep, Dima clicked the light off and took the precaution of strapping himself into his bunk, for the empty tanker had begun to bob and roll uncomfortably in the increasingly restive sea.

After Lundquist's update, Stig returned to his cubicle and booted up his PC. He typed in the URL for Cargoview, a commercial vessel tracking service used not only by the shipping lines but also by government agencies and security services around the world. Cargoview offered its customers a variety of knowledge services, including the ability to monitor the whereabouts of vessels in real time through satellite tracking. Another point and click feature allowed users to bring up data on any ship targeted by the user in the system. Stig felt confident that Cargoview's positioning information would locate the *Smolensk II*. He worried, though, whether it had already reached its home port of Murmansk, placing the two sailors identified by Anna outside the reach of INTERPOL. Extradition of persons from the Russian Federation had proven to be nearly impossible in recent years; on the other hand, the legal procedure for detaining a person of interest for questioning outside of Russia was very straightforward. The latter was what Stig was aiming to achieve.

Stig entered his password, clicked onto the website's search box, and typed in the *Smolensk II's* international registry number from the case notes he received from Anna. The powerful search engine took a few moments to troll through its database and conjure a live aerial satellite view of the ship on his screen. To Stig's relief, it still was on the high seas, approaching Norway's Varanger Peninsula. With three clicks he zoomed out to enlarge the map to measure how far the vessel was from land. Through the GPS's time and distance calculation, Stig read that the empty ship was within the Norwegian economic zone and steaming at peak speed of about twenty-four knots, suggesting she only had at most fifteen hours left on the open sea before reaching Russia's territorial waters. Stig next clicked onto the website's doppler radar view and with dismay eyeballed a heavy bank of clouds descending fast from the Arctic northwest. It looked as if the ship might be overtaken by an early snowstorm. He assumed the ship's captain was also tracking the fast-moving storm and surely felt the swelling of its high waves. This sector of the Artic was notoriously storm prone. With the system's intensity glowing on his radar screen, Stig realized that the ship's captain would push hard to reach safe harbor from the treacherous waters as quickly as possible.

It would be close, but Stig was determined. He went back to Anna's office, and together they walked to Gunnar and Eva's offices for a quick chat. He hoped they would all agree to call Officer Bjornsson in Stockholm to arrange an arrest warrant for Mostov through INTERPOL. Bjornsson would need to convince a Swedish prosecutor to issue an INTERPOL red notice, the form used by all member countries of INTERPOL to officially demand the arrest of a wanted suspect or criminal.

Napping in his bunk, midshipman Mostov had no appreciation for just how much he and the lifeless rat had in common.

CH. 19

"Bjornsson here."

"Officer Bjornsson, this is Eva Dahlqvist in Gothenburg. Captain Bodin and officers Renell and Peng are here as well. Do you have a moment?"

"Of course, Detective."

"I just emailed to you a file on Dima Mostov, a crewman on the tanker *Smolensk II* which left Gothenburg last Tuesday. She's sailing off Norway's coast, *en route* to her home port in the Russian Federation, it appears. We believe there is sufficient cause to detain this man for questioning in connection with the sabotage of the Port's oil facilities. A review of all non-Nordic crew from ships with access to the underground storage cavern and who took shore leave in the last two weeks boils down to this prime suspect. We hope you also concur there is sufficient cause to file a red notice with INTERPOL. But we need to move quickly. The *Smolensk II* is approaching its home port of Murmansk."

"I understand. The immediate issue is how to provisionally arrest and detain Mostov when we have no jurisdiction. He's aboard a Russian-flagged ship, and I don't see the Federation readily cooperating to hand over one of its citizens to Sweden. They'll want him as much as we do, he may have protection for all we know. Moreover, Sweden's stance on most matters relating to the Federation has been one of neutrality."

Lieutenant Dahlqvist spoke up. "Mostov is on a Russian ship alright, but that ship is still in Norwegian waters. What if we were to request another country to file the international red notice? Basically, take Sweden out of the equation."

"It would need to be a government having a legitimate interest in detaining Mostov," Bjornsson advanced, thinking out loud.

Stig volunteered, "That's easy. Companies based in Norway, the U.S., Denmark and other countries *own* the oil in the underground cavern at Tor Harbor; their economic interests have therefore been injured, providing jurisdiction which INTERPOL will recognize. Whichever country we ask just needs to have an interest in a drop of oil in the Port's cavern and agree to cooperate."

"I like it," Bjornsson offered. "We might as well ask the Americans. They have the pull and frankly I am not sure the Norwegians will want to issue an arrest warrant for a Federation sailor any more than a Swedish judge would. The last thing they would wish for is an international dispute with Russia involving oil. I'll call the U.S. Embassy and explain the situation as soon as we hang up. We've worked well with the Americans in the past. Anything else?"

"Yes, there is," Stig said. "A severe storm is bearing down on the ship as we speak. Not only will the Americans need to file a red notice with INTERPOL fast, but they will also need to stop the ship and board her under some very adverse conditions."

"That will be up to them to decide. I'm signing off now and will get back in touch as soon as I learn anything," and with that the call ended.

It was late in the day on Friday, and time was running out. Bjornsson rang over to the U.S. Embassy and identified himself.

"You're in luck," the operator said. "Our commercial attaché just walked in the door an hour ago. I think he would be the right person to speak to," as she patched Bjornsson into Daniel's room.

Daniel picked up the call on the second ring and listened intently to Bjornsson's summation of the facts. Daniel was especially concerned about the strategic threat posed by the microbes, apart from any commercial considerations.

"I am quite sure my government will be keen to lend assistance in this case, Thor. I live in Gothenburg and have been reading about the turmoil at the Port and the ongoing investigation. I'm also liaising with several of the oil majors and their insurers to keep them up to speed with what I can get from our local sources. The situation sounds awful."

Daniel continued. "Thor, it's one thing for the U.S. to file the red notice with INTERPOL and arrest a fugitive. It's barely lunchtime back in Washington, and urgent cases can be filed 24/7 with the Office of International Affairs, inside the Criminal Division of the Justice Department. I can email Mostov's prints and other personal data you send me to the Duty Attorney in the Fugitive Unit who will process the provisional arrest warrant, pronto. However, Mostov is still in Norwegian waters, if I understand correctly, so we will need other support to detain him and the ship. The closest military command we have in Norway is assigned to NATO's Joint Warfare Center in Stavanger, at the old naval base on the west coast of Norway. The Center is subordinate to the Supreme Allied Commander in Norfolk, Virginia, giving us a strong advantage. After I speak with the OIA Duty Attorney, I'll contact Norfolk and let them know we'll be following up in Norway on an INTERPOL arrest. The Russians will squawk, but we can manage the heat so long as the arrest is made in Norwegian waters."

"Thank you, Daniel. My government greatly appreciates your assistance. Using NATO as cover is both brilliant and defensible. Russia will bristle but won't risk provoking an incident over a sailor with a criminal background. They'd look bad, something they don't want in this case. Once Mostov is taken into custody, my office will naturally wish to participate in his questioning along with your Justice Department," Bjornsson said. "If it is clear he is involved, we would seek to prosecute him in Sweden, where the evidence presumably would be based. Do you see any issues with that?"

"It's not up to me to decide whether or not the U.S. would waive extradition, Thor."

"Very well, I understand. Those discussions will take place later. We also need to be prepared to make other arrests if he is willing to name accomplices. The key is for your government to make the first move. If you can detain this person and ward off the Federation's protests, the Swedish government will have a freer hand in making any other arrests that are warranted. When can we speak again?"

"I'll call you in an hour with an update."

"OK, I'll be waiting."

Daniel looked at his watch. He'd need to work quickly to avoid delaying his dinner with Karin. He asked the operator to dial the OIA Duty Attorney at the DOJ and reviewed the urgency of the situation with her. An expert in both international arrests and seizure logistics, she assured him that a U.S. warrant would be issued within the hour, and that INTERPOL would be notified immediately afterward. The Duty Attorney told Daniel the OIA would request INTERPOL to only notify the Norwegian and Swedish governments, since Mostov's whereabouts were known. Otherwise, a blanket notice to the nearly two hundred members of INTERPOL would alert the Federation's Ministry of Emergency Situations. Notice from INTERPOL to Norway and Sweden would help give them the diplomatic cover in case the Federation got nasty, she said. Sweden particularly needed the cover, as it had only just become a member of NATO. She also told him that the Norwegian Defense Ministry could be counted on to permit U.S. assets assigned to the NATO base to be used to apprehend a suspect on the *Smolensk II*, if the ship was within Norway's exclusive economic zone. If the ship got too close to Federation waters, they would not risk a confrontation. She further advised Daniel that the Commander at Stavanger's naval base would receive orders from Norfolk to lend all required support to the operation. He would know what to do from there and report back on the progress of the arrest. Daniel thanked the lawyer for her work and then called Officer Bjornsson to update him. If all went as planned, in a few hours, the *Smolensk II* would be forced to yield the first person of interest in the investigation.

CH. 20

With an umbrella in one hand and his mobile phone in the other, Daniel left the side entrance of the Embassy and walked along the harbor to the Grand Hotel. He tapped Karin's number into his phone.

"Hi Karin, I'm on my way. How are you?"

"Hi Daniel. I'm well, looking forward to seeing you."

"Same. I'll be at the Grand in five minutes. Shall I meet you in the lobby?" he replied.

"Yes, that's fine, I won't be long."

Daniel entered the hotel and took a seat in one of the ottomans opposite the reception desk. Although Stockholm's busy tourist season had already ended, the hotel was completely booked with conferences, trade fairs and the like. Over the years, Stockholm had become one of Northern Europe's favored meeting destinations.

At exactly 20:00, the elevator doors slid open, and Karin stepped out. Daniel rose immediately, and his eyes lit up as he saw her. He took her hand in his, the brief hug that followed conveying both warmth and anticipation. Their embrace was short, but in that moment, they both felt a quiet thrill—an acknowledgment that something was shifting between them, though neither dared say it aloud just yet.

"You look lovely," Daniel said softly, his eyes lingering on her as the words slipped out naturally.

Karin's cheeks flushed, a warmth spreading through her at the unexpected compliment. She wasn't used to feeling this way, so effortlessly charmed by someone, and for a moment, she hesitated, unsure how to respond.

"Thank you, Daniel," she finally replied, her voice softer than she intended, her smile growing as she met his gaze. The simple exchange held more weight than she anticipated, and she found herself wondering what else this evening might hold.

He helped her with her coat and after putting on his own, the two walked out of the hotel and down the red-carpeted stairs facing the *Gamla Stan*, Stockholm's old town, a medieval island linked by roads and walkways to the rest of the city. They stopped briefly to take in the expansive view of the Royal Palace opposite the hotel. It was dramatically lit up by spotlights whose rays gleamed in the water's reflection.

They crossed the bridge to the *Gamla Stan*, the old town's cobblestone streets winding beneath their feet as they meandered past quaint, lantern-lit boutiques and cozy eateries. The air was crisp, carrying the faint scent of cinnamon and roasted chestnuts from a nearby vendor, mingling with the saltiness of the harbor. Karin clasped Daniel's arm as they walked, the warmth of his body providing a comforting contrast to the autumn chill. Above them, the soft glow of lanterns illuminated the weathered facades of centuries-old buildings, casting long shadows that danced with the flicker of the candlelight spilling from the restaurant windows.

When they reached the restaurant, he opened the door, helped her remove her coat and passed it to the obliging attendant. The two were escorted to their table by the maître de. Atop the linen covered dining tables, candles emitted an amber constellation of warm, glowing illumination across the room. They arrived at their table in the back corner of the restaurant's second level. Daniel centered her chair as Karin settled in. Sitting across from her, he noticed how her string of pearls glistened, as did her lips and eyes against the softness of her skin.

"What a great idea, holding the firm's client dinner at the Wasa Museum," Daniel said, his tone appreciative, but his gaze lingering on Karin longer than the words implied.

Karin smiled, warmed by his compliment. "It's definitely a departure from the usual venues," she replied, but her mind was already drifting ahead to the rest of the evening. She found herself wondering if this dinner, so different from the typical client dinner she was used to, might hold a different kind of potential. Something personal, perhaps, and her heart beat a little faster.

"Yes, the Wasa Museum provides an intimate setting to converse with clients and catch up with their spouses. The firm not only handles their accounting needs, but in some cases, we also handle their personal tax matters. So, it's a good way to solidify relationships. No pressure, just a relaxing evening with good food and conversation."

"Like tonight", he replied with a smile.

"Indeed," she laughed.

Standing nearby, their waiter tendered the wine and meal menus and they decided to order the *prix fixe* special of four courses including a main course of lightly cured cod with pear and parsnips in a white wine sauce. Each course was paired with a wine selected by the chef.

They talked about their careers, with Karin confiding in Daniel her angst over whether she would be asked to take a senior partnership interest with the firm. Her review was up this year, and she hoped she would have that option, although she was not even sure she would accept it due to the financial investment that was expected along with the pressure to bring in ever more client accounts. A part of her yearned for a chance to switch to a business development role in one of Sweden's premier multinationals. Daniel sympathized, confiding that he never had the desire to join a law firm, but preferred to work in-house where he could get a good mix of business and law at the start of his career. Otherwise, it would take several years toiling as an associate and, with luck, finally as a partner before he got substantial client exposure and the ability to lead on client matters. He knew he lacked patience for that. In his last year of law school, one of his professors in Washington had arranged an internship for him at the State Department, and he soon realized the agency offered the best of all worlds — an immediate transactional practice and the opportunity to carry out foreign policy work. His manager valued his skills and offered him a position after graduation, working on bilateral free trade deals in Latin America. He was hooked.

As dinner continued, their conversation flowed easily, shifting from work to family. Daniel found himself opening more than he expected, confessing that he had been married once, but the demands of his career had strained the relationship until it eventually broke. "It's not easy to balance everything," he admitted, his voice tinged with a hint of regret. "I was so focused on the next deal, the next negotiation or crisis, that I forgot to pay attention to what was right in front of me." Karin listened quietly, understanding more than she let on. She had made sacrifices of her own—long hours spent building her career had come at the expense of relationships that never quite had a chance to take root. And yet, here they were, both successful in their own ways, both searching for something more, wanting to find a sympathetic partner.

Coffee was served along with the final dessert course, a warmed blackberry crumble accompanied by a dollop of cardamom-laced whipped cream. Karin pressed her spoon into the berries, crushing their drupelets and creating a lavender-hued infusion with the cream. She then scooped up a spoonful and offered the first taste to Daniel.

"Oh, that's amazing," he said moments after Karin removed the spoon from his mouth. She beamed.

As dinner drew to an end, Daniel asked for the check and paid while the attendant brought over their coats. The two began their stroll back to the Grand Hotel, as an autumn chill tinged the air. Once again, Karin reached for Daniel's arm, and he drew her near, entwining her arm with his.

"That was a lovely evening," she reflected aloud as they approached the Hotel's canopied entrance.

Daniel spoke next. "I have the day free tomorrow before the event at the Museum. There *is* an urgent matter I am working on involving the oil mess at the Port of Gothenburg. But it appears to be under control for now, and unless things change, how about if we take a little time off together to visit Skansen to see the period homes, or take a boat to Drottningholm for a palace tour?

"Either would be wonderful," Karin gleamed. "But I really love the palace gardens, and they'll be in opulent decline right now. We could bring a picnic lunch; I'm sure the hotel's restaurant can pack up something."

"Great. I'll bring some wine and a blanket. Shall I pick you up at 11:00? A boat departs every half hour from there," he motioned to a small ticket booth at the end of a quay.

"Perfect. I'm looking forward."

As Daniel leaned in to kiss her cheek goodnight, Karin moved subtly, turning her face just enough for their lips to meet. The kiss, though brief, held a surprising intensity, a spark neither of them expected but both welcomed. His hand gently cupped her cheek, prolonging the moment as their breaths mingled in the cool night air. When she finally pulled away, her lips still tingling from the warmth of his touch, she smiled softly, her eyes catching his. 'Goodnight,' she whispered, and with one last glance, she ascended the stairs, leaving Daniel standing beneath the awning, his heart racing as he watched her disappear into the hotel.

The soft sensation of her kiss on his lips was a warm reminder of the unexpected connection that had unfolded between them. He lingered there for a moment longer, staring out at the shimmering reflection of the Royal Palace across the water, just as he did earlier when their evening began, knowing that something had shifted tonight. There was no turning back now—only the promise of what might come next. And as he turned to leave, a sense of both excitement and uncertainty settled in his chest, propelling him forward into whatever the next day might bring.

CH. 21

Gnady was in a silk robe, tending a cigar and relaxing in a club chair under a palm in the glass-domed winter garden of his luxury townhome situated on Moscow's Christie Prudi Boulevard. It was only a short drive from his neighborhood to the Kremlin, which made it a favorite residential zone for ARBs – anonymous Russian billionaires - who wanted to make their home inside the city.

Earlier that Saturday morning, Gnady returned home refreshed from a sauna and massage at the palatial Sandunovskye Banya in the center of Moscow. *Banyas*, or saunas, served as an ingrained part of Russian life from time eternal. The Greek historian Herodotus had written about the people of the steppes who stewed in wooden steam huts. It was there that they cleansed themselves and passed the time away, resting their weary bones or chatting about family, communal or business matters, while immersed in the pleasant smell of heated fir or aspen wood. It was believed that those who partook also received medicinal benefits from their steamy sessions, curing arthritis, coughs, low blood pressure, depression and a host of other ailments.

Gnady had no need for any such cures *per se*. Yet he felt sublimely relaxed from his sauna experience. His skin was smoothed and still nicely scented with oil applied by his favorite masseuses, twins nicknamed "Fire and Ice" who had attended to him with considerable agility and charm under the marble arches of one of the private steam rooms. The girls, former ballerinas, had each received a handsome gratuity for their bodywork, more than they could have earned from a month of giving dance lessons at one of Moscow's famed ballet studios.

He rose from his chair and surveyed the top of an art deco buffet which offered generous portions of salmon, piroshky and blini, along with red and yellow berries, fresh squeezed juice, dark bread and honey. He poured himself a cup of tea in a tall, clear glass, adding a splash of cream in the English manner and watching with captivation as the white clouds mushroomed like miniature atomic explosions in the murky liquid. With a gilt-washed spoon he stirred the tea to a consistent amber hue and returned to his chair. Sipping, he began to peruse *Neftegaz,* a journal that covered the Russian oil and gas industry. On the cover page, an article confirmed the mysterious contamination of oil in the Port of Gothenburg's refinery and its adjacent storage facilities. The story mentioned that an investigation was underway, its writer explaining that the cause of the loss was unattributed for the time being.

The news of our activities is traveling fast, Gnady smiled inwardly. He felt a wave of relief, as his firm's options contracts were now approaching a break-even point. With a little more of the coaxing that he planned, they should be back in positive territory in a matter of days. Gnady put down the journal and phoned Axel who recognized the number on his mobile phone's display.

"Gnady, how are you?"

"Never better, Axel. I just returned from some splendid waters this morning. You should join me some time, the Russian saunas are marvelous, and as a Swede, you would greatly appreciate them."

"I hope to one day. But without the birch branch beatings, if you please. But now I think we need to meet here instead. Our operation has progressed to the point where we need to speak in person about our next steps. It's time to turn up the heat. Have you been watching the news?"

Gandy turned serious and was mindful of the need for circumspect conversation. Secure communications could not be assured.

"Indeed. Just now I was reading about the developments in a *Neftegaz* news article. It seems the market is finally primed for adjustment. So, I agree we should meet. I can still catch an afternoon flight and join you for dinner this evening."

"Excellent. I'm *en route* by train to Stockholm. Fly directly there and book a room at the Grand Hotel, where I am staying. On Sunday we'll get a small conference room after breakfast and work through the afternoon. I have a draft of a Manifesto for you to review concerning our little project. But this evening I'm attending a dinner hosted by Persson & Frandberg, my accounting firm. It's a great opportunity for me to network with their clients, drum up contributions. You should join me. I can bring a guest."

"Yes, I would imagine they should be happy to meet a potential client."

"Bring a jacket and tie," Axel added, "And drive straight from Arlanda airport to the Wasa Museum. Cocktails begin at 20:00. I'll see you there."

"Very well, I will be pleased to accompany you. I'll take a flight home at the latest on Sunday evening, to be prepared for the opening of trading on Monday. We can work together on Sunday morning and wrap up by noon. Understood?"

"Yes," Axel replied.

"See you tonight, then," Gnady said. Then he speed-dialed his security chief, told him about the last-minute trip and ordered his driver to stand by for the drive from his townhome to the private passenger terminal at Sheremetyevo airport.

CH. 22

At 11:00 on Saturday morning, Daniel bounded up the stairs of the Grand Hotel, his heart quickening as he spotted Karin seated gracefully on one of the lobby's plush sofas. She looked radiant in her dark green jacket and apricot pashmina, the colors accentuating her natural elegance. For a moment, he paused, taking her in, marveling at how effortlessly she commanded his attention. How does she always manage to look so perfect? he thought. A plastic bag with the Hotel's logo was on the floor at her side. She rose to greet him, and he gave her an enthusiastic good morning kiss.

Then he stood back for a moment. "You look lovely this morning", he proclaimed, and Karin blushed.

"Oh Daniel, thanks again for dinner last evening. It was rather romantic, don't you think?" Karin's eyes sparkled mischievously as she teased him.

Daniel chuckled, a slight blush creeping up his neck. "Romantic is one way to describe it. Perfect is another. I could definitely get used to evenings like that with you."

Karin raised an eyebrow, her lips curving into a sly smile. "The food or the company?"

He grinned, leaning in slightly. "I'll let you guess, but the company definitely had something to do with it."

"Well, that's good, because I have you all to myself today, and we have a picnic prepared by the hotel," pointing to the bag near her chair. "So, you're in luck. Let's go!"

Daniel smiled and placed the wine bottle he was carrying in the hotel bag. The two then left the hotel, turning right and strolling along the quay to a small booth that sold tickets for a variety of tours around Stockholm's archipelago. He bought the tickets and put his arm around Karin as they waited to board the glass-roofed boat for the hour-long trip to Drottningholm, the Rococo royal summer palace inspired by Versailles. The boat gently rocked as it chugged steadily along, making the cruise feel splendid. Sunshine and colored autumn foliage punctuated the islands and shoreline along the way.

After disembarking at the Palace, they wandered along the gravel-strewn pathways of Drottningholm's gardens, the crunch of the stones underfoot mingling with the soft rustle of leaves in the autumn breeze. Fountains bubbled gently in the background, their sprays glistening in the sunlight, while the sweet, fading scent of roses in decline hung in the crisp air. The gardens, lined with perfectly manicured box hedges and tall juniper topiary, felt like a sanctuary, a peaceful retreat where time seemed to slow down just for them.

At the end of the formal gardens, the grounds abruptly opened to a meadow where ancient oaks poetically dotted the landscape in no apparent pattern. Looking out across the parterre, they had a bucolic view of the palace and decided to unfold their blanket under the protective canopy of one of the immense oaks standing mutely nearby. The tourist season had already passed, so they had the park grounds largely to themselves.

After they unfolded their blanket, Karin removed two lunch boxes from her bag and opened them up. Inside were shrimp and egg sandwiches, chips and a pear, and finally she removed two bottles of sparkling mineral water. Daniel took out the wine bottle and poured some of its contents into their paper cups.

Finished with lunch, Daniel rested with his back against the tree, and Karin nestled closer to him, her head resting lightly on his shoulder as they gazed out at the serene expanse of the formal gardens. Daniel wrapped the blanket around them, the warmth from their shared closeness making the autumn chill almost unnoticeable. His fingers grazed her hand softly, and she responded by slipping her hand into his, their fingers interlocking naturally. As the breeze rustled the leaves above, they sat in comfortable silence, a quiet sense of belonging washing over them.

After a while, he broke the silence. "I'm looking forward to your party tonight. I wonder if I'll know anyone there."

"It's possible. We have a lot of clients who do business with the U.S. I hope to see several friends there and introduce you to them. I've told some of them about you, you know...."

"Oh, have you? And I wonder what it is that you have said?"

"Nothing really, just that I've met a hopelessly forlorn American, in need of introduction to Swedish high society!"

"Ha! And that would be the rarified world of accountants and tax advisors you inhabit?" he teased. "But you have a point; my social life is a miserable one for sure. All work and no play, which is why I was so happy to get your call about tonight's social affair. It will be nice to meet some new people, including your colleagues."

Karin checked her watch and looked up at Daniel. He was quick to read her mind.

"Looks like it's time to start packing up," he said, and stood up. Then he took Karin's hands and pulled her up. He took a moment to kiss her while brushing her hair back with his hand.

"I noticed your hotel chef failed to pack a dessert, so I thought I would take the liberty of improvising", he said, smiling.

Karin blushed momentarily and said, "A kiss is the best dessert ever, totally keto. I could get used to that!"

Then they gathered the blanket and empty boxes and started walking back to the palace courtyard where they entered one of the outbuildings that had been converted into a gift shop. With time to kill before the boat ride back to Stockholm, they stepped inside and looked at the royal reproductions displayed attractively for sale on tables spread out through several rooms.

"Hey, look at this," Karin pointed to a display rack that held butane candle lighters with handles shaped as *Dala* horses. She selected from the stand a white one with red and blue accents along with the monogram letter "K" painted on it, and she handed it to him. He unfolded a metal tube that served as a wick and easily flicked its trigger, causing a thin flame to shoot out.

"It works well enough," he commented.

"Great. I'd like this one, a nice memento of our trip, and anyways I'm always out of matches for candles."

She took it to the sales attendant who said, "Good spotting! These just arrived. You're one of the first to buy one!"

Karin smiled and placed the lighter in her purse after paying for it.

Then they strolled over to the pier where they waited in a queue for the return boat ride to Stockholm. After disembarking, they walked back to the Grand and agreed to meet again in the lobby at 19:45. It was already past dusk, and this time on the stairs of the hotel it was Daniel who took Karin by the hand and spun her close for a tender kiss, goodbye.

They paused at the base of the hotel stairs, the world around them fading as they stood in the soft glow of the lamplight. Daniel gazed into her eyes, his heart pounding as he realized how much she had come to mean to him in such a short time. Without thinking, he reached for her hand, pulling her gently closer. "I'll see you tonight," he whispered, his voice low and full of meaning.

Karin smiled, her gaze never leaving him. "Can't wait."

And then they parted. But as she walked up the stairs, Daniel stood rooted at the spot, and he knew—without a doubt—that they were both falling fast, and there was no turning back. Then he set off for the embassy to get ready for the evening ahead.

CH. 23

The Varanger Peninsula juts out between the low fjords and inlets in the extreme northeast of Norway, opposite the Russian Federation's Kola Peninsula to its east. About a hundred kilometers to the south, one can reach yet a third border, Finland, where three time zones meet. Only a few such places exist in the world.

Within the larger Varanger municipality sits Kirkenes, a town of some 3,000 inhabitants whose livelihoods depended historically on whatever trade could be eked out of the drab and austere Barents region. Fortunately for its residents, the pace of commerce had quickened in recent years due to the increase in oil exploration.

The military garrison located at Varanger also provided lifeblood to the region since World War II, when the Luftwaffe built two runways there for conducting bombing runs against the Soviet Union. During the post war years, Varanger's Hoybuktmoen Airport was built nearby the ruins of the defunct Nazi airstrip. Several times each day, members of the Norwegian infantry regiment based there patrol the 150 km border separating Norway and the Russian Federation. Conscripts assigned to the regiment's six border stations, many of them local Samis, must have stamina for enduring the bitter cold and dark evenings on foot patrol during the long winter months.

At 2315 hrs., NATO's command at Stavanger placed a secure call to the military base it also maintains at Varanger. The outpost's radio operator patched the call through to base commander Colonel Winslow Duke III, USAF, who was resting in his quarters but sprang to attention.

"Duke here."

"Good evening, Colonel. This is Commander Walt O'Connor, at Stavanger. We have orders from INTERPOL to intercept the *Smolensk II*, an oil tanker navigating just off your coast, and to detain one of its crew. We'll send you the coordinates for the vessel and a file on the seaman. Your helos will need to scramble fast; it's gonna be a tricky mission. We are *not* giving the ship's captain any advance warning. Radio him just as your helos approach. Hopefully, when he's confronted with two combat helos displaying U.S. insignia, he'll get compliant pronto. One of the helos will have to land on the ship's helo pad and then take custody of the sailor. But we are *not* looking for a confrontation this close to the border, understood?"

"Roger," Duke replied before hanging up and punching the alarm near his desk for the five-minute ready crew.

The USAF choppers assigned to NATO and stationed at Varanger were state-of-the-art weaponry — Lockheed Jolly Green IIs specially equipped with dipping sonar for detecting Russian or Chinese subs and a small fleet of Boeing Grey Wolfs. They also featured standard air to surface missiles and countermeasure capabilities along with over-horizon detection sensors, like the small detachment of US patrol aircraft parked nearby.

Dressed in an impermeable, battery-heated flight suit and buckled in the cockpit of the lead helo, mission commander Major John

Annarino, USAF, scowled, knowing that if they somehow managed to detain the seaman, he would need to be firmly restrained on the return flight by Capt. Jerry "Ace" Berman, USAF, his tactical co-ordinator and copilot. Berman, a former Navy seal, third degree black belt and student of krav maga, was up to the task.

The last thing we need is a seadog thrashing around behind the cockpit, or worse, upchucking in my beautiful bird, Annarino thought.

Annarino started contemplating the mission as he began the start sequence, ensuring the engine had time to warm up. Cleared by the tower and with all instruments green, Annarino nosed his Grey Wolf up and broke hard right like a rocket ship toward the open sea. A Jolly Green II flew in trail by fifty meters to the right. A low ceiling of thick gray clouds flowed in an easterly direction overhead. A few moments later, his helmet-mounted visual display indicated the *Smolensk II* on the horizon approximately 160 kilometers away, bearing Southeast down the coast toward Murmansk. The ship was being tracked through coordinates fed minutes earlier to the helo's detect-ID system which was locked on the vessel. It would take only about forty-five minutes of flight time to reach the target. A good thing, too, for the *Smolensk II* was being quickly overtaken by the early arctic storm detected by the helo's snout that registered it as a large opaque mass on one of the cockpit's numerous color LCDs.

CH. 24

Still relaxed and quaffed from the morning's spa experience, Gnady was waived through Swedish Customs after exiting the sleek MD 80 jet that flew him to Stockholm's Arlanda Airport. His waiting chauffer, a former Iranian refugee driving a custom black Volvo S-90, eyed Gnady in the rearview mirror and didn't say a word as they whisked through the quiet streets. At last, they reached the Wasa Museum, whose entrance was lit up by blazing torch lamps. There was a small line of vehicles outside the museum, but eventually it was Gnady's turn to exit. He stood back to behold the edifice, admiring its contemporary, ragged lines and the sloping roof which glistened in the light of the harbor's embankment. A coat checker helped him with his coat and sealskin hat. A security officer then confirmed his appearance on the guest list and handed him a name tag that he immediately pocketed.

As he stepped further inside the cavernous building, it took Gnady's eyes a couple of minutes to adjust fully to the dimly lit, cavernous chamber that opened before him. The room had the air of an ancient Catalan church, dark and haunted, surfaces covered in moss, unlike French churches with all their glitter and polish. Inside the stadium-sized room in mournful repose lay the fully reconstructed 16th Century Swedish galleon known as the *Wasa*, so named after the Royal House of Sweden. The warship, decked out with sixty-four bronze cannons, sank abruptly within minutes of her maiden voyage launch. According to eyewitness accounts, the first gust of wind that caught her sails caused the top-heavy ship to list and roll unceremoniously over. The King and his court looked on from the shore, mortified, as its passengers swam for their lives to reach the shore.

In the 1950s, the slumbering *Wasa* was rediscovered in the brackish, cold waters of Stockholm's harbor, and a team of marine archeologists floated her to the surface. Despite her indisputably flawed design, she was truly a wonder, brought further to eerie life by the trove of jetsam recovered from her belly and put on tragic display in glass cases throughout the museum's several floors.

After completing a casual walk around the ship to inspect her more intimately, Gnady heard the muffled echo of his name being called by Axel. Gnady turned as Axel approached, and the two gave each other a powerful shoulder embrace.

"Quite something, isn't she?" Axel said, gesturing toward the Wasa ship.

"An extraordinary prize," Gnady nodded in unaccustomed reverence.

"There's nothing like this anywhere in the world," Axel declared, gazing admirably at the haunting hulk. "She's nearly intact. I have been to this place at least a dozen times, but I never get tired of the experience. And to think, she was green, powered by the wind alone."

"That helps to explain your admiration, Axel."

"Yes, I suppose it does. It's good to see you again. We have a lot to do now. Our work so far has been a complete success, and we must keep it that way through the finish."

Gnady spoke cautiously in a low tone, for the room was conducive to echoes. "Yes, but powerful interests will line up around us, and we must stay ahead of them. Our plan is a good one, however. If we stick to it, we cannot fail," Gnady said with confidence.

It was nearing 20:00 and the museum was beginning to fill with new arrivals. Karin and Daniel were among them. They headed for the open bar, and Daniel requested two flutes of champagne.

"*Skol*," he said, as they clinked their glasses and sipped, acknowledging each other with a nod afterward, as was the Swedish toasting custom. They took some time strolling on the various levels of the museum. During their rounds, Karin introduced Daniel to several of her clients and partners, enjoying the lively and cordial conversations stemming from Daniel's experience as a U.S. trade official. Daniel exchanged business cards with several people he met and made mental notes of trade ideas that popped into his head from some of the more practical conversations.

Like many of the guests, Daniel and Karin were eventually drawn closer to the Wasa by the sheer pull of its size. As they walked closer to the ship, Karin recognized Axel near its midsection, speaking with another guest. She took Daniel by the arm and guided him over to say hello.

"*Hej* Axel. It's great to see you here. This is my friend, Daniel Lake."

"Hello Karin, it's a pleasure to be here. Your firm has done a terrific job representing the Foundation. Let me introduce you to Gnady Pankov, one of our benefactors."

After they all shook hands, Axel spoke first.

"So, Karin, how goes life at the firm? I suppose it's a challenge these days, keeping track of changes in accounting rules, new regulations and such."

"It certainly is. As you know, not even tax-free foundations like yours are immune from scrutiny these days. Well, at least it provides a little job security for my fellow bean counters," Karin said, and they all gave a laugh.

"In Russia, where I come from, taxes are always a topic of conversation." Gnady offered. It's a kind of sport between our over-zealous tax collectors, many of whom are corrupt, and the taxpayers who can be extremely creative in response. I need an army of accountants just to survive, so should your work ever dry up here in Sweden, you will find ample opportunity in Russia."

"Thanks for that tip, I'll remember it," Karin replied. "And it's great that you support the SBF, Gnady. We have been the Foundation's accounting firm since nearly the beginning. Are you in a similar line of work?" she inquired.

"Not exactly. I'm involved in oil trading and investments. As you know, it's the first business of the Federation. I'm based in Moscow. My firm buys and sells in the securities and futures markets. As part of our social responsibility, we help worthy foundations, like Axel's."

"I can imagine the accounting aspects in Russia are complex, especially if you are also trading in foreign markets," Karin sympathized.

"Daniel, what do you do?" Axel inquired.

"I'm a commercial attaché with the U.S. Consulate in Gothenburg. Like Gnady, we support trade as well, all types, including oil. As a matter of fact, I met earlier this week with some U.S. oil companies I am sure you know, Gnady. I suppose you have read about the mysterious loss of oil at the Port of Gothenburg? It's taking up more and more of my time."

Gnady nodded and then looked down for a moment at his glass, collecting his thoughts on how to reply.

Axel was quick on the mark and filled the brief but noticeable pause in conversation. "Based near Gothenburg, I've been following the news coverage with interest. Some of my Foundation's activities center on researching applications that could be useful in sea conservation and finding alternative energy sources, from kelp oil to ocean wave technology. I was therefore intrigued by the rumor that some type of microbe is involved. Have you heard any more about this?" Axel inquired.

"Not much more than what I've read in the papers, like you," Daniel replied. "Naturally, though, the oil companies are scrambling to locate alternate facilities for storing their oil. To say they are concerned with the safety of their holdings would be an understatement. So, right now, we are developing information on depots having spare storage capacity," Daniel replied.

"I wish them luck," Axel said, "To begin with, it's a pity they do not support more environmentally friendly types of energy. Oil is such a dirty business, and thankfully, one day the world will run out of it, with apologies to my friend Gnady, here. For the most part, I find big oil and governments behave in total ignorance of the future supply situation. And they only pay lip service to environmental protection and renewable energy sources. All the while, they continue to foul the air and oceans as they please. As far as I'm concerned, this business at the Port of Gothenburg should be a wake-up call for them. Don't you agree?" Axel said with a bit of testiness in his voice.

The muscles in Gnady's jawline began to tighten, the strain revealing his discomfort with where the conversation might lead. His unease was not lost on Daniel, who, diplomatic as ever, tried to diffuse the situation.

"I actually do agree with you," Daniel replied. "Oil is a blessing but also has elements of a curse. And so long as ships can be registered under flags where the laws are weak and controls are lax, we will continue to see spills in the ocean and a variety of other environmental transgressions. Supporting alternative energy sources and sustaining ocean life are huge challenges. My government takes this subject very seriously."

Axel was surprised with Daniel's reply; he apparently was not a blind shill for U.S. trade interests after all. For his part, Gnady thought it best to cut short the conversation which had gone far enough, and he saw his opening.

"It is getting late now, and I am only here for only one night. This evening I still need to review our positions in the U.S. market, so please excuse me. It was a pleasure to meet you both. Thank you for your hospitality at this fine event, Karin. I enjoyed viewing the Wasa ship in her splendor. If I could buy her and take her home with me, I would." No one doubted his words. "Axel, do you care to join me?" Gnady asked pointedly.

"Yes, I suppose it's time to leave. Karin, thanks once again. This evening was a great chance for me to meet some potential donors for the Foundation. I really enjoyed it and hope the two of you have a good rest of the evening. Daniel, you're welcome to visit my Foundation whenever you like, we're located on Marstrand," Axel said as he fished a wad of cards from his pocket and handed one to Daniel. "Here's my card. I'm sure we have several common interests when it comes to trade and the environment."

"Thanks Axel, until we meet again, then," Daniel replied and raised his glass to Gnady and Axel as they turned to walk toward the coat check.

It wasn't much more than a ten-minute walk to the Hotel, and after they had left the museum, Gnady confronted Axel. "What was that all about, carrying on with the American about our enterprise? Have you lost your senses?"

"Christ Gnady, he has no clue about what's going on, don't be ridiculous. There is no way he could suspect anything from our conversation."

"Oh? And inviting him to meet again, what is the sense of that? How close with fire do you wish to play?" Gnady asked indignantly.

The two continued walking together in silence until they reached the hotel. The silence persisted uncomfortably as they waited for the elevator.

Once inside, Axel said with resignation, "I guess we've both had enough for one night. Let's meet up tomorrow, start fresh after breakfast. Say, 09:00 in my suite. We'll begin with finalizing the Manifesto for publication by the main news wires. We need to send it to them by an encrypted email tomorrow afternoon, so the markets have digested it before they open."

Gnady listened in steely silence, miffed and disturbed inside, but he had no alternative other than to go along with his naïve, insolent host. He reasoned that Axel was probably right about one thing, the likelihood of any future cooperation between them was next to nil after Pankovneft's options inevitably clawed their way back to profitability. And the sooner, the better, he swore.

The elevator doors opened.

"Excellent. Until tomorrow, Axel," Gnady said as he exited the elevator and walked to his room in quiet contemplation. Once again calm and philosophic, Gnady pondered to himself, *Who am I kidding? This was and always had been a marriage of convenience, if not necessity.* Ever mindful of cutting his exposure, he thought, *What a fool I was to think our association could ever be more than short-term.*

CH. 25

Major Annarino flew for miles over the dark green ocean, scouring the frozen emptiness for a visual of the ship. He was prevented from doing so, however, by a heavy mix of clouds, mist, and snow that began to hem in his flight path. The gale force winds buffeting his craft didn't help and forced the two pilots to watch their instrumentation as much as the sea below. He relied instead on radar to guide him on his approach to the *Smolensk II*. Annarino and the other helo approached the tanker from its stern, flying his bird at wave-top level to avoid detection by the ship's Litton air search radar unit which scanned the sky in front of the vessel's tower. When they were positioned over the tanker's bow, Annarino radioed his intent to the other helo to search for the helipad and land his craft on it. The pilot in the Jolly Green confirmed and steadied his helo aloft. Both craft slowed to fifteen knots, mimicking the speed at which the *Smolensk II* was traveling. Due to the measured speed, however, freezing sleet and ice had begun to stick to the airframe and blades of both helos. To compound matters, turbulent gales made it difficult for Annarino and the other pilot to keep their birds steady.

After Annarino maneuvered to forty feet over the ship's bow, Berman flipped the chopper's forward searchlight switch on and quickly peered down at the deck below. They were still far enough away from the supertanker's bridge at the stern that the dense snow flurries totally eclipsed the spotlight, allowing them to operate undetected. The spotlight pierced the darkness and then dissipated in the milky white confetti which swirled in the pounding air below. Berman raised his visor to try to get a clearer view. From what little he *could* see through the murky light, they were hovering directly over a series of large pipes that ran along the deck's surface from bow to stern. He also could make out a patchwork of smaller pipes that crisscrossed the deck's surface. Some of them were partially obscured by small drifts of snow that had begun to collect under them. He motioned Annarino to glide the helo slowly forward, and a few moments later, he spotted the landing pad amidships, in an area where the large deck pipes disappeared below deck into one of the ship's stowage tanks and then re-emerged from another tank nearly forty yards further up. It would be a difficult, tight landing. Berman pointed down and quickly followed with a "thumbs up" to Annarino before killing the spotlight.

Annarino nodded and started his ascent back to two hundred meters where the other helo joined him. Now that the landing pad was sited, the next phase of the operation to detain seaman Mostov could proceed.

The two craft edged ahead in parallel and hovered fifty meters shy of the ship's bridge. Then they began flying carefully in reverse, a difficult maneuver in the choppy air. With his radio on, tactical coordinator Berman locked on to the ship's frequency. Then he linked up with Colonel Duke's command post at Varanger. On signal, both helos turned on their spots and lit up the ship's bridge, whose startled occupants were blinded by the sudden wall of white light, magnified by the churning snow. Having gotten the attention of the bridge, Berman and his counterpart refocused their spotlights to the decks directly above and below the bridge, exposing the gunships' imposing profiles to the crew on the bridge.

A translator sitting beside Colonel Duke spoke calmly in fluent Russian. "This is Colonel Winslow Duke, representing NATO. Do you copy?"

Just the tanker's astounded radio operator was on bridge duty with the ship's captain when the call came in and broke the air. He looked over to the equally astonished captain. The captain momentarily looked away and raised his arm to shield his eyes. The next moment he fumbled to remove his headset from its holster and grabbed a mic from its operator.

"This is Captain Leonid Voitchenko, what is the meaning of this intrusion?" he barked.

"Captain, we have orders from INTERPOL to arrest one of your crewmembers, Dima Mostov," the translator replied on cue. "He is wanted for questioning in connection with the sabotage of the Port of Gothenburg's oil storage facilities, which your ship recently departed."

Captain Voitchenko was a hardened veteran and highly experienced, as only the best captains are allowed to train for supertankers like the *Smolensk II*. He quickly found his wits. "I understand. But do you have an arrest warrant to support your claim should I decide to hand a member of my crew over?" he demanded.

Colonel Duke's translator spoke. "Yes, you will receive INTERPOL's warrant during the arrest of Mostov. The helicopter crew will provide you with a copy." For added measure, Duke added "Let me remind you, Captain Voitchenko, that you are navigating in Norwegian waters. If you refuse to cooperate with this valid warrant, you will be named as an accessory in the investigation, and I can assure you that you will never again sail any vessel outside the Federation's waters without risk of your own arrest by INTERPOL."

Inside the helo, Annarino and Berman grinned and nodded as they listened to the simulcast exchange.

With his confidence flagging, Captain Voitchenko paused for a moment. Then he said, "And what about the safety of my crew and ship? We are fighting for our survival here in the middle of a storm, in case you are not aware. I must maintain full speed if we hope to reach safety in port beneath the path of the storm. The deck is beginning to take on ice, and the ship is heaving in the swells. If your helicopters wish to land under these insane conditions, they can be my guest, but I will not slow down and endanger my crew. If I did, I would lose at least an hour's time, and I do not have a moment to lose. Your arrest warrant is not valid so long as it jeopardizes the safety of my ship and crew. One more thing, I am not sending Mostov out on the open deck. If you want him, your crew must take custody of him from *inside* my bridge, where I can securely remand him to you. Whatever happens after that is your responsibility."

That was his final gambit, but it was too weak to dissuade Colonel Duke from his orders. "Affirmative, Captain. Standby to be boarded," Duke replied.

CH. 26

Guests at the event soon began to leave, and Daniel retrieved his and Karin's coats from the cloakroom. As they stepped out of the Wasa Museum and into the cool, damp evening air, Daniel instinctively put his arm around Karin, drawing her closer. There was a quiet intimacy between them now, a comfort that hadn't existed just days before. He couldn't help but smile at how natural it felt to be by her side. Karin leaned into him slightly, her hand brushing his as they strolled along Strandvagen Avenue, both enjoying the shared silence.

"That was an impressive and enjoyable event. I'm so glad you invited me," Daniel said.

"You were a hit with several of my clients. For a moment there, I think you gave out more business cards than me," she jested.

Daniel smiled. "You can hardly blame a fellow for trying to expand his network." Then he added, "Your friend Axel was a rather curious fellow, so passionate about his cause. What more can you tell me about his Foundation?"

"Well, it's focused mostly on biotech and ocean research, working out of a small lab facility on Marstrand. We helped him set the Foundation up as a non-profit, since that allows him to maintain tight control with only minimal public disclosure. If he sticks to his mostly scientific charter and applies any excess funds to the SBF's declared purposes, the tax authorities basically leave him alone. The only people he answers to are his sponsors, but in reality, they have little say. I would imagine most simply write their checks and are satisfied with their tax deductions and clean consciences."

"Very nifty," Daniel replied.

"He's a great client. I actually brought him into the firm. We grew up in the same district and went to school together. I was one grade ahead of him, but everyone at school knew one another. I remember a lot of the girls were swell on him, too. He was idealistic and had dreamy, intense eyes to match, though not as nice as yours!" she said.

"And wasn't Gnady straight from central casting? Come to think of it, they're rather strange bedfellows, both working at opposite ends of the oil spectrum," Daniel observed.

"It's true. But we see more and more of this these days, as energy firms back alternative fuel sources. There's a strong need to diversify. The intersection of interests in the energy sector is something our energy practice consults on quite a bit," Karin noted.

It was too early in the evening to retire for the night. As they approached their hotel, neither spoke but they felt hungry for each other's company.

"A nightcap?" Daniel asked, his voice soft but filled with intent.

Karin smiled playfully, her eyes glinting in the low light of the hotel entrance. "Your place or mine?" she teased, knowing full well where the night was heading but savoring the thrill of the moment.

He chuckled, leaning in slightly. "I think your place sounds perfect," he replied, the excitement of being alone with her again quickening his pulse. Without another word, they headed inside, the unspoken understanding between them electrifying the air.

She inserted her card key into the elevator slot and after reaching her floor, she gestured with her head to the right and led him to her room near the end of the hall.

"Let me take your coat," Daniel said as he peered about the dimly lit chamber. The room was basic, a small desk, queen bed, a nightstand with a phone.

She flicked on the small desk lamp and knelt to open the minibar, deciding which of the little bottles of *snaps* to remove. But before she could make a choice, she felt Daniel's presence behind her—close, magnetic, irresistible. When she rose to show Daniel the choices, she inhaled softly as he tenderly pulled her toward him, using her hips for leverage. Smiling, she placed her arms across his shoulders as he held her waist and leveled his eyes softly at hers. She used the chilled bottles she was holding to playfully tease the back of his neck with them, causing tingles down his spine. He traced a line with his finger from her lips to her breast, cupping one of them and squeezing its nipple lightly, followed by the next one with his other hand. With an assenting nod, she molded her body into his and kissed him deeply while he unzipped her dress and glided it off her slender shoulders. Standing before him, Karin opened his belt and pushed his trousers to the floor. The next moment she hopped to his waist, and they fell into the down-filled duvet where Karin maneuvered on top of him.

Daniel's breathing quickened and so did his pulse from the sudden sensation of her weight pushing against his groin. He unclasped her bra and drew Karin near once more, her breasts melting as they touched his lips. She was flush with ecstasy and responded with a low murmur and fluttering eyes.

They moved together in a slow, steady rhythm, their breaths mingling in the soft darkness of the room. Each touch, each caress was filled with something deeper than desire—there was an unspoken understanding, a sense of vulnerability that neither had expected. As their bodies intertwined, so too did their emotions, and for the first time in a long time, Daniel felt truly connected, not just physically but emotionally.

Karin's whispered sighs filled the room, her touch gentle but sure, just so, and with every movement, they both sank deeper into the moment. Finally, still, Karin lay beside him, her head resting on his chest, the rise and fall of his breathing matching her own. In that moment, they were no longer two people joining together—they were something more.

Spent, Karin pulled away and sank back into the bed next to Daniel, her eyes closed toward the ceiling, her reddened lips parted.

For the first time in years, Daniel felt the emotional intimacy he had long craved but had never found. This was more than the fleeting satisfaction of physical closeness; this was something real, something alive. He glanced at Karin, her hair splayed across the pillow, her breathing soft and steady.

He had been alone for so long, but now, with her beside him, the loneliness that had once been his constant companion seemed to dissipate. The weight of his past— the broken marriage, a string of meaningless encounters— suddenly felt lighter. Maybe, he thought, this is what I've been waiting for.

Karin stirred slightly, a soft smile tugging at her lips as she nestled closer to him.

He looked over the tousled duvet to Karin and sighed contentedly, "That was like heaven." She smiled at him and moved to his side.

There was nothing more to be said in the reverie of the moment. Daniel cradled her in his arms for several minutes more. The last thing he remembered was watching her breathing become more and more deep as the two finally drifted off in the diffused moonlight that bathed the room.

CH. 27

On Sunday morning the rain and cold from the Arctic storm 2,000 kilometers to the North bore down on Stockholm, and bursting skies hurled sheets of rain against the windowpanes shielding the bedroom where Karin and Daniel still lay asleep. The persistent pinging noise eventually caused Daniel to rouse, and Karin, lying in his arms, seemed as if she too was beginning to stir. Hoping not to disrupt her slumber, Daniel quietly slid away and tiptoed into the bathroom, closing the door behind him. He fidgeted with the water temperature until it was just right, and before he stepped in the shower, grabbed a soap bar that Karin had opened plus one of the little shampoos and razor packages from the vanity. The warm shower felt soothing, its heat enveloping his body and steam filling the small room.

A few minutes later, Karin appeared in the doorway with the bed sheet wrapped around her. She surveyed Daniel for a few moments as he stood with his face turned up toward the showerhead. She quietly opened the glass shower door and crept in behind him, her hands reaching around to his chest, providing a surprise embrace as she playfully bit into his shoulder. He turned and smiled, pulling her into the stream of water with him.

"Hey, there's already a lot of steam in here," he teased.

"Just you wait," she said. "There's plenty more coming if you can stand the heat!"

"Try me," he said, and kissed her on her neck. It had been a long time since either of them had made love in a morning shower, and they both enjoyed themselves.

Before toweling off, she whispered in his ear *"Ett liv utan kärlek är som ett år utan sommar."*

"Translation?" he asked.

"A life without love is like a year without summer."

In one of the hotel suites a few floors higher up, Pankov looked self-satisfied standing before the floor length mirror as he adjusted his alligator belt and smoothed down his slick dark hair. He applied balm to his deep crimson lips and his rugged, dark facial stubble already looked bristly and heavy. He'd been up since 5:00 and had already jogged, showered and spent an hour on the internet catching up on the news and sending a flurry of market instructions to his traders. He finished packing his carry-on and left a generous tip on the bureau before leaving his room to meet Axel in his suite.

Axel peered into the peephole of his door upon hearing a knock and took a deep breath before opening it to greet Gnady.

"Good morning, Gnady, hope you enjoyed your rest. I'm sorry for pissing you off last night during our talk with that damned American. It's hard for me to control my feelings sometimes. You know my passion for the environment, and how I abhor the damage to it caused by big oil."

"Don't worry Axel, all is forgiven. But be more mindful in the future, we need to remain calm if we are going to get through the next couple of weeks without detection."

"You're right. I won't let it happen again."

You bet, Gnady thought.

"Let's enjoy brunch; room service just brought it up."

"Good, I am hungry," Pankov replied.

A sumptuous spread was arranged on the breakfast cart. Axel poured a cup of black coffee for himself and tea for Gnady, while Gnady dug into a plate of gravlax and sprinkled some flax seed over the sour milk he had ladled into a bowl. He helped himself to a glass of vitamin juice and avoided the carb-laden bread and pastries. The two walked over to an alcove in the suite where there was seating and a desk, and they began to eat.

After a few swallows, Axel dabbed his mouth with a linen cloth, frowned at the inclement weather outside and turned his attention to the business at hand. "I've taken the liberty of preparing a draft of our Manifesto, Gnady. Here it is, tell me what you think," Axel said as he handed Pankov a typed page that he removed from a folder.

"I appreciate your initiative," Gnady remarked, resuming his concentration and starting to feel a twinge of remorse over the rebuke he had given to Axel the evening before. As he walked over to the desk, Pankov removed a pen from his shirt pocket and began pacing as he read the text slowly, tracing each line with the pen's gold nib.

To the Citizens of the World:

> *For too long, mankind has ignored the growing and undeniable body of evidence of global warming and environmental damage caused by its reliance on fossil*

fuels for energy. The situation is fast approaching crisis levels at which we will lose all control.

Action is urgently needed to secure not only mankind's survival on this planet, but also the survival of all life forms that share the world with us. To date, governments have shamefully failed to agree on sustainable solutions to our unnecessary and perilous dependence on fossil fuels.

In any event, the day of reckoning will soon be at hand, for we have already entered the period of Peak Oil, and rationing will begin to occur in a matter of years.

We can no longer afford to stand by idly and must act now to save the planet.

Accordingly, an anonymous coalition of concerned environmentalists intends to start neutralizing oil production and storage facilities around the world to force a reduction of oil production and usage. This will also accelerate the use of alternative, clean energy sources as oil prices rise, if we begin to ration oil as we must. A rapid changeover to sustainable energy is the only option that will let us survive as we exit the planet's Peak Oil producing years.

The plan of our coalition is to force a reduction of human-produced carbon emissions by 50% from current levels in ten years' time. It can be done voluntarily if

governments agree on prompt measures to reduce oil
usage and utilize clean technology to manage pollution.
Or, we will intervene as required.

To show our determination and capability, we recently
neutralized Scandinavia's largest oil depot in Gothen-
burg, Sweden and a storage tank at a nearby facility.

All petroleum sources around the world are vulnera-
ble to elimination through a natural process we have
perfected. The next site we have targeted is a large oil
installation in the Western hemisphere.

There is nothing that can be done to stop us. The just
and equitable phaseout of fossil fuels must begin in
earnest. The future must become low carbon. Heed
our warning in an orderly way, or we will destroy the
world's supply of oil on a schedule of our choosing.

Pankov put his pen down and smiled. "This is perfect, Axel. A bit
of fear along with a measured warning, meaning that the markets
will be at least able to price in the cost of cutting carbon output
over ten years. I'm confident this will create the market effect we
both wish to achieve."

"I'm happy you approve. Take our Manifesto back to Moscow
with you," Axel said, handing Gnady one of the copies he brought
with him.

"I'm flying back this evening," Gnady confirmed. "My chief security officer will send it anonymously to the news wire services.

Like the stratum of a *matryoshka* doll, his layers of encryption are untraceable even by the top Western intelligence agencies. Servers upon servers upon servers. We'll arrange for the media to have it on their desks a few hours before trading begins on Monday, for maximum effect. Panic will grip the traders as rumors spread and they rush to cover their positions. We'll see the spot market for Brent crude rise in London by ten pounds if it gains a shilling," Gnady wagered. An even higher fortune in profit would soon be at hand.

And with that, Gnady returned to the service cart, pinched one of the tasty shrimp tea sandwiches off a plate and greedily popped it in his mouth, chewing and grinning at the same time, his destiny once again secure.

CH. 28

Normally, Annarino would have utilized a standard hoist and basket operation to pluck up Mostov while hovering from a safe distance above, but there was no reason to believe the seaman would at all cooperate once he left the bridge, and the winds were way too strong for a rappelling maneuver. Moreover, the ship's captain had already shown his uncooperative intentions. Instead, Annarino prepared for the landing. In the near white-out conditions of the snow squalls, it was difficult for Annarino to position the helo above the landing site in advance of the descent to the deck. He had at most twenty-five feet of clear visibility below, and he hoped that would be enough. Ice on the blades had begun to affect the helo's flight capability. Its wide blades were starting to lose their bite, and Annarino was feeling it through his controls. The tanker was still cruising at near top speed below, and its deck heaved up and down in rhythm with swells the size of three-story apartment buildings that buffeted the ship. The task of landing on a bouncing helipad while trying to remain stable in turbulent gales would be a challenge even for Annarino, an ace pilot. And Annarino was not one to disappoint.

Tactical coordinator Berman normally would have used the flare dispenser to provide extra illumination and visual depth for the landing, but doing so on an oil tanker was obviously out of the question. The best he could do was to keep the six under-fuselage searchlights at his disposal fixed on the landing pad, as he tried to get a visual of the deck through the chin bubble below his seat. Without a horizon to reference, it became difficult to hover. Once again, he calmly lifted his night vision visor which was grainy from the swirling snow caught in the downwash of the main rotor.

Annarino flared the helo's nose down to gain a better view of the deck below. The surface was congested with a tangle of pipes and metal scaffolds. Eventually, the helipad came into view.

"Watch for wires or any other obstructions," he cautioned.

"Roger that," Berman replied as both strained to maintain situational awareness. When mishaps occurred, they were usually the result of a lack of crew coordination.

"Easy right. Easy back and left 20 feet. 10 and hold," Berman coached his pilot. "Start your descent." They were hovering 25 feet over the helipad.

On the ship below, Captain Voitchenko called his security officer on a walkie-talkie, avoiding the vessel's intercom.

"Gregori, meet me on the bridge, I have an urgent matter to discuss with you."

"Yes Captain," was the prompt reply.

Gregori Chelmnov was a burly man with a barrel chest, shaved head and hands as big as baseball mitts. As husky as Chelmnov was, he was also quick and well-coordinated. Per the Captain's orders, Chelmnov was the only other crewmember allowed to carry a sidearm, which he often displayed in a shoulder holster for the benefit of any new crew who signed on. All in all, he was an imposing figure who the crew feared more than the captain, and with good cause. When Voitchenko hand-picked Chelmnov some ten years earlier, he gave the security officer just one command: to always maintain strict discipline and order on board. In the ensuing years, the loyal and dutiful Chelmnov had not let the captain down.

Chelmnov entered the bridge and walked briskly to a side console where Voitchenko waited.

"Officer Chelmnov, there are two NATO helicopters shadowing us overhead, and I have reluctantly given one of them permission to land. They claim to have a warrant from INTERPOL to arrest seaman Mostov for committing an offense while on shore leave in Gothenburg. If he did anything so foolish, as far as I am concerned, they can have him."

"*Da*, Captain," the dispassionate Chelmnov replied. "Shall I apprehend Mostov, or will they?"

"I only gave them permission to board, not search the ship. So, we must restrain Mostov and turn him over. After I inspect the warrant and approve Mostov's arrest, you will hand him over to them here on the bridge, after you secure him."

"Understood. But the landing conditions will be most adverse," Chelmnov noted.

"True. But I will not reduce speed, as it would take us at least twenty minutes to reach a crash stop in full reverse, plus another thirty minutes to reach top cruising speed again. They can have Mostov, but I am not required to deliver him on a silver platter. It will be their choice whether they wish to land, and if they can do so safely. I expect them shortly, so proceed now."

"*Da*, Captain." Chelmnov pivoted toward the water-tight door, opened the latch and loped down the several flights of stairs to the crew quarters beneath the bridge. There were no locks on the doors, but custom called for an advance knock and permission to enter before opening a cabin door. Chelmnov felt no such compunction and burst into the room where Mostov lay in his bunk. Mostov sat up when his door unexpectedly opened, and then he froze at the sight of Chelmnov bearing down on him. Reflexively, Mostov curled up into the corner of the bed and coiled his legs close to his chest, hoping to kick-strike Chelmnov as he approached. Chelmnov didn't break his stride and reacted to the pathetic sight of his quarry by swearing and grabbing the rail of Mostov's bunk. Able to curl fifty kilos, Chelmnov quickly jerked the bedrail upward and Mostov tumbled out of the bed with a thud. Chelmnov threw the bed to the side and snared the stunned Mostov by the back of his neck as he squirmed near the floor with his face pushed against the wall. Chelmnov pressed his knee into the back of his prey for good measure, and the mismatched brawl was effectively over. Pinned to the corner of the room and breathing with difficulty, Mostov accepted his capture with a muffled cry of surrender.

Chelmnov eased off Mostov and brought him to his feet.

"Comrade Mostov, Captain Voitchenko has requested the pleasure of your company, and I am your escort. But first, tell me where you've stowed your ID," Chelmnov said.

Mostov motioned to the top shelf of a row of built-ins, and Chelmnov held Mostov against the nearby wall, still gripping his neck. After riffling across the shelf with his free hand, Chelmnov found Mostov's wallet and stuffed it into his pocket. His passport was already being held in the ship's safe, along with those of all the other crew. Then he shoved the sullen seaman into the hallway while pinning Mostov's arm behind his back. With one false move, he could have snapped it from his shoulder socket.

Eventually, they made their way up to the bridge where several other staff and officers had gathered.

Captain Voitchenko spoke as the crew stood around in silent witness. "Midshipman Mostov, I will shortly receive an INTERPOL warrant for your arrest. Because we are not in Federation waters, I have no choice but to comply and hand you over to the authorities who will board us at any moment. Have you anything to say which might cause me to reconsider turning you over to them? What do they want from you? What did you do during shore leave?"

Mostov's head was spinning, and he stood stunned and speechless before the assembled officers.

Realizing the gravity of the situation, he suddenly cried out, "Captain, I have done nothing wrong." He was terrified at the thought of being arrested yet again. As grim and difficult as life was in Murmansk, he had no desire to spend any more time in a jail cell, even one in Sweden.

"I bought some food and walked the streets. I met a local man, and we talked about the ship, nothing more."

"Tell me more about this man," Voitchenko pressed.

He was no one, we just talked at a restaurant, that's all," Dima lied. Then he desperately blurted, "You cannot let them take me!" in a quavering tone.

It was all the seasoned Captain needed to hear to conclude that Mostov had committed a serious infraction or violated an important trust during his encounter with the Swede. The Captain felt no sympathy for Mostov.

"You are a fool, seaman Mostov. Now I'm ordering you to remain silent. Security Officer Chelmnov will hold you until such time as your arrest, which I expect will be imminent," the captain said. Chelmnov then cuffed Mostov and stuffed the midshipman's wallet and passport into his pants pocket.

Overhead, Major Annarino began to spool down to the *Smolensk II*. The occupants on the bridge strained to watch its approach through the bullet-proof, thick plexiglass. In turn, Annarino glanced at the brightly illuminated bridge and saw a group of figures at the controls and two more standing beside each other in the port bridge wing. He assumed one of them was Mostov. As he descended, Annarino began to feel vibrations from the drag and loss of lift caused by icing on the blades, so he adjusted his torque to compensate. He resolved to land, apprehend Mostov and climb above the howling storm as quickly as possible.

"Can't allow more than fifty percent of the leading edge of the blades to get ice-covered," Berman cautioned on the intercom, "or we risk getting stranded on the tanker or falling from the sky." There was also the chance of ice entering the engine and causing a flameout if the particle separators in the turbines began to choke.

As he nosed the bird toward the landing spot, Annarino activated the switch for the automatic landing program and let the helo steady herself as she approached the ship's deck with her landing gear extended. With only ten feet to touchdown, the automatic landing program failed due to its inability to gauge the distance and slope of the rolling surface below. Normally, a slope of over fifteen or twenty degrees off vertical would require manual landing. The alarm sounded and a red caution light blared overhead. Caught off guard, Annarino grabbed at the controls to regain manual operation.

With only five feet to touchdown, the deck rose up in a large wave swell and slammed into the landing gear under the tail, producing a loud cracking noise and causing the cockpit's instrument panel to light up like a Christmas tree. The kick from the deck catapulted the helo back up in the air as the stunned craft trembled from the throbbing effect of a bent tail driveshaft. Both crewmen grimaced as they felt the blow course up their spines.

"Dammit," Annarino swore and instinctively pulled on the collective, attempting a straight climb and hoping that he could abort the mission at that point. But the feeble torque from the damaged tail rotor spun the helo toward the open sea as if it were an errant shuttlecock. Just as Annarino managed to regain control, the helo encountered a blast of air flow that accelerated off the sea and up the side wall of the ship. The gust buffeted the main rotor blade, and the windswept helo yawed backward. As Annarino strained to recover yet another time, his luck ran out. Helicopters are inherently unstable, and the airflow around the rotor blades and fuselage is highly complex. The bucking helo's crippled tail rotor dipped low and struck the deck railing. Both crewmen gritted their teeth as the rotor blade sheered into the deck in a staccato of clangs and screeches.

With nothing to counter the torque of the main rotor, the helo gyrated uncontrollably, and despite Annarino's frantic efforts, it began a slow and reluctant descent down the side of the ship. Moments later, the doomed craft touched down on the craggy breakers that nearly clawed over the oil tanker's gunwales.

In the agonizing final seconds of their struggle to save themselves, no opportunity presented itself for the stricken crew to signal a mayday alert. After losing radar and voice contact, the remaining helo searched in vain in the darkness for a flare or other sign of life, to no avail. The co-pilot took note of the crash site coordinates and programmed the flight computer to maintain position in case a flare or other signal appeared. Only thirty minutes of fuel was left to find the downed pilots before the solo helo would be forced to wave off and head back to base.

Captain Voitchenko, surveying the concatenation on the deck below, coolly remarked, "Midshipman Mostov, it appears you have been temporarily reprieved. Although I did not receive your arrest warrant, I am ordering you to spend the remainder of the voyage in the brig. You must thank the Holy Mother you were not aboard that cursed flying machine."

Mostov appeared both relieved and resigned. Officer Chelmnov once again took him by his arm and led him toward the stairwell. When they were out of range, Captain Voitchenko addressed his communications officer.

"Have the radio operator contact fleet command and put the call through to my cabin in five minutes. I wish to report this incident."

Then he turned to his skipper. "Only fools invade Russia in wintertime. To home port, full speed ahead."

CH. 29.

Monday morning, television news anchors began reporting on the story of an anonymous Manifesto being distributed by the newswire services. The social media networks promptly picked up the story, and on-line postings went viral with it while tweet volume buzzed as well. Thousands of groups around the world began to follow the news phenomena. But there was little follow-on news to confirm or deny the wide range of rumors swirling around the message. The effect on the market was predictable, and crude futures in Chicago had jumped by eight dollars per barrel on average, a huge move by historic standards. This would equate to roughly a dollar or more for gasoline and diesel at the pump. Oil prices in Japan opened dramatically higher and were climbing in steady increments as traders lost nerve and speculators moved in, smelling blood on the floor. In the U.S., the Dow futures indicated an 800-point drop at the opening of the market. The Footsie and CAC markets were opening soon and showed similar losses at the open.

Karin and Daniel had already checked out of the Grand Hotel and were aboard the first-class compartment on one of the early trains headed for Gothenburg. Karin catnapped while Daniel kept busy answering email pings on his iPhone from the State and Energy Departments which fed him more intel on the story. There wasn't much to go on. In one email he learned that a joint State, Defense and Energy task force was formed on national security grounds. Another email instructed him to transmit a status report later in the day covering anything and everything; even the most miniscule details on news and leads were requested. Such details often bore significant fruit.

He phoned his office, and his secretary Heather answered.

"Hi Daniel, how was your weekend?" Heather inquired.

"Magical. I'll fill you in when I see you. Have you heard the news about the oil supply threat, that Manifesto? I'm getting bombarded with emails from home asking for any news I can relay. I'm going to have to come up with something fast. The oil companies and their trade associations are peppering me too. We're going to have a busy day, and I don't expect to get back to Gothenburg until just before lunch. Karin and I are on the morning train."

"Is there anything I can do?" she asked.

"There is. Please call over to Sweden's Office of National Security in Stockholm and set up a phone conference for 14:00 with Thor Bjornsson for me. He's an intelligence officer; I'll text you his contact info. This weekend, through INTERPOL, I helped him issue an arrest warrant for a suspect who they believe may have contaminated the Port's oil. But now I'm going to need Thor's cooperation, and let's just say he owes me. Ask him to convene a briefing later this afternoon with the Port police so I can get up to speed with their investigation. I can meet them at their office."

"Okay. Anything more?"

"Call Langley's staff operations officer at the Embassy in Stockholm and tell him I need anything they can get on one Gnady

Pankov, an oil trader from Moscow. Spelled P-a-n-k-o-v. I met him at the client event hosted by Karin's firm last night and found him rather interesting, to say the least. While you are at it, see what there is on one Axel Carlsson, who runs a biotech and marine research foundation on Marstrand. And ask the same of Officer Bjornssson, perhaps he'll have something he can share."

"Sure. Anything else I can do?" Heather asked.

"That's it for now, other than keep my appointment calendar as free as you can for the rest of this week." As he glanced over to Karin, he said "Karin and I plan to grab a quick lunch in Gothenburg. I'll come to the office afterward. But give me a call if I get any important calls or messages. Thanks, Heather," he concluded.

"Of course. I'll get right on this and see you in a bit," she replied.

Daniel put his phone down and looked over at Karin, who was now awake and had listened to the call.

"Christ, Karin, things are heating up. An anonymous threat was published this morning about the oil contamination at Tor Harbor and the Port's refinery. It's the first real break we have. Here, you can read it on my phone."

With a few clicks Daniel's phone screen opened to the Manifesto, and he handed the mobile to her. She mouthed the words as she read.

"How awful. What kind of people could do this? *Can* they do this?" Karin asked.

"Good question, we plan to find out. Whoever they are, their threat appears to be credible. They've struck at least twice now. It looks like the real deal. I'm going to have a busy afternoon, but my meetings won't start until after lunch. Why don't we have a bite to eat when we get back to Gothenburg? Do you have time?"

"I'd love to. I also need to get back to the office this afternoon. There's a conference call on a Romanian cross-border lease deal I need to sit in on."

"Great, I'm famished!" he said.

Trains are often late in Sweden, but this one rolled into the central station at Gothenburg on time. The couple hailed a taxi, and Daniel told the driver to take them to Smakling, his favorite haunt. The driver threw their luggage in the trunk, and they sped off.

Klaus was behind the bar and hailed Daniel as the couple entered.

"*Hej* Daniel, welcome! I see you have a guest, table for two?"

"Thanks Klaus, please meet my friend Karin," Daniel said, and Klaus came out from behind the bar to shake Karin's hand.

"The pleasure is mine," Klaus said, his eyes sparkling upward to her as he gave Karin a formal bow. "Come this way, I have a quiet table toward the back of the restaurant that you can have." With that he stowed their luggage and escorted them to their table, two menus in hand.

"I like this place a lot," Daniel offered. "As comfortable here as wearing a pair of old slippers. You'll find some classics on the menu, and I can definitely recommend the meatballs."

"Count me in," Karin replied.

Daniel ordered for the two of them, and Klaus dutifully marched into the kitchen with their order.

"I asked a government intelligence officer in Stockholm to call me later this afternoon, Karin. One of the things I asked for was a file on Axel and his Foundation, the SBF." Daniel said.

"I know, I overheard," Karin replied. "I wish I could help you, however the privacy laws and our firm policy prohibit my sharing anything on either of them that's non-public. Do you understand?"

"Of course," Daniel replied and added, "but I need to inform my government that the SBF's auditor is your accounting firm. My report must include all available details. You are Persson & Frandberg's account manager with the SBF, so this could become a little awkward."

"I understand," Karin replied. "But we aren't at the point of any conflict of interest yet, are we?"

"I don't think so. But we must be careful since there's a limit to what we can discuss."

"I fully agree," Karin replied.

A moment later, Klaus approached their table with two plates of meatballs on his arm and he placed them in front of his patrons. Another waiter followed with two serving bowls brimming with lingonberries and *gurken* salad.

"Anything else I can get you?" Klaus offered.

"No, we're fine. But we're on a fairly tight schedule, so please bring the bill on your next round," Daniel said. Klaus nodded.

Karin reached over the table and took Daniel's hand. A studied look appeared on her face, and she spoke earnestly.

"I had a wonderful weekend, Daniel, in every way. You were a dear. I can see you're going to be extremely busy during the next several days, and the last thing you'll need is any distractions. So don't worry about me, focus on your job and know that I'll be here when you can find the time. No pressures."

Daniel squeezed her hand and nodded as he listened. He felt a sense of relief and appreciation for Karin's assurances. On the train he had fretted about how he would balance the demands of the coming week with his desire to be with Karin. She had let him off the hook, and the thought floated in his mind that *she* was the dear one.

CH. 30

They parted company outside the restaurant. Daniel called a taxi and sped off to the Consulate, where a crisply dressed Marine searched through his bag and waved him through security. Heather noticed him on the office's closed-circuit lobby camera. She greeted him as he entered the reception area where she sat at one of the desks. Heather detected a twinkle in his eye.

"Welcome home. I can see you must have had a nice time."

"Back to reality," he said as he put his carry-on luggage next to the coat closet.

"Is there ever too much of a good thing?"

"I won't bet you on this one!" he smiled.

"So, a good time was had by all. You can tell me more later if you wish. By the way, your call with Officer Bjornsson starts soon, I'll patch you in. Also, Langley came through with a file on Mr. Pankov. His dossier is in the blue wrapper, on the top of the inbox on your desk. They had nothing on Mr. Carlsson, but I copied the English pages from his firm's website for you. Quite the idealist, it appears."

Daniel sat down at his desk and thumbed through the mail and messages. He glanced at a credenza where a stack of customs paperwork lay in another box, ready for his review. They would wait. He sat back, opened the blue folder and removed the file on Pankov. The pages revealed he was forty-five years old, born in Moscow and divorced. Undergraduate education at St. Petersburg State University with an executive MBA in finance from Columbia. Parents deceased, no siblings. His first job was with the Barings Bank New York office, which later became the ING Group, and a couple of years later he transferred to its Moscow office. He became a partner and eventually the firm's Moscow office manager. After the firm imploded in the 1990s, he opened his own trading firm with personal and borrowed funds. He had multiple entry visas to the U.S., with entry points from countries including Brazil, Mexico and various OPEC states. Occupied a townhome in central Moscow. Public ownership records showed Pankov held 25% of Pankovneft with the other 75% held by a Cypriot trust since 2009, after the global market crash. As did a lot of companies, Pankovneft likely needed recapitalization during those dark days, Daniel speculated. A local Cypriot attorney was named as trustee. The firm's financials were lacking, and without a permanent U.S. establishment, no U.S. income tax filings were required by Pankovneft. Old personal income tax records from his stint in New York while at Columbia were still available, according to the sheet Daniel read from. But there wasn't much of interest from that period and little else in the file.

"It's 14:00, I'll place the call now," Heather said from her desk. In a few moments, the intercom light on his phone lit up, and he picked up the handset. Officer Bjornsson's deep voice was on the other line.

"Hello Thor. Thank you for being available."

"No worries," Thor amiably offered.

"Were you able to get any information about the two persons of interest I met up with by chance this weekend, in Stockholm? My secretary Heather called in with the names earlier this morning."

"Yes, we got her inquiry," Bjornsson acknowledged.

"Good. I'm confirming that the first is Axel Carlsson, who resides on Marstrand. He runs a foundation called the *Svenska Biomarina Forskningsinstitutet*. The other is one of his connections by the name of Gnady Pankov, a citizen of the Russian Federation. He operates an oil trading firm known as Pankovneft. Were you able to find anything on them?"

"Daniel, Swedish privacy law is rather strict on what I can tell you about these individuals. If it involves State security, however, I have a little more leeway. If so, to save time I can accept an official request from your Embassy after we speak. Can you arrange that?"

"Yes, Thor."

"Very well. In that case, I will begin with Mr. Carlsson and his Foundation. The Foundation he runs is privately owned, and as you already know, it is based on Marstrand. He is its sole founder, owner and director. It has an operating budget of approximately 10 MEu per annum and has reported funds on hand of 60 MEu, invested conservatively, judging from its tax returns. It gets its revenue from a mix of sales of environmental spill solutions, consulting fees and donations. It is annually audited as required by law. The Foundation appears to be above board. The problem, however, is with Mr. Carlsson. He has been on our radar screen for some time. We first noticed him when he was just seventeen. He was arrested and jailed while protesting at a G-8 summit in Madrid. The Spanish are lenient on these kinds of things and released him the following day on the condition that he exited the country in 24 hours. Our Madrid Embassy helped to make departure arrangements for him. It appears we escorted him from jail and put him on the next SAS flight out, unfortunately to a hero's welcome at home among the anarchist crowd and Greens. During college he turned his energies toward environmental causes and joined the Young Greens, a radical group with ties to the global environmental movement. You may recall that some of these jerks trashed downtown Gothenburg in 2001 during an EU conference. It is believed that Axel bailed them all out, probably for old time's sake. Today he's a brilliant and respected scientist, on the cutting edge of genetic engineering. According to our security branch, he usually keeps a low profile on environmental causes, but he nevertheless is still thought to hold extremist views. So, there's clearly a dark side to him when it comes to the environment. Just like a dog returning to its vomit, he can't help himself from time to time."

"Alright, thanks for that rather ugly picture."

"By the way, have you received any news on the arrest of Mostov?" Bjornsson inquired.

"I haven't heard anything yet this morning, but I'm expecting an update soon. As soon as I learn something, I'll let you know. It'll be interesting to see how long it takes for Mostov to talk. Russian mob associates, even at the lower levels, are known to be as loyal as guard dogs. Fortunately, we have an ex-GITMO interrogator waiting for him at the base. If anyone can make a detainee talk, it's him," Daniel said.

"I'm sympathetic," Bjornsson said. "But I would advise you to refrain from mentioning the GITMO connection to any of my colleagues, since GITMO is still a toxic subject to many Swedes, including those in law enforcement."

"Understood," Daniel replied. "From now let's assume our interrogator is a former Boy Scout."

Bjornsson chuckled, "Off the record, I wish him luck. I'll expect your call soon." Then he hung up.

CH. 31

The Divine Providence that saved seaman Mostov from arrest was also working to protect flight crew members Annarino and Berman. One of the huge swells riding up the side of the *Smolensk II* caught the helo and cradled its fall until the chopper reached a valley between the waves some thirty meters below. It sat momentarily like a lame duck, its bay doors wide open and exposed. As the frigid, black saltwater flooded in freely, the helo's nose started to slip beneath the water line.

The bobbing helo was soon caught in the wake of the swiftly steaming ship and nearly tipped sideways. Working on pure adrenalin and cognizant of the waning moments of buoyancy, Annarino opened the latch to his door and motioned Berman to follow his lead. The two men pushed out of the partially submerged helo and floated onto the surface. Moments later, the helo got absorbed into the vast expanse of the sea as inconsequentially as the myriads of swirling snowflakes that blanketed it.

Both men were excellent swimmers, and when they reached one another, they held on tightly in the surf. Each kicked his legs powerfully to stay afloat, aided by an automatically inflating life preserver that unrolled from the collar of their harness. Both wore rubber-lined exposure suits underneath their flight suits. The exposure suit functioned like a diver's dry suit, keeping them warm in the frigid water. Batteries powered the suit, but the life of the batteries could last for perhaps thirty to forty minutes. At that point they would weaken to the point where hypothermia would set in, sealing the wearer's fate. Every extra second of the search would be crucial.

"See those lights?" Berman yelled, pointing at a 30-degree angle.

"Yes," Annarino nodded.

"She's coming around for another pass. Activate your helmet light," Berman shouted, as he reached to activate the distress light mounted on his helmet. Annarino followed suit. Twin high beams pierced the darkness, and their columns were silhouetted by the falling flakes of snow. They were uncertain if the lights would be enough.

The pilots next checked the status of the signal beacons embedded in their suits. When an airman ejects, his sonar beacon automatically engages, allowing rescuers to pinpoint his position. Both beacons were operating. The downed airmen were also aware that the helo searching above had thermal reading equipment that without doubt was scouring the water below for them.

With so much rescue technology at work, it took less than a minute for the pilot overhead to lock onto the struggling crew. A few more moments passed when Annarino tapped Berman on the shoulder, pointing to the approaching headlights of the other helo. They watched as the pilot deftly steered the chopper to a hover point forty yards or so above them.

"He's taking his good ole time," Berman scowled while Annarino grinned at their good fortune.

Meanwhile, the co-pilot of the Jolly Green II radioed the base at Varanger and told the operator they were now on a rescue mission for the downed crew.

Colonel Duke was in the command room monitoring the mission when the call came in.

"Jheezuz Christ!" he bellowed. "I want those airmen rescued pronto, do you copy?"

Raising a stranded body safely into a helicopter takes skill, effort and training, plus hooks, lines and hoists. As if on cue, one of the two back-enders in the Jolly Green II activated the helo's external rescue hoist cable which he steered using a hand controller. The rescue hoist spiraled down toward Annarino and Berman. It was equipped with green and red LEDs for increased visibility needed in covert operations. Without the LEDs, the floundering crew could not easily time their catch in a nighttime sea rescue mission. It was of no practical help that the hoist was painted neon yellow.

The hoist swung around them in the wind like a pendulum as it bumped along the surface of the water. It took a few passes for the rig to come within an arm's reach of the stricken crew. Annarino lunged at the swiftly bouncing hoist but missed it on its first pass by just a second. It came around again and on the next pass, Berman caught it firmly around his arm. He checked his grip to avoid getting potentially jolted as the line went from slack to taught to slack again by the helo's movement. Berman took the hoist and helped Annarino onto it. The two crew working in the cabin watched the operation and activated the winch motor to begin the extraction after Annarino gave him an animated thumbs up.

Halfway to safety in the helo, the cable carrying Annarino began to spin in the violent downwash created by strong wind gusts of 50 knots that were enhanced by the rotor motion. He soon felt disoriented and nauseous from the effects of spinning and tried to work himself free of the hoist, but to no avail. As he spun faster and faster, he lost hold of the line and rotated around like a whirligig, losing consciousness. Meanwhile, up in the hoist assembly housing, some of the individual strands of the cable started to fray from twisting around and rubbing violently against each other. The tension from the buckling wire caused the assembly to vibrate and jolt as the limp crewman reached the cabin of the helo, where a serviceman wearing a safety harness reached over to pull him on board. After dragging Annarino clear of the cabin opening, he worked Annarino out of the hoist and then pulled him to a fold-up seat and buckled the stricken pilot snuggly in it. Annarino lifted his head, shook it, and slowly began to return to his senses.

Berman waited below for what felt like a lifetime. Meanwhile, the serviceman attempted to send the hoist back down, but the winch motor creaked loudly, and the line refused to unspool. He looked up into the housing and realized that a large segment of the cable's wire strands must have ratsnested. There was no way to get into the hoist housing to cut the frayed strands away, and even if he could, the distressed cable was no longer safe to use.

He returned to the cockpit to inform the pilot that the hoist was busted. The pilot, a seasoned pro and cool under fire, radioed Varanger to give an update on the situation. He spoke over the helo's intercom so the other three crew members could hear.

"We've recovered one of the crew, but the hoist is now FUBAR. It's just a single hoist, not a dual. So, there's no way to recover the other crewman. We have about ten minutes more of fuel before we need to cut out and reach the coast in time. Waiting your instructions." The dispirited pilot looked grimly at his fellow co-pilot.

Before joining the USAF, Colonel Duke worked for several years on his daddy's cattle ranch up in Pagosa Springs, Colorado. As a farmhand, he had plenty of ideas of how to move loads using his ingenuity and a rope.

"For fuck's sake, boys, you know we never leave anyone behind! On the double, now! Unstow one of the auxiliary nylon ropes and make sure you have your gloves on. You're gonna tie a signal lamp to one end of it and secure the other end of the line to the bar that holds the hoist assembly. Then just lower the rope down to the target. When he grabs hold, your crew will work in tandem to pull him up faster than a one-eyed dog in a meat market! And don't forget to turn the goddamned lamp on, like it's Christmastime!"

"Roger that," the re-energized pilot replied.

The pilot activated his auto hover button, and the two back-enders scrambled to carry out their orders. In seconds they attached the rope as instructed and guided it to the ocean's surface below. Berman saw the beam of the light swinging at the rope's end; the crewman above tried countering the rope's movement to steady it as much as possible. It took a few tries, but Berman eventually caught the signal lamp with a strong grip. He realized there was a problem with the hoist, so he improvised for the journey up to the helo. With some of the nylon rope's slack, he fashioned a bowline knot for his foot and stepped into it. The two rescue crewmembers felt his weight on the rope and in tandem began tugging Berman toward them. Berman swayed in the wind and held on for life, knowing what had happened to Annarino during his ascent. He held his body's mass toward the center axis of the rope to help reduce the torque of the wind. Fortunately, the adrenaline-fueled crewmen pulled Berman up faster than the action of the methodical winch, and the spinning effects of the wind were largely averted. Berman clambered aboard the chopper unassisted as the two panting servicemen caught their breath.

"What took you boys so long?", Berman shouted as he shook their hands, grinning widely. "A few more minutes and I'd have had to call me a Uber!"

The whole search and rescue team chuckled in relief and prepared for their trip back to the base, with no time to spare.

Berman then took the seat beside Annarino and began to check him over as he began to come around. Annarino made the sign of the cross and Berman nodded. The two death-cheating men were silent as they fist pumped and secured themselves for the merciful flight home.

CH. 32

The late afternoon meeting at the Port of Gothenburg police headquarters was scheduled to begin promptly at 16:00. Gunnar, Eva, Stig and Anna arrived early and waited impatiently around the conference table. Daniel walked in exactly on time and introduced himself to Lieutenant Dahlquist and the inspectors. Professor Gisslen arrived late, clutching his hat and jacket in one hand while fumbling with a briefcase and umbrella in the other. He had a security tag hanging upside down from the lapel pocket of his tweed sport coat, cracked his knuckles and pushed his glasses up on the bridge of his nose. Stig sighed.

"Sorry I'm late," the Professor murmured apologetically as he opened his briefcase, took out a stack of papers and thumped them on the conference table. He wiped his brow and took a seat, breathing heavily from the dash he hadn't yet recovered from.

"It's okay, Professor," Anna offered. "Pour yourself some coffee, and please try to catch your breath." Then she reached for the speaker phone and dialed Thor Bjornsson in Stockholm who was waiting and answered on the first ring.

Eva nodded thanks to Anna and then spoke in a matter-of-fact tone. "Welcome to today's call. With us here at your suggestion,

Thor, is Daniel Lake, the U.S. commercial attaché based in Gothenburg. He works on a U.S. government task force which is investigating what we now believe is a major threat to the world's oil supply, as reported in the news this morning. Also joining us today is Professor Gisslen who you met at last week's meeting. I suggest we go around the room and give an update on what we have learned since our meeting last week. After we are done, Professor Gisslen will fill us in on what "Peak Oil" is all about. You'll recall it was mentioned in this morning's infamous environmental Manifesto. It very well could be the key to understanding the background of the person or persons behind the attack on the Port's oil facilities."

Gunnar went first. "Needless to say, security has been beefed up across the entire peninsula, focusing on the refinery, storage areas and the Port's loading docks. It's a huge challenge since the entire area is unfortunately accessible to a determined intruder. Security cameras are being installed as quickly as we can source them. Luckily, there is just one road artery that services the Port, running parallel along the coast, so the cameras we're installing will soon be able to monitor all vehicles coming and leaving. We'll soon have more road cameras up than central London. In addition, security patrol dogs from Poland and Romania are being flown in; it seems they are plentiful there. The coastline is a little trickier to monitor. Patrol boats are sweeping the waterfront on irregular schedules, and shore leave for foreign crews has been suspended. Everyone has been cooperative. If there is another incident, the hope is that it won't be on our turf. If it is, though, we are in near lockdown condition so there's a good chance we'll catch anyone foolish enough to return to the refinery, or any other oil facility, for that matter."

Anna was next. "After the Manifesto was published this morning, it became clear that we were likely dealing with eco-terrorists or enviro-anarchists. They usually work in independent, small groups. Many are very capable, and at the top of their chain have advanced university degrees. They are difficult to track as they stay low and off the grid. When they communicate, they are careful to do so in dark rooms on the web. These places are very difficult to access, we therefore could use some help from your NSA, Daniel, to analyze the data we've amassed. I've also been working on developing a profile from which to begin searching criminal databases for potential suspects. And now I am beginning to think that the seaman I earlier profiled doesn't fit the..."

Just then Daniel's phone rang, and the read-out was a number at the State Department, one of the task force members. He excused himself and walked out into the hall.

"Bad news, Daniel," the caller said.

"What is it?"

"INTERPOL's arrest of Dima Pankov went sideways. Unfortunately, he's still on the tanker and will arrive in his home port of Murmansk soon."

"What happened?"

"The chopper went down with its crew in a storm. No details yet about how it happened."

"Are there contingency plans?" Daniel asked.

"We are working on it. One of our properties has been dispatched to Murmansk to hopefully tail Mostov, to see who tries to contact him, if he gets picked up, or whatever. If we get lucky, we'll get photos of his handler. That's about it for now. Oh, there's some talk of opening a channel with Russian security, given the media and political uproar over the threat. We are hoping they'll be cooperative and let a Swedish officer interrogate Mostov. They'll never allow an American near him. We're thinking a good candidate might be your Officer Bjornsson. He's as up to speed as anyone at this point. Whoever these bastards are, they are playing with fire, and everyone from the OECD to OPEC is under pressure to shut them down fast."

"It so happens I'm on a phone conference with Bjornsson now," Daniel said.

"Alright, work your charms, and let me know if you hear anything else."

"Will do," Daniel said as he signed off the call and re-entered the conference room.

All eyes turned to him as he sat down.

"It turns out all our efforts through INTERPOL to arrange Mostov's arrest were for naught. The NATO helo went down at sea before he could be arrested. No word on the crew's status. Mostov will be likely be picked up by the FSB as soon as he disembarks at the port. A tragic outcome."

"I was just mentioning that Mostov's profile had slipped in my ranking of suspects," Anna said, hoping to downplay the obvious setback and re-energize the dispirited room.

Daniel continued, "There may be other opportunities to track down the manifesto; my government is working on it through back channels. Separately, security in other port facilities around the world is being ramped up, just as in Sweden. There are gaps everywhere, it seems, based on a false sense of security over the low risk of old school industrial sabotage. It seems everyone's attention these days has been centered on cyber security, while traditional security precautions have not been kept up. But private industry is kicking into high gear on this now. Our NSA is also following the trail of the press release issued by these zealots. It could take us some time to determine the origin of their email, based on the sophistication of the encryption. But suffice it to say that we are good at rooting out where web communications originate. Last but not least, Thor and I have been doing background checks on a rather odd pair I met by coincidence this weekend. Gnady Pankov, a Russian oil trader, and Axel Carlsson, a local marine biologist with a history of supporting Green causes. I met them at a social event so it was not possible to speak with either of them in detail, but I plan to follow up the conversation with Carlsson on the types of people who could conceivably be behind this extreme case of sabotage. Maybe we'll get some good leads."

Eva cautioned, "With no jurisdiction over this man, Daniel, your questioning must be informal. In case you believe you will need to take formal statements, please bring Anna with you if Thor is not available to join you."

"Perfect. For now, assuming he'll cooperate with our request for an interview, the plan is to just gather background information from Carlsson," he said.

From such off-the-record talks, helpful information was often developed.

"Thank you all for your updates," Eva concluded. "Now let us learn more about Peak Oil from Professor Gisslen."

CH. 33

"As you recall, I am a marine biologist," the Professor began as he adjusted his glasses, "so a colleague in the geophysics department of Chalmers provided me with an overview on the theory known as Peak Oil. It's well outside my area of expertise, but at the same time it is not very difficult to understand. I've brought along some detailed articles on it in case you wish to delve deeper into the subject," pointing to the stack of papers on the table to his right.

"To begin with, any beer drinker will understand the concept as his glass drains. At some point, the glass goes from full to half empty. At the half-way point, the amount of beer -- or in our case, oil – begins to dwindle and will eventually run out. Thus, Peak Oil originally stood for the idea that sometime around the year 2000, roughly half the world's recoverable oil would be produced. By the way, already in the late 19th century there was great fear of the industrial age grinding to a halt over a belief that the world's supply of coal had peaked. But, as we now know, the world has at least a 500-year supply of coal."

"Who came up with the Peak Oil theory?" Stig interjected.

"An American geoscientist by the name of M. King Hubbert, working at Shell Oil. He predicted that oil production for a given area was finite in nature and resembled the shape of a bell. The top of the bell was the "peak" for the area's oil production. In the 1960s, he posited that American oil production would peak in 2005, but he was clearly wrong given advances in extraction technology and recovery levels. Also, he didn't anticipate marginal fields producing much more today than they did in his time, or the new extractions made possible by fracking and shale oil processing. Moreover, there has been a great amount of exploration in previously unreachable areas such as the deep seabed. New technologies and discoveries inspired by the profit motive have enabled the oil markets to maintain their long-term supply and downward price trends. Still, he had a point, and his concept has been accepted by the scientific community at large.

"We've seen the concept already apply closer to home, in Denmark, for example, where oil production has been on the decline during the last ten years, despite continued investment. Denmark increased its recovery rate to about 30% from perhaps 15% in the 1990s. But overall, Denmark's glass of beer is shrinking, and there is no more easy oil to be found in its part of the North Sea. No one can say for sure, but the Danes might be able to squeeze oil out of their dense limestone fields for another fifty years. The same will eventually happen to the Saudis, I might add, though the Kingdom keeps its true reserves a well-guarded secret."

"I hear pretty much the same views in the oil industry meetings I attend," Daniel confirmed. "Even our own President Jimmy Carter told our nation that we could exhaust the world's proven oil reserves in a decade. The authors of the communiqué seem to have their facts straight even if no one knows how much oil is left on the planet. The amount is finite, and these bastards are clever to twist that message to strike as much fear as possible over dwindling supplies. So, their call to action and demand to limit carbon consumption is compelling to a lot of people. Even our own governments and UN committees routinely call for lower carbon output, though nothing is as radical as this. I'm concerned with the political implications. Will Green parties in Italy and Germany rally to tip a change in their ruling coalitions? Will panic oil buying grip the markets? Will the global economy go into recession due to this threat? Will China become more aggressive in securing oil reserves, given its reliance on external oil supply? Could fear over supplies cause another war in the Mideast? Will OPEC take advantage of the situation? Will Iran become more aggressive as its revenue spikes? The possibilities are endless, so there's a lot riding on discovering who is behind this extortion plan and stopping them before things get out of hand."

"You are right", Dahlquist said, removing her glasses. "My team has been focusing on the crime itself, but there are much larger political issues involved," she said as she waived the glasses in the air, revealing their well-chewed temple tips.

Gisslen continued. "To be fair, there is another part of the story that runs a bit inversely to the Peak Oil one. I'd be remiss if I did not tell you a little about it."

"What is it, Professor? Dahlquist said.

"Some people in the oil industry have been discussing a new concept that the world will soon reach a point of peak *consumption* of petroleum-based energy. They say that after decades of growth in demand for oil, the demand for it will soon begin to fall. Several variables are driving this phenomenon of peak demand. Chief among them is the switch to natural gas and renewables, plus increasing electric vehicle acceptance. Widespread EV adoption alone will shave millions of barrels a day off global demand. The toughness of new regulations and speed of developing economies are two more factors. When and how these factors all coalesce and result in peak consumption is just as difficult to predict as the decade of reaching peak oil. The two theories are the flip sides of the same coin. Both events, peak oil and peak demand, are competing with each other for now. No one knows which of the two stories will become dominant over time, but I think we can all agree that reaching peak consumption is in everyone's common interest."

Anna spoke next. "Thank you, Professor. Your update was fascinating. I can see how these themes are driving some of the fringe groups we fear may be behind the sabotage of the Port. Daniel, I would like to accompany you when you visit Carlsson. My knowledge of sociopathic political groups in Sweden and around the EU would be helpful during your questioning. Meeting with Carlsson could help me expand the inventory of suspect categories I've been developing."

"Perfect," Daniel said. "And it would be odd for him to refuse to fully cooperate, knowing your credentials as a Port police officer. I'll see if he can meet with us tomorrow morning and text you if it's a go."

"Alright, I'll pick you up and we can discuss our approach while we are driving."

"Anna, could you tell us more about the categories of suspects you mentioned?" Dahlquist inquired.

"I've divided them into main classes. What they all have in common is a vision of the world switching toward a future with less oil. On the one hand are the crazies, absolute anarchists who spread terror and chaos for sheer nihilist gratification. Nutty as they are, they are extremely capable and difficult to pinpoint or monitor. Next are those with a geopolitical axe to grind. For example, the Iranians might be behind this, trying to raise the value of their oil exports to the few countries willing to buy from them. For that matter, any company or country sitting on a stockpile of petroleum could have the motivation to spook the markets and thereby reap a near-term profit. Environmentalists and Green proponents make up yet another category, as we previously discussed. They are obsessed with global warming and have the willpower and means to execute their various threats. They flourish when there is chaos or crisis stemming from fossil fuels, arguing the extinction of homo sapiens is close at hand. Yet, they know they hold a minority view for now, so they are in it for the long term and try to score incremental successes. Sweden has many such players. This group also relies on politics to reduce the world's reliance on carbon, for example, advocating for electric vehicle subsidies, fuel and road taxes, emission standards, barriers to drilling and the like. Their problem is that they let their fantasies about decarbonizing get in the way of reality. Most of them are simply alarmists, however a determined splinter group or Green party offshoot just might have the nerve to move the process along through, in effect, a terrorist act. So, in conclusion, there's your overview of the main types of people or groups who would likely be behind the sabotage we've seen so far, though other suspect classes surely exist.

"I'll bet it's the environmentalists, due to the demand to reduce carbon emissions," said Stig. "They have the drive and the sophistication to get this done. It smells like something they'd cook up."

"Let's not get ahead of ourselves, Stig," Dahlquist cautioned. "Each group will remain in focus, and we need to develop a strategy for identifying and weeding out the main suspects. That will be this office's focus in the coming days. There is tremendous pressure to find who is behind this, as Daniel mentioned. So, let's adjourn our meeting now and we will reschedule another meeting for early next week. Thank you, Professor Gisslen, for bringing us up to speed on what could be the driving motive behind what is clearly an act of environmental terror, whoever is behind it."

CH. 34

Before the markets in Europe opened, premarket trading numbers flashed red for stocks and green for most commodities around the world. When Axel's Manifesto hit the newswires, the early numbers for West Texas Intermediate light, sweet crude surged higher by 8% on the New York Mercantile Exchange. North Sea Brent crude on the ICE rocketed over 10%, while gold prices spiked 12% on the Comex. In the age of electronic markets, any short positions were quickly covered, magnifying the price explosions. Panicked whispers were ricocheting around Wall Street to the effect that the President's cabinet was meeting to consider options, including releasing more oil from the U.S. Strategic Petroleum Reserves. Euro-zone leaders were also scheduled for a conference call to coordinate their response with Washington. A bailout for Greece was on the table, after it became clear the country would be hard-pressed to afford its winter supply of fuel. To say that the world was watching with fear as oil prices climbed would be an understatement.

Gnady traveled to his office early that morning and sat perched on the edge of his chair, intently viewing the three screens propped upon a large, macassar partner's desk made by the exotic art deco furniture designer, Émile-Jacques Ruhlmann. The irony, of course, was that Gnady had no true partnerships with anyone. Just the jackals who crept in and out of his life at opportune moments.

The first screen, a Bloomberg terminal, showed all the indexes Gnady tracked. It also displayed a range of oil resources, including industry insights and research, news and company data. The next screen focused on up to the minute derivatives pricing and the status of Gnady's many positions and trades. This screen was the only one that now showed green numbers. The third screen was split into 6 frames with various news outlets, each of them displaying pundits opining on the oil crisis that was quickly shaping up or interviews with grim-faced politicians.

Ten months earlier, Gnady went long and bought futures contracts, putting up only 5% of the total position value. He fully expected the leverage to magnify his returns. If crude oil rose just 5% in the months ahead, as he expected, he stood to make a 100% return on his firm's investment. But Gnady expected an even higher return on his investment. Returns of 3X to 5X or more were possible and often realized. His private equity firm had built its reputation on such trades.

Over time, large purchases of crude oil futures contracts by speculators had, in effect, created additional demand for oil and driven up the price of oil for future delivery. This was the momentum play that Gnady's firm had largely relied on to reap outsized profits. As far as the market was concerned, the demand for a barrel of oil that results from the purchase of a futures contract by a hedge fund or a speculating private equity firm like Pankovneft was just as real as the demand for a barrel from a refinery or other user of petroleum. Gnady had fully expected the normal momentum, as measured by the forward 200-day trading average of oil assets, to continue. He had always played the favorable odds and won. But just a few weeks earlier, his positions were on track to expire worthlessly, wiping out most of his firm's capital. The sudden reversal of fortune was stunning, even to Gnady.

He surveyed the screens with serene satisfaction. His net trading position now showed a gain of 240%, though that figure had been bouncing around with the day's volatile trades. He was confident the upside remained huge. He smiled, knowing the big players in oil futures trading, including Goldman Sachs, Morgan Stanley and JP Morgan, would be going ballistic, frantically trying to unwind their short positions in the hope of stemming further losses. With all the recent political developments, they had expected the price of oil to keep falling below the price at which they were contracted to deliver that oil. Gnady now had a valuable asset that he could play: the right to receive crude at a bargain price any time before his contacts expired. With each passing hour, the value of his contracts climbed higher.

The silence inside Gnady's office was broken by a hasty knock on the door by his assistant.

"Sir, you have a phone call from Sergei Mikhailov, the auditor from the National Settlement Depository. Shall I connect you?" she asked.

Gnady frowned. *This shithead can't keep his powder dry for one minute, thought Gnady. I look forward to the day of his untimely demise.*

"Yes, yes, please do connect him," Gnady said with resignation.

"Sergei, to what do I own this honor?" Gnady smirked.

"Oh Gnady, it is I who have the honor," Sergei answered with false praise in his voice. "For I am watching the record volume of trades being made as oil prices skyrocket, and I'm thinking that you have once again won the lottery with your prescient options contracts over the past many months. You are truly a clairvoyant. You have reaped a huge fortune overnight."

"I wouldn't overstate it, Sergei. Any so-called gains are merely on paper," Gnady demurred. "I just have confidence in the long-term rise in oil prices, that is all," he added with disdain. "Our investing strategy is simple. We're of the belief that there is always eventually a bull market. Patience and discipline pay off. Rule your emotions, Sergei, don't let them rule you."

"Such modesty, I am truly humbled," Sergei offered. "In fact, I was a bit emotional, in light of the trust account recently registered in my daughter's name in Cyprus. So, the real reason for my call today is to thank you for that, and to ask when funds might become available."

Gnady winced at the brazenness on display.

"Our line is not a secure one. Besides, I really do not know what you are talking about," Gnady curtly deflected. *Accounts could be closed just as easily as opened,* Gnady thought to himself. *This insufferable ass has just dug his own grave, enough is enough, already.*

"We shall see, my friend," Sergei suddenly fumed. "I look forward to continuing our discussions in person, then. You may be winning in the market today, but from where I sit, that does not mean a winning streak will continue forever."

But I know when yours will end, Pankov smiled inwardly. *Time to start tying up loose ends.*

CH. 35

Early the next morning, Daniel stood in the lobby of his apartment building. Anna pulled up on time at 9:00 a.m. driving a well-maintained 900-series Volvo, just as he fished from his wallet the business card given to him by Axel that Saturday evening before. As he hopped in her car, Anna handed Daniel a paper cup of cappuccino, and he took a sip. The two headed northwest, against traffic, on the 6-lane highway leading out of Gothenburg and along the archipelago that led all the way up to the Norwegian border.

"Good morning, Anna. Thanks for the coffee. I debated whether we should call Axel in advance of our visit, but in the end thought it would be best to simply show up, unannounced," Daniel said. "It's an unofficial visit, so it's best to keep things low key. A small gamble, but let's hope he's there. When I met him last weekend in Stockholm, he was rather talkative, and I'm willing to make a bet that he'll continue to spill his guts to me. After all, he did invite me to his Foundation, so I'm merely following up on that. Let's see how it goes. Let me take the lead in introducing you to him."

"Ok. We need to feel Axel out on the types of people or groups who could be behind the threats we've been seeing. Perhaps he can provide some specific names the team can follow up with," Anna added.

"Yes, it struck me that he knows more than he was intimating when he and I spoke. I met him at a social event hosted by my friend, Karin Lofgren, who's known him since their childhood. Now her accounting firm does Axel's numbers. He does not have a CFO, so her firm plays a big role with the SBF's finances, too. When I met him, Axel was accompanied by that dubious fellow, Gnady Pankov. An unlikely pair. Axel was intense. And it was curious to see him with Pankov, an oil trader. After all, Axel is strongly opposed to carbon energy. Why would he pal around with Pankov, even if he donates to the Foundation, something Karin shared with me. You've seen the file Thor shared on Pankov. I felt some tension between him and Axel; something just doesn't add up with those two."

They soon found themselves exiting the highway and driving on the bucolic, winding 2-lane road leading to Marstrand and the parking area opposite it, where the passenger ferry shuttled to and from the island. After buying tickets at the convenience store, the two boarded the waiting ferry. There was a brief trip across the channel, and the pair disembarked onto Marstrand. Anna and Daniel walked along the cobblestoned quay and then turned uphill along a path that passed several quaint homes. They finally stood in front of a nicely maintained structure having a small placard that read, "Biomarina Forskningsinstitutet".

The two looked at each other and Daniel raised an eyebrow as he rang the doorbell.

In a few moments, Axel opened the door and stood back, visibly surprised at seeing Daniel.

"Well, this is unexpected," Axel said, arms opening, trying to be cordial. "Please come in."

"I'm sorry I did not call you in advance," Daniel said apologetically while following Axel down a hall to the main lab chamber.

Small, darkened offices were noted to the left and right as they walked along.

"I thought I'd take you up on your offer the other night in Stockholm to visit your Foundation, learn more about its activities. You do recall?"

"I certainly do," Axel said with coolness and a not hint of regret. But deep inside, he felt perturbed by the unannounced intrusion. In truth, Axel was an introvert who knew how to turn on the charm in public settings but preferred working alone in the lab, or with a few trusted colleagues, or sailing in isolation on the open seas.

The main hallway opened onto a brightly lit room that functioned as a laboratory. Daniel and Anna looked quickly around, impressed with the equipment and pristine countertops. Everything was spotless and white, apart from a number of stainless steel or chrome instruments.

"I'd like to follow up on our discussion about the environment," Daniel said. "You've doubtless seen the big, new story on the Manifesto that was published. As a consular and trade official, I'm trying to understand its implications, and which groups might be behind it. I've brought with me Anna Peng, a behavioral scientist. She's begun to develop suspect group profiles, but there are several gaps we hope you can help us with."

Anna spoke up, "Nice to meet you, Axel, you have an amazing place here."

"Thank you, it's modest compared to other labs, but we do important work here, in a focused way. One of our specialties is clean technology. Another is research on organic and inorganic molecules and organisms that have the potential to reverse man's damage to the environment. That's it in a nutshell. We have many interesting projects going on at once."

Anna saw an opening and said, "I also have a scientific background, but it's more on the behavioral side. I only wish I could work in a lab as neat as yours!" Axel took the compliment well, and Anna inched ahead. "My work is on the outside, mostly criminal cases. They get very messy, as you can imagine."

"Oh, we have messes to deal with here as well, you'd be surprised, Axel said, warming to the conversation. "I do work in the real world. Come, let's have a seat over here," as Axel motioned to a sitting area with a coffee machine, "and I'll tell you about one of them."

Daniel and Anna took a seat first while Axel made some espressos.

Axel continued, "Some time ago we got a call from Sydney, Australia, asking our assistance identifying a microbe that was wreaking havoc near Lord Howe Island, an area including the world's southernmost coral reef. Not only was the reef bleaching, but anyone snorkeling in it developed a nasty rash. Our team of scientists, working with the University of Melbourne, isolated a rogue organism whose secretions were toxic to both the reef and humans."

"Great work," Daniel said. "How was it found?"

"We believe the microbes somehow travelled from the bottom of an extinct volcano where they lived harmlessly, contained in a microenvironment. Perhaps an underwater tsunami pushed a plume of them out into the open ocean, and they infected the reef, floating about, feeding on its delicacies. The part of how they got there, we're not exactly sure about."

"And then?"

"We quickly developed a cocktail of viruses designed to feed on such bacteria. It took a few weeks of focused trial and error. Eventually, the right blend of bacteriophages was created. And then we had a GMP facility in Sydney grow enough of the virus cocktail to fill a bulk carrier ship, which was dispatched to the reef. Viruses have a long shelf life, so they easily survived the voyage to the reef nearly 100% intact. The ship seeded the virus all along the reef area using camera-guided hosing, and voila! Within a week, the offending bacteria was stopped cold, and the reef began to return to its normal state."

"That's amazing," Daniel offered.

"And it's not all. The Aussies were so pleased, we received a generous grant from the National Office in Canberra to study the bacteria in their natural habitat, the bottom of the volcano. It's unlikely anyone has studied in that environment, so the possibility of finding a variety of new species is great. Once we isolate them, we can research if they have any other traits, for example pharmacological uses."

Anna reflected for a moment and saw an opening. "I'm also trying to crack a case with toxicity that is rather unique. The Manifesto Daniel mentioned demands a 50% reduction in carbon-based energy. So far, whoever is behind it has somehow neutralized two large repositories of oil in our region."

Axel appeared unfazed and listened patiently.

"Since our city was chosen, Anna continued, I theorize that the perpetrator of this enviro-crime must come from our area, or more broadly, in Scandinavia. I'm hoping you might be able to shed some light on the types of people or groups who might have been involved. Do you have any thoughts you could share with us?"

Axel chuckled softly.

"Are you amused?" Anna said.

"Not at all. It's a very serious matter. But your characterization of it as an "enviro-crime" — *that* was amusing."

"I beg to differ. Millions of barrels of oil have been destroyed, and they will now have to be carefully disposed of, at great expense. And let's not fail to mention the blackmail," Anna said.

Axel bristled. "Well in my view the bigger crime is that the oil companies continue to deceive the world about their impact, and indeed the implications, of climate change. Their conduct has been far from innocent. What about their crimes, why aren't you investigating them?"

"We both believe the legal system can determine any liability for what the oil companies have done, just like the tobacco companies have paid for the consequences of their actions. In the meantime, we cannot just have terrorists, or zealots, or whoever they are, taking matters in their own hands, can we?" she said.

"That's exactly what should be happening, as the politicians and oil giants are way too powerful to stop. It will be years before the world sees any accountability, and by then, the damage to the environment from global warming will be too great to reverse." Carlsson appeared indignant.

"Even for a smart scientist like yourself?", Daniel interceded, trying to cool the discussion down. Anna studied Carlsson's body language carefully.

Axel continued, "We are almost at the tipping point. This is not the same as the harm done by cigarettes which target individuals. What oil companies do affects us all. Their crimes are unique and of epic proportions. Don't you agree?"

Daniel said, "I see your point, but I respectfully disagree. There is hardly a consensus on mankind's effect on the climate, or a tipping point, as you say. I don't believe it's that clear cut. In any case, we cannot have individuals or groups sabotaging the world's energy supply."

"And therein lies the problem, Daniel. You can't see the forest for the trees. Carbon is literally choking the earth, and you don't even acknowledge it. I'm afraid my patience with this conversation has come to an end. There's no point in trying to convince you otherwise. Anna, with all due respect, I am not about to help you on this matter. And for the record, I have no clue who is responsible, but someone ought to give them a medal, as far as I'm concerned."

"I'm very sorry you feel that way, Axel. But thank you for your openness on this topic. The zealotry you revealed is rather helpful, in a way."

"And what way is that?"

"It reveals the irrationality of the mindset we are likely dealing with."

Caught off guard by the pointed dig, Axel stood up and fumed, "Get out," pointing to the door. Anna had been prepared for his response and, smiling, said "No need for a police escort."

CH 36.

Anna and Daniel left the Foundation and walked silently until they had rounded a corner and approached the waterfront once again for the trip back to Gothenburg. They spoke softly as the ferry approached.

"Christ, can you believe that? That was some rise you got out of him. What a jackass! He's awfully touchy."

"Sorry things got out of hand," Anna said, but you are exactly right. I felt I had a chance of getting him to blurt out a confession, an old Perry Mason trick!", and the two of them laughed.

"That's ok, and like you said, we know a little more about the mentality we are dealing with. Don't you agree Axel is way too defensive? This is how he behaved in Stockholm the other night. I'm pretty sure he knows more than he's letting on," Daniel said.

"I think you're right. Remember, he's been an active supporter of extremist groups for years now. As far as I'm concerned, he's back on my list of persons of interest, more than before."

Back in Gothenburg, Anna dropped Daniel off in front of the Consulate before she drove to her office.

In the lab, Axel let out a cry of exasperation as he paced back and forth.

"Shit, I can't believe that bitch got me all worked up!" The next moment, he made an agitated, spontaneous call to Pankov, who answered it with an unusually buoyant tone.

"Is this the smartest scientist in Europe, or perhaps even the world, that I am speaking with? Maybe so, judging from the gains made by my company's portfolio of option contracts so far this week." Pankov, who was usually serious, sounded giddy.

Axel almost immediately regretted making the call. Pankov was still the same greedy bastard as ever; even more insufferable than the bureaucrats Axel had just evicted.

"Seriously Gnady, is money all you can think about? I'm sitting here taking heat for you while you are trumpeting about with your latest market gains."

"What are you talking about, Axel?"

"I was just paid a visit by some kind of police shrink, plus that arrogant American we met at the Wasa Museum last week, Daniel Lake. Now I wish I had never gone."

"Holy Mother, what in the hell did they want? I knew it was a mistake for you to give him your card and invite him to your Foundation. Just because the Wasa sank once, doesn't mean we should tempt history with a similar fate."

Axel paused before speaking and chose his words carefully.

"The officer wished to speak with me about the profiles of individuals or groups that could have been behind our Port and harbor efforts. I didn't get the feeling they suspected me in any way, at least. Still, the visit was unnerving, even as I tried my best to stay calm."

Gnady, sounding sober now, said "And did you? Remain calm?"

"Not entirely. At one point, they provoked me with some non-sense about comparing climate change to cigarettes, can you imagine? After that, I couldn't stand their presence anymore, so I made them leave."

"What?" Gnady stammered. "How could you have done that? For fuck's sake, why can't you control yourself? Have you no mindfulness or discipline? Look, there are no such things as coincidences in this world. They *must* suspect something, other-wise I don't believe they would have visited you. For certain you can't trust those Americans, they constantly stick their noses in other people's business. From now on, be smart about our af-fairs. Remember, you created a scene at the Wasa Museum too, what are they to think? *Sóvo ne vorobéy, vylétit – ne poimáyesh.* Words are not sparrows, Axel, once they fly out, you cannot catch them."

"I don't give a damn what they think," Axel replied. "Don't you see the impact we have had; they are running scared. As a matter of fact, we need to double down now, prepare some more targets to hit. I'm ready to move on to a new one, this time in the land of the free and the home of the brave, Florida, to be exact. It will convince the Americans to finally get serious, more than any hurricane, about the climate. If we strike there, the green coalition in California and Massachusetts will be able to overwhelm Congress with fuel economy legislation, pipeline moratoriums and on and on. And whatever the U.S. does, the rest of the world eventually follows."

"What in God's name are you talking about, Axel? Your Pro-methean obsession on behalf of the environment must stop. We have already accomplished what we set out to do. Oil prices have spiked! Can't you be satisfied with that? There's nothing more to do. With higher prices, people will now start to conserve energy. Have you even thought about *that*? It's time to become *invisible* and let the market's momentum run for a while. Take the victory."

"I disagree. We need to drive a final spike of fear into the world's cavalier mindset. Back our Manifesto with some real teeth."

"What you are saying is needlessly risky. Making a point in your little hometown of Gothenburg is one thing, but do you really think you want to take on the Americans in their own backyard? What you are proposing is foolhardy. Don't cross this line with me."

"The time to press ahead is when the opponent is on the ropes, and I find it hard to believe you of all people don't understand this," Axel said in disbelief. A stand-off, and after another moment of silence, Carlsson quit the call just as Pankov started cursing him on the other side.

CH. 37

It was just after lunch, and at the office, Daniel hunted around in the kitchen for something to eat. He checked the fridge and found a tray of shrimp and curried chicken wraps, leftovers from a meeting earlier in the week. A bowl of fresh fruit was available on the table, and the chicken wrap and a banana were speedily devoured. At 1:25 pm he sat at his desk and dialed in to a three-way video conference call set up among the State and Commerce Departments and Homeland Security. Arranged by the President's Chief of Staff, it was meant to be high-level; the start of a task force meant to assess the threat to the world's stockpile and reserve of oil and contain the risk. Each participant was allotted up to five minutes to speak. Daniel released the mute button on screen and waited for the operator to signal the meeting was starting.

The first speaker, from the Office of Countering Weapons of Mass Destruction, welcomed the participants. He wasted no time in providing an overview of the potential devastation of a global release of the chemical agent or organism responsible for the damage reported in Gothenburg. The effect of such a release constituted a terrorist act, in the speaker's views, and generally would be treated as such by the world's judicial systems. Both the FBI and CIA would remain involved, lending crime-solving assistance and resources to Sweden and members of the European Union. The hunt was already on to find out who was behind the acts of sabotage and the Manifesto. He expressed confidence in finding the culprits.

A pair of experts from the Cybersecurity and Infrastructure Security Office spoke next. The first said its resources were working on learning more about the origins of the emailed Manifesto, but she conceded it could take several weeks to discover where it originated. Lots of technical talk ensued, but the gist of it was that if the sender used an anonymizing service like a proxy server, they might never be able to trace the email sender. The second speaker gave an update on security measures being implemented at major refining and storage operations. New safety regulations were being drafted by the EPA. For all refineries and storage depots, increased security patrols were being recommended, and surveillance systems were being checked and enhanced. The speaker conceded that the expanse of energy infrastructure was so great within the U.S. that it was simply not possible to eliminate the risk of a contamination event from occurring. Pipelines sat open and exposed for hundreds of miles in practically every state. In discussions, a consensus developed that this weakness posed an insurmountable risk to the nation.

Eventually, it was Daniel's turn to speak. The operator introduced him.

"Good morning, everyone. As you may know, I'm based in Gothenburg. It's still early in the investigation of the events. I've teamed up with Gothenburg's Port Security and police personnel who meet regularly to manage the risks of another occurrence and solve the two incidents at the Port. They've isolated a new bacterium that they believe is the agent that neutralizes the oil. So chemical agents are ruled out for now."

A research scientist from the Office of Health Security chimed in. "Can we get a large sample of them? Enough to send them out to various labs, the NIH and so forth? Several liters should do. We need to independently examine the genetic structure of the organisms and start developing a virus, chemical or other means of neutralizing them. Maybe a genetically modified version of the bacteria can be developed. Kind of like TIL therapy in battling cancer, where we use the organism's own DNA to fight against it. We have cutting edge research on this we can quickly plug into."

"I'll ask. I don't see a problem with getting you a large sample, with vats full of them available. If so, we can send it on one of the private company jets that routinely fly to DC. I'll arrange for an embassy guard to accompany the courier."

"Excellent. Please keep me informed of progress," the scientist concluded.

More questions.

"Is there any progress in identifying suspects?" someone asked.

Daniel replied, "Some of you may already know of the Navy's attempt to carry out an INTERPOL arrest warrant of a Russian Federation suspect identified by the Gothenburg Port Police. Unfortunately, the attempt was made off the northern tip of Norway yesterday, but it failed due to stormy weather conditions. Thankfully, I recently learned there was no loss of personnel. The person of interest presumably disembarked at port in the Federation, and so it's next to impossible for us to get him extradited to Sweden. He's probably been taken into custody for questioning, and the Federation will deny any outside access to him. The Russians rarely hand over anyone they hold, let alone one of their own citizens. As a result, that very good lead is closed for now. Separately, one of the Port officers has been developing a list of specific groups that could be involved. She's a behavioral scientist, very capable. Some groups and individuals she's identified are local, and others are from the region. Prime suspect groups are extreme environmental actors and anarchists, as both groups are motivated. I'll ask for her list so our resources can go to work on the names. No promises, as the Swedes are consumed with privacy, and it would look bad if they outed some of their citizens to us. Still, I will try and offer her some assurances about our involvement and cooperation, if needed. Lastly, we are gathering stats on the greater regional economic effect of the event plus the impact on the energy market in the Scandic region. Both are a cause for concern, as we have already seen some market turmoil, and panic is starting to set in. The Greeks in particular are worried. Oil and gas prices are already sky high there. In addition, economic growth in Scandinavia has been tepid for some time, the Krona is weak, and it won't take much to put the economy into a recession that could easily spread to Germany and the UK. And then, all bets are off."

The call went on for another forty minutes, and it concluded with a member of the White House Chief of Staff saying that an emergency meeting of the G7 was scheduled for Friday in Gothenburg. There was a chance it would continue into the weekend if necessary. A working group of mainly policy, security and trade experts would be in attendance. He informed Daniel to clear his calendar to attend the meeting as one of the United States representatives. Some other meeting attendees were also informed they would need to attend. Another Zoom meeting to prep for Friday was scheduled before the phone call ended.

Daniel hung up and walked over to Heather's cubicle where he told her about the G7 meeting which would take priority over any other pending Consulate matters. Colleagues would be catching evening flights to Gothenburg and having side meetings at the Consulate in the coming days. The prospect of a very hectic Thursday, Friday and beyond made Daniel think about Karin, and he wanted to see her before he got preoccupied with the meetings. One part of him longed to run away with her somewhere, Rome or Prague. Paris, for the romance.

"Heather, would you please make reservations for two at Smakling for 8 p.m. this evening?" he asked. "Gotta fortify myself somehow for the busy days ahead, and nothing's better than a hearty plate of Swedish meatballs," he winked as he returned to his office to sift through the pile of documents that had stacked up on his desk. It was also possibly his last chance to see Karin for a while. Then he placed the call.

CH. 38

"Hey stranger, how goes it?' Karin said. "I didn't expect to hear from you so soon."

Oh, it's going, alright!" was the reply.

"I've missed you," she came right out and said it.

"I've missed you, too. Let's do something about it, I have a break tonight and then I'm tied up again nonstop in meetings for the next few days. You'll be hearing about them, a G7 working group will be in town. I'm attending with a slew of people from home. But I've made reservations for Smakling again, 8 pm. Not the most romantic, but it should be quiet there, midweek, we'll have a chance to get caught up. Can you join me?"

"One moment, I'll have to check *my* calendar. Oh, I see it's clear, so I guess I'll see you there," she teased.

"Perfect."

For the rest of the afternoon Daniel plowed through the paperwork on his desk while Karin went home from the office early and took a luxurious bath and washed and dried her hair. Then she straightened her apartment, what little was required, put on fresh sheets and organized the bathroom countertops. She pulled out a lowcut blouse and short skirt from the closet and applied some light makeup to color her cheeks a bit. Checked her look in the mirror and before she knew it, she was heading out the door to Smakling where Daniel had just arrived.

As soon as Karin stepped into the vestibule, Daniel pulled her close, his arms wrapping around her waist, and their kiss hello felt both new and familiar, like starstruck kids falling in love all over again.

Klaus, who was tending to the bar and reading the *Dagens Nyheter*, raised an eyebrow and cocked his head. He looked back down into the paper, in which different articles about the oil disaster at the Port were scattered among the first few pages. Lots of breaking news and speculative stories filled with quotes from "anonymous sources".

He looked up. "Ahh, you two again! Two days in a row now, either you are desperate for food or truly love our chef, which one is it?" "A little of each," Daniel said while looking at Karin, "And I think there's even more love to go around!" They all enjoyed a good laugh.

Klaus threw his towel over his shoulder and said, "Walk this way," as he ushered them to Daniel's usual table at the back of the restaurant. Daniel slid a chair out for Karin and helped seat her after handing their jackets to Klaus. Klaus fished in his apron pocket for a candle lighter but came up empty. Karin saw him searching his pockets in vain and quickly opened her purse, removing the white Dala horse lighter Daniel bought her at the Drottningholm gift shop. Klaus picked up the candle as she lit it and took a gracious bow of thanks after placing it on the table.

"I'll be back in a few minutes," Klaus offered, "The specials are written on the blackboard, as usual."

"We'll be here," Karin replied, her eyes twinkling from the dancing candle flame in the middle of the table. "So, tell me what you've been up to. It seems like it's been forever."

Daniel took a moment before he began. "Well, for starters, you won't believe who I visited."

Karin thought for a moment. "I haven't got a clue," shaking her head. She assumed it was a business magnate or visiting official.

"I'll tell you in a moment, but I've been in one meeting after the next. I can't tell you everything, but a ton of resources are being gathered to try to identify whoever is behind that environmental Manifesto. It's a major challenge due to the encryption. Also, oil infrastructure at home and practically everywhere else is next to impossible to secure, it's hopelessly vulnerable. So, we have our work cut out for us."

"I figured you've been really busy."

"Up to my eyeballs, but I enjoy the bustle. A lot more interesting than manning another trade fair booth," Daniel said.

So, just who is that mystery person you visited?" "Almost forgot! This morning, I drove out to Marstrand and stopped to see your old friend and client, Axel Carlsson, at his lab."

"Oh, I never would have guessed that!" Karin said, somewhat taken aback.

"His name, and that of his Russian sidekick, Gnady Pankov, came up at a meeting I attended yesterday."

"A most unlikely terrorist......or?!" Karin mused.

"Not to me, but it turns out an inspector from Stockholm dug up some info on Axel's past involvement with radical Green groups. It's mostly public info, so I'm not revealing anything you couldn't learn on your own. And a behavioral expert with Port security wanted to meet him to help her work up a list of possible leads to check out. She was hoping he would volunteer some assistance, building profile categories. Since I had his card and invitation from last Saturday night in Stockholm, I offered to accompany her on a visit to his Foundation. Nothing to lose, it seemed."

"Wow, and how did it go?" Karin asked.

"Not all that well, to be honest. The expert ruffled Axel's feathers a bit and he became incensed. He lost his cool and asked us to leave only 15 or 20 minutes into our visit. We got an impressive tour before that, though. His place is small, but world class, I'll give him that."

Karin leaned forward, her brow furrowing slightly. "I've replayed our conversation with Axel and Pankov a few times in my mind, and something about it just feels off. I can't shake the feeling that there's more going on than we realize."

Daniel's expression grew serious, matching her concern. "You're not the only one. Something about the way Axel reacted when we visited his lab…it didn't sit right with me either. It's like he was hiding something, and whatever it is, it's big."

Karin nodded. "Exactly. I've known Axel for years, and he's never been like that before. It makes me wonder—what if we've only seen the surface of what's really happening?"

"And I still do not get how Axel can stomach hanging out with that Russian oil trader. Something feels odd with that, too," Daniel said.

Klaus walked up to their table. "What can I get you this evening?"

Karin pointed at the menu. "How is the grilled perch filet tonight?"

You'll love it, served over a bed of diced apples and beets, with the same mashed potatoes as our friend here will get with his meatballs, I presume?"

Daniel laughed. "You know your customers."

"All good, then?"

"Let's have some wine, a Sancerre for Karin, my lovely friend, and a burgundy for me. Plus, a carafe of your finest city water while you're at it. Some lemon, too."

"Coming right up. Pleased to meet you, Karin," Klaus said earnestly as he turned and headed for the kitchen. "Leave room for dessert, it's on the house," he trailed off.

Back to business.

"I think Axel is a dead end for us now. But Anna, the Port Security behavioral expert, plans to keep an eye on him, that's for sure. He rubbed her the wrong way."

Dinner came and the two exchanged more thoughts on Carlsson's odd behavior. It troubled Karin more than Daniel, and he eventually steered the conversation to a weekend trip to Paris that he thought they would enjoy. But Karin's mind was still on Axel, something about him made red flags flash in her mind. She drifted in thought, but then Klaus stopped by with two rhubarb tartlets spiced with cardamom and some espressos, and she was back in the moment.

"Enjoy, the rhubarb is the last batch of the season, picked at a family friend's place in the archipelago." The two wasted no time in devouring the flavorsome confections.

Daniel took the bill. "Delicious as usual," he said while shaking hands with Klaus on their way out. Klaus handed off their jackets and the two decided to walk off dinner a bit.

The air was crisp and moist, a chilly evening breeze had moved in. The two walked closely together for warmth as they strolled the cobblestone streets of the Haga district, peering into shop and gallery windows as they went. Karin eventually steered them in the direction of her apartment and opened the lobby door.

They climbed the stairs to her first-floor apartment, and Daniel was not surprised to see a tasteful, art-filled space when he entered. Karin meanwhile was using her phone app to turn on her Sonos sound system, and in a moment a soft melody with Gabrielle Chiararo's soothing voice started playing.

"Your place is gorgeous," Daniel said. "I'd be embarrassed to show you mine. I've done nothing with it since moving here three years ago. A man cave, of sorts."

"No worries. I'm happy to help with a design intervention any time. My parents loved art, and I guess I'm carrying on the family tradition. There are lots of auction houses nearby where I've found most of the things here, inexpensively. It takes time, but I love finding a good bargain!"

"This one's cool," Daniel said as he pointed to a vibrant blue and yellow print.

"Oh, that's Ellsworth Kelly, one of my favorites, an American. This piece was published in France. It's one of his early graphic works," Karin said.

"One of my favorites now too, the lines are so simple, seems like anyone could do it."

"I've heard that before," Karin said, "but he was the first one to do it, so he gets the credit. The lines are crisp, the color fields so distinct."

"Perfect for an accountant, very orderly!" Daniel jested and Karin smiled.

"Touché!"

Karin moved closer, her fingers gently tracing the back of Daniel's neck as she tilted her head up to meet his gaze. The moment stretched between them, charged with quiet anticipation. Without a word, Daniel pulled her into his arms, their bodies pressing together as they kissed. The kiss was slow at first, a gentle exploration, but soon it deepened, and they both found themselves smiling against each other's lips. The world outside disappeared, leaving only the two of them tangled in each other's warmth, and they stumbled into the bedroom where he slowly unbuttoned her skirt. He slid his thumb underneath the elastic of her panties and pulled them off as she worked his belt and pants. He threw her bra on a lounge chair, and she found his shirt easy to unbutton. Karin massaged his thighs under the covers while Daniel pressed his lips against her breasts. A tumble of movement, then a bite on his shoulder. In a few minutes, he held his breath, and hers exploded. He pulled away, and they stared up at the ceiling, drained. Then Daniel sat up on his elbow.

"Hmmm…. I was thinking of staying the night, if that's ok?"

"I had hoped you would ask!" she replied.

Daniel reached down to the floor and found his phone in his pants pocket, and he set the alarm. Six a.m., a sigh. Then a moist peck from her, this one on his cheek, and the two fell asleep, their bodies entwined, another soft jazz number lulling them into oblivion, courtesy of Sonos.

CH. 39

The next morning, Karin made of them each a bowl of skyr with fruit and nuts and a cup of *mellanrost* Gevalia before Daniel hurried apologetically from the apartment to return to his place. She wished him luck as he left, and they exchanged a quick kiss at the door. After a fresh shower and a change of clothes at his place, he met a familiar contract driver who opened the limo door in front of his apartment, and they sped off to the Consulate.

A few new faces, experts from D.C., Atlanta and Los Alamos, were already congregating in the conference rooms, preparing for the meetings that would start with a working lunch. The remaining personnel drifted in over the next hour.

As the chief trade rep for the Consulate, Daniel worked the rooms, introducing himself and getting to know the many new faces. Pre-meetings began at 9:30 and were efficiently led by expert moderators. The participants had split into security, trade and energy teams. U.S. policies and concerns were prioritized by each of them. These three topics had been pre-assigned by the staff of the G-7 based in Germany, whose turn it was to lead the G-7. Each member country would also be working on these topics. In the end, it was hoped that a consensus would be found on behalf of the G-7, although a common criticism of the G-7 was that it frequently failed to implement any of the meaningful policies it yielded.

The clock was ticking and morning sped by. A working lunch began in the Consulate's main conference room, with all three teams meeting to report on the results of their discussions and the positions they would propose at the G-7 meeting. Each team used the other two as sounding boards for its proposals.

The only substantive area of disagreement came from within the energy group, which covered energy infrastructure, energy security and supply. Some of the team recommended a kind of counteroffer to the Manifesto's demand to reduce carbon output over ten years by 50%. They felt that engaging the issuers of the Manifesto in this way would show good faith and help move the global economy toward the goals the US had already promoted in other venues like the United Nations and the World Economic Forum. A side benefit, to be kept confidential from the other G-7 members, was that this approach would give the U.S. security apparatus time to flush out whoever was behind the Manifesto by listening in on communications and negotiations. This faction felt it was inevitable that the culprits would slip up and get caught. The opposing camp felt the Manifesto should be rebuffed on its face as blackmail. They believed the U.S., much less the world, should not give in to the pernicious anticarbon forces as a matter of principle. To do so would just be the start of a slippery slope that would have a systemic adverse effect on the markets. That would be much more worrisome and sustained than any extra oil disruptions the perpetrators might cause. A group discussion weighed input from the trade and security teams and ended with agreement that the US position would be to explicitly reject the Manifesto's stretch for a 50% reduction of carbon output. However, the door would be left open for closer co-operation to reduce overall carbon consumption. A "we share your concerns" approach on the environment. The leader of each group then participated in a Zoom meeting with teams in Washington, and, by the end of the evening, a set of U.S. positions for the G-7 meeting was formulated. Points on increasing surveillance were agreed upon and so were supply and trade measures like adding to the U.S. strategic oil reserve and encouraging supply capacity from OPEC. More levers for cutting oil consumption and acting on climate change were prepared. Daniel was the last to leave the Consulate that evening. A bus took the visiting representatives to the Elite Hotel at the top of the tree-lined Avenue, where they would call home to their loved ones, answer emails, check how the markets closed and watch either CNN or Fox News, depending on their preference, before nodding off.

The venue for the G-7 meeting on Friday was an 18th century Gustavian manor house called Vossared, located roughly 40 minutes south of Gothenburg. Overlooking a freshwater lake and situated on a huge tract of land that had remained intact since the 1300s, it was owned by a large Swedish firm that used the retreat for high level, internal meetings, but occasionally the company lent it out. The barns and outbuildings had been converted into state-of-the-art meeting and conference rooms, and privacy was guaranteed by a difficult-to-find, private four-mile gravel approach road with checkpoints along the way. A helicopter pad sat on the property and sometimes helos shuttled guests directly to the property after arriving at Gothenburg's Landvetter Airport. At 7 a.m., the Consulate arranged for a small convoy of sleek Volvo V-90s to drive its guests to Vossared. They assembled outside the hotel and were whisked to the meeting site.

Delegations from Germany, Japan and England were already seated in the main conference room at Vossared, with some of the attendees busily munching on colorful licorice found in bowls on each table. The remaining teams including the Americans all arrived in plenty of time for the meeting to start at 8:30 a.m. The air was filled with the smell of coffee and cinnamon rolls heaped on plates in the reception area outside the meeting hall. At the sound of a bell, a rep from Sweden's Office of Foreign Affairs welcomed everyone. He announced that assistance from the Prime Minister's office was available for anything that might be required to help the meeting succeed. He turned the meeting over to the team leader from Germany who reviewed the security, trade and energy concerns of the G-7 from a high-level standpoint, with a few Power Point slides. His presentation concluded with an image of the Manifesto left on the screen behind the podium from which he spoke. It was to remain up for the duration of the meeting, so a somber tone was set by the Germans at the outset.

One by one, each country's delegation spelled out its positions on the three given topics. It became clear over the course of the morning that both Italy and Japan were the most jittery over losing access to oil; for them, potentially losing a steady supply of oil was an existential threat since their economies depended so much on oil and coal imports. They were ready to make quick concessions publicly, to ensure their supply of carbon energy, even if it was supposed to taper off over time. The U.S., Canada and the UK positions were all similar as these countries willing to take more risks in dealing with a possible disruption in the world's supply of oil. The U.S. reiterated its position that giving in to blackmail was not acceptable. An alternative response was needed.

After each team leader presented the concerns and positions of his or her nation, the meeting went into an open forum session where attendees could express any thoughts based on what had been presented. With his trade and legal mindset, Daniel articulated a way to not give in to blackmail but at the same time reiterate the G-7's willingness to meet the main goals of the Manifesto.

"Hello everyone, my name is Daniel Lake, and I wish to begin by reminding everyone of the commitments each of our countries have already made as signatories to the 2015 Paris Accords. I think we can provide a workable response to the Manifesto by announcing a combination of actions, such as setting more ambitious emission reduction targets and fully funding the 2010 Green Climate Fund to help small and developing nations adapt to climate change and reduce their emissions. I believe we need to demonstrate to the blackmailers that the G-7 stands ready to translate its long-term net-zero goals into the short-term policies that are necessary to realize them. If we can do that, the carbon usage target set by the authors of the Manifesto will realistically be reached without the need for explicitly agreeing to their attempt to blackmail the world."

His approach gained almost universal support from the participants. Discussions followed based on his outline, with some additional ideas like pressuring China, India and Brazil to commit to using greater renewables and cleaner energy. By evening time, a consensus had grown in which the G-7 would issue a press release that responded with substance to the demands of the Manifesto while not appearing to cave in to its specific demand of reducing carbon output by 50% in ten years. Some technical analysis was still needed to ensure the multi-prong plan was acceptable to each nation from a domestic political standpoint. The attendees agreed to meet again on Saturday to finalize a joint report and draft a press release for consideration by the G-7's leadership.

As the attendees were packing up and preparing to leave, a few members of the UK and Canadian teams asked the Americans to join them at the bar at the Elite Hotel for drinks, and Daniel decided he would join them. The mood was good, fueled by rounds of Swedish *snaps* which tasted more like rocket fuel than vodka. A Swedish Foreign Office rep who had been observing the meetings joined them. He toasted the end of the day with a hearty "skol," and everyone reciprocated with a raised glass. The lead U.S. negotiator then turned to Daniel and thanked him for his contribution to the success of the meeting. More "skols" in Daniel's direction, and then the affair ended. The group retreated to their rooms in the hotel while Daniel made the short walk to his apartment through the empty, familiar streets where he fell into a deep and satisfying sleep.

CH. 40

The lines of criminal and state activity blur and frequently merge inside The Russian Federation's prison system. Corruption, violence and all kinds of criminal activities meld together there. Whenever one is caught, an assassin's connections can be deconstructed with patient efforts, first snaring the driver, then the gun supplier, the higher-level fixer and so forth, all the way up to the instigator of the kill. It is a rare detainee or prisoner in the system who succeeds in sealing his mouth. It is simply a matter of time for the truth to out itself, with the right amount of encouragement, and there are plenty of persuasive techniques available, depending on the detainee. Everyone eventually yearns for a shot at redemption, the promise of early release, or more benevolent treatment.

"So," Boris Yanovich pointedly asked Mostov, "Explain once again, cockroach, what you did to warrant such interest by the United States FBI authorities acting in concert with Norway and Sweden? You have created quite fuss for everyone concerned." Yanovich was the prison's gruff warden. He was overweight, with bulging eyes and a flat, misaligned nose courtesy of the years he spent doing youth boxing. Five minutes inside the interrogation, his shaved head was already glistening with sweat. Dima slumped in his chair, with his wrists chained to a steel table. He moaned a few incomprehensible words. His cheeks were red, his eyes were puffy while drops of blood and spittle had congealed in the corners of his mouth and glistened in the crevices between his teeth. The interrogation room had a fetid, metallic smell that made Dima feel nauseous and added to his misery. Mercifully for all, the air was cold and dry, otherwise the holding chamber would be suffocating.

"Again, cockroach! Louder!" Boris boomed, opposite Dima.

"I just did as I was told," Dima whispered hoarsely. He had not had anything to eat or drink since the captain of the *Smolensk II* handed him over to a waiting FSB security team who took him straight to a holding tank in Murmansk's main prison. The warden of the Murmansk prison was pleased to have control over this interesting inmate.

"*What* were you told?" Yanovich demanded. The more information Yanovich gleaned, the more handsome his reward.

"To simply add some more oil to the ship's hold, that's all. What could be so bad about that?" Dima sobbed.

"Shut up, you *slaboumnyy*. It is *I* who will ask the questions. And exactly how did you do this?"

"I just squeezed the oil out from a container, that's it. Into one of the main pipes leading to the hold."

"And where did you get this oil container, who gave it to you?"

"I don't know any name, I swear!" Mostov said. "The bag was left next to a park bench for me to pick up, that's all," Mostov lied, and Yanovich sensed it.

Yanovich motioned, and another slap was delivered from one of the attending prison guards. Dima wailed. A second guard laid a pair of pliers on the table. Boris picked it up and with a wicked grin began to playfully snap it at Dima's trembling fingers. Terrified, Dima sat up at the table and made fists to avoid the scare tactics.

Yanovich changed his line of questioning. "If you value your fingernails, and your fingers too, you'll now tell me who enlisted your services in your foolish venture. Surely you know the name of your mafia handler. Tell me his name now, or else!"

Yanovich knew the *systema* as well as anyone. He'd followed it from his post in the prison, aware of the complexity of its many components, its levels, and its compensation from hundreds of prisoners over his many years as an interrogator. He knew the *systema* involved elements within the FSB and even the prosecutor's office. It was a system of control from the highest levels, including all the way up to the Kremlin. There was a certain order to the *systema*, and he did not wish to run afoul of it. Boris was keen to learn exactly which level of the *systema* was involved, for he did not wish to go any higher than necessary or ruffle the wrong feathers. The name of Mostov's mafia handler would be a good place for him to glean further information. By delivering information higher up the chain, he would be rewarded by a *krysha*, a higher-ranking official who would take the greatest cut of money, for as it travelled up the chain, the information became more valuable. Up to a point, and then it could become dangerous to whoever knew it. You could steal or blackmail under the *systema,* but only so much.

"Tell me then, who recruited you to do this?" Boris opened the jaws of the pliers menacingly, and the muscle-bound guard squeezed the tendons on the sides of Dima's wrists until his fingers popped open like *moules* dropped in a scalding broth.

Their teamwork had the desired effect.

"Alright, enough! I'll tell you! Dima cried out from the torment. He whispered out the name of his handler in the *Bratva*. It ranked as the largest organized crime group in the world, higher than the Japanese Yakuza and the Mexican Sinaloa cartel in terms of revenue.

The *Bratva* could not exist without the tacit complicity of the Federation. The Russian civil service, parliament, law enforcement, business, military and above all, the secret services had links to it.

"Good, cockroach. You have made the right decision." Boris got up and left the holding cell with the name that with further investigation would yield a mid-level fixer who would be traced to Gnady's organization, then Gnady himself and eventually to Axel and the sabotage of the *Smolensk II's* cargo. It would not take very long.

Dima was unshackled and led to one of the prison's several barrack-style rooms where about 100 other inmates were held and lived by their own rules, with little involvement from the guards. It was a Darwinian existence there, and tiny fish like Mostov could be swallowed up without warning. They either learned their place quickly or suffered the consequences. Dima entered the room clutching a pillow and a blanket, wearing his newly issued prison uniform which fit him loosely like a pair of oversized pajamas. He shuffled over to his assigned bunkbed, with a hundred pairs of watchful eyes following him closely. He tried not to sob as he buried his swollen face in the pillow to both soothe the welts and hide his shame and terror.

Sixteen hundred kilometers to the West, at nearly the same time Mostov was being interrogated, Officer Bjornsson arrived for an appointment at the Russian Embassy in Stockholm. At the meeting he intended to press for access to Mostov, the primary suspect in the Gothenburg Port sabotage affair. Bjornsson was not sure how much cooperation he could expect from the officials in Murmansk. But he carried with him the authority of Sweden's State Office of National Security, and that counted for something. A good start, he thought, as he received the respect due to his office from a Cossack-like security officer who greeted him in the Embassy's reception hall. The Embassy official who Bjornsson had his appointment with would have direct ties to the FSB and the Ministry of Justice. Bjornsson passed through security and was led to a comfortable conference room where he was met by a coiffed agent with rectangular spectacles that framed thick black eyebrows.

"Welcome, Officer Bjornsson," the smooth-talking Federation representative said. He was just a mouthpiece and therefore didn't mince words. "I understand you wish to learn information about a Federation citizen who is being held in custody?"

"That's correct. I wish to speak with your Ministry of Justice branch in Murmansk. I understand you have clearance to make the call."

"Of course, you have been cleared to speak with our Ministry branch in Murmansk. Just one moment while I place the call."

The officer dialed, some words were exchanged, and the call was placed on hold until a voice reentered the call. The speaker in Murmansk confirmed that Mostov had been imprisoned the day before.

"So, it is my government's position that Dima Mostov is the primary suspect in the sabotage of the Port of Gothenburg's oil facilities. An extradition request is being prepared, and it will be sent to the Ministry of Justice main office in Moscow," he said.

"You know, it will take months for your request to receive due consideration, and I can assure you it will be turned down, even then," the official on the other end of the call intoned. "We do not easily give our citizens away to foreign governments. Nothing is for free."

The negotiation had begun, and Bjornsson countered.

"Even so, Russia and Sweden are committed to cooperating with each other in police matters," he said. "There is plenty of precedent for sharing information on wanted criminals. We have reason to believe Mr. Mostov committed several crimes on Swedish territory. Even if the Federation will not agree to extradite him, we nevertheless wish to interview him to learn if he had any accomplices in Sweden. We need to learn how he came to sabotage the Port's facilities, as we suspect. Surely that would not be an issue, would it? In fact, we don't want him; you can keep him. We only want information relevant to his alleged crime. An interview should suffice, that's what I'm officially requesting, just so there is no misunderstanding or delay."

In truth, Bjornsson held the final cards on this request, as the Russian Federation was more in need of information on criminal matters involving its citizens than were the Swedes. There simply were more Russian criminals fleeing across the Finnish and Swedish borders to escape whatever their offenses were in Russia, real or perceived. No one was leaving Sweden to go to Russia. And for the most part, the Swedes were cooperative in returning true criminals who had fled the Federation, except in capital cases. The senior Federation security officer in Murmansk understood this well and knew better than to jeopardize this channel of basic cooperation.

The officer hesitated and then said, "Officer Bjornsson, you may have permission to interview Mr. Mostov at his prison so long as a Federation witness is present. You may have up to one hour to learn whatever it is you are after. Of course, final permission for your visit must be approved by my superiors, so you must wait until then."

"How long might that take?"

"If I knew that, I would be a member of the Duma," came the steely reply.

CH. 41

Pankov got an early start to his day on Friday, as he was anxious to see how certain tranches of his firm's futures contracts might settle before the weekend. In some cases, there was a tendency for the contracts to become more valuable as the trading day ended, since as the hours ticked off, buyers bid up prices if they expected oil to rise over the weekend, which appeared to be the case. In the final 30 minutes of trading there might be some selling pressure that could send prices lower, but no matter. Gnady planned to hold his options until they expired in two more Fridays, for maximum gain.

At 10:30 a.m., a sumptuous tray of food was rolled in on a cart, and Gnady helped himself to a plate of blinis topped with sour cream and red raspberries. He took another plate and filled it with smoked whitefish, some glistening caviar and a few slices of thinly sliced rye bread. Once trading began, Gnady enjoyed monitoring the Bloomberg screens until he heard a knock on his office door. It was Gnady's Secretary, and she poked her head in a few moments later.

"Mr. Pankov, you have a visitor in the waiting area, that same gentleman from the National Settlement Depository, Mr. Mikhailov. He seems rather agitated. Do you wish to meet with him?"

A burley hand appeared in the door above the Secretary's head and pushed the door open.

"He *will* see me," Sergei brusquely announced, "And for the record, I'm not agitated, if you must know. I'm simply *concerned*," Sergei said as he strode into Gnady's office.

The secretary looked shocked at Sergei's effrontery while Gnady appeared flustered.

"You have some serious *yaichki* to barge in like this, my friend," Gnady said, placing his coffee cup in its saucer. He motioned to his secretary that everything would be alright, and she retraced her steps to her desk, looking frustrated.

"Not as large as yours, I believe," Mikhailov replied bluntly as he closed the door. As he walked toward Pankov's desk, he stopped momentarily to look at the gleaming Fabergé egg sitting atop its amber stand. "A little bird, and not one of the ones in your most beautiful, decadent egg, has chirped the most interesting information to my ear."

"And what might that be?" Gnady said, smirking. "And please, no riddles, speak plainly."

"Very well. Yesterday I received a most interesting phone call from the warden of the main prison in Murmansk. He has suggested that an audit of your firm may be in order. I listened to his story and thought about what he said long and hard, and guess what? I tend to agree."

"How could such a person take an interest in Pankovneft?" Gnady scoffed. "We have nothing to do with whatever occurs in his jurisdiction." Pankov was nonplussed, as there was no plausible connection in his mind to anything Sergei was rambling about.

Sergei met the challenge. "Well, perhaps not yet; we shall see. But apparently, a fresh inmate there revealed to the warden a rather fabulous tale of how he was hired to taint a delivery of oil being offloaded at the Port of Gothenburg. Surely you know about this affair, the port that's become famous in the past week. This warden apparently did a little further investigation. It appears the inmate's handler in the *Bratva* pointed his finger in your direction. That could very well explain the spectacular appreciation of the options contracts you bought several months back. Nothing escapes my eyes in the market, my dear Gnady. I've seen much in my time, and I must say that such a scheme appears to have your fingerprints all over it. If in fact it is yours, you have deeply impressed me." He hesitated a moment before saying, "So, what are we to do?"

Pankov's face looked ashen, but he was quick to recover.

"Well, Inspector, I have no idea of what you are talking about. But let's make believe what you say is true, just for a moment. How embarrassing would it look for your office to have missed such a monumental market flaw for so many months? Or, shall we say, the "coincidence" that my firm has opened a bank account in your daughter Viktoria's name in Cyprus?"

Mikhailov stroked his chin for a moment. He now regretted he did not make the effort to set up a private company as the owner of the account, instead of his daughter, who was the more expedient option at the time. *Oh well, in for one kopek, in for a thousand.* A bit more tempered, he said "I appreciate your point, but the fact remains that something must be done with this new information and the little jailbird who is singing about you, Gnady. If we fail to act on his information, someone else will, as sure as Lenin's body lies in his glass tomb. The warden is expecting to be paid for his information. So is his *krysha* protector. I think we have more to lose than to gain if we fail to work together, don't you agree?"

Pankov replied, "The warden does not know what he has gotten himself into. He has overstepped his bounds and yes, he must be dealt with. The *Bratva* will not be pleased with his interference with its investment in my firm. The same goes for you to, Sergei, remember that well."

Sergei winced. The game of chess continued.

"So, what do you propose?" Sergei asked.

"I think the little singing bird, as you call him, is going to suffer a permanent case of laryngitis. Tell the warden that the inmate was falsely accused by the Americans, wishing to blame the Russian Federation for the oil fiasco whose origins were one of their rogue and sloppy germ labs in the Ukraine, funded by the CIA. They have many of them there, doing all sorts of illicit activity, it's a known fact. Microbes, bacteria, it's all the same. Therefore, tell the warden he must release the prisoner. An unfortunate misunderstanding, that's all. Let the warden also know that he will be generously compensated for his discretion and for being malignly inconvenienced by the Americans. Can you manage to do that? The little bird will meet his fate after he is released, I'll see to it," Gnady said.

Mikhailov stroked his chin again. "All this is possible, my friend," he said. "Blaming the Americans to help clear up matters is sheer brilliance! And what of the warden? A loose end that also requires attention, no?"

"I see your point, it's good to be cautious. *Beda nikogda ne prihodit odna.* When there is one problem, there is usually another one. He certainly has it coming, jeopardizing the Bratva's investments, as he has brazenly done," Gnady rationalized.

"If that is your conclusion, I will not second guess it."

"Then we are in agreement, Sergei?" Pankov asked, tired of the conversation.

"Not entirely," Sergei pressed ahead. "You've conveniently forgotten your partner, haven't you? I have a vested stake in your options contracts now, Gnady. We have become associates in this endeavor. I checked your holdings this morning before coming here, and to be sure, you stand to gain upwards of 10 billion rubles. That is just from their appreciation on the Russian exchange. Heaven knows how much you will profit in the weeks ahead on the foreign futures markets."

Gnady smiled in admiration, for as much as he detested Sergei, the man had a point. Gnady was about to become fabulously wealthy, perhaps even a billionaire. The markets had a way to run.

Sergei counseled, "The account you've opened in Cyprus for my daughter. With your massive gains, Gnady, you can well afford to be generous with her, no?"

"That depends on what you mean by generous."

"A small sum, just a rounding error on your profits will be enough. I believe the sum of 10 million Euros will suffice." Mikhailov folded his arms on his puffed-up chest, appearing unwilling to budge. His ploy worked.

Gnady swore. "Your greed knows no bounds. If I do this, it will be the last such payment I make, do you understand?"

Pleased with his negotiation, Sergei pursed his lips and nodded his head to signal his agreement. "I do. Just make sure the funds arrive in Viktoria's account on Monday at the latest. Meanwhile, I'll tell the warden he has a lavish reward of his own coming to him if he follows through with releasing the prisoner. Don't worry, if you do your part and act quickly, you won't have to transfer a ruble to him. The story will end there."

Gnady shook his head; he could not recall the last time someone had ripped him off so elegantly. True, a piece of bad luck, but the price to resolve the unexpected snafu in Murmansk was tolerable, he reasoned.

"Farewell, my friend," Sergei said. He turned and walked toward the door, stopping once again in front of the magnificent Faberge egg. He picked it up carefully and, in a flash, placed it in a black velvet bag that he shook open from the pocket of his suitcoat.

Gnady watched and stood frozen, shocked by what he just witnessed. "Stop!" he stammered. "What the *fuck* do you think you are doing there?"

Sergei turned and said, "Exactly what *you* would do if you were in my shoes, my dear Gnady. I'm taking this as collateral so that you perform your end of the bargain. It's a long weekend waiting for those Euros to be wired to Cyprus, and I want you to remain focused. You'll get your precious egg back as soon as the funds clear. You know the saying, *'Doveryay, no proveryay.'* Trust, but verify. Once again, it has been a pleasure doing business with you," Sergei said with a defiant tone as he briskly exited the office.

And it will be your last such pleasure, Pankov vowed under his breath.

CH. 42

By lunchtime, Gnady had regained his usual composure. His CFO, a trusted and well-paid graduate of the Skolkovo School of Management, would see to funding Sergei's daughter's Cyprus account for the final time. The money would route to GP Pankovneft's local law firm in Cyprus which would then pay it to a local consultant, who would then deposit it in his company bank account and transfer it a final time to the local bank account indicated by the law firm. The money would be held in a trust structure, utterly shielded from scrutiny. It was all legal under Cyprus law, but as a form of money laundering, it was not in most other jurisdictions.

Another interruption, this time it was Gnady's personal cell phone, protected with scrambler software. Carlsson was calling, and he spoke first.

"Gnady, how are you? I've been watching the markets the past few days and surmise you are pleased with everything?"

"Yes Axel, all is going according to plan. Glad to hear from you." *It's good this fool has no appreciation for the fortune I've just made, one scrounger is enough for today.*

"I am very excited for you, and for me as well. It's public knowledge that the G-7 is meeting now to develop a response to our Manifesto. I'm expecting substantial compliance from them. And whatever they agree to do will be supported by second and third-line countries. We'll have done more than anyone before us to truly make the world begin its transition to renewable energy in earnest," Axel beamed. "And all it took was a little initiative, a little organism, to be exact. Had you not gotten the idea for my designer bacteria and funded the project, we wouldn't be where we are today."

"I'm glad you are pleased. Maybe you'll receive the Nobel Prize yet. But I've had a rough morning here, there's something you need to know. It seems that crewman, the ex-con who you met in Gothenburg, was taken in by Federation security as soon as he got off the tanker in Murmansk. The ship captain apparently called him out."

Axel listened in silence.

"Somehow the damned Americans connected him to our little Tor Harbor demonstration, and they teamed up with the Norwegians and Swedes to arrest him through INTERPOL. Their efforts failed, thankfully, so now we have the chance to silence him before he makes any more trouble. He's already prattled on about his involvement with us to the warden in the prison where he is being held. I'm handling it."

"Do what you feel you must. I'm not going to be involved in any killings, do you understand? Not in my name."

"So now you have become a saint, is that right?" Gnady said.

"Look, murdering humans was never part of our arrangement. So, don't involve me."

"But you *are* involved, Axel. What I must do now will protect your precious reputation, and that of your egotistical Foundation.

You won't be able to continue your work if we don't see eye to eye on this. Both oil *and* blood must be spilled, and both will most certainly spoil on your behalf. Just so you know."

"And I won't be able to continue my work once you are caught. You'll be forced to implicate me in a murder I had no part of. It's inevitable. The risks you are talking about now will take us both down. Just let the seaman go, for God's sake. No one will believe his crazy stories."

"I'm afraid someone already has. The head auditor of the National Settlement Depository visited me this morning. He's blackmailing me with the information he received from the prison warden about the seaman's involvement in our plans. He's expecting a large payment, which I am taking care of, also on your behalf. The auditor wants no loose ends either, it's been settled. So, I'm doing what must be done. And that's final, discussion ended."

Axel realized it was impossible to dissuade Pankov from carrying out his intentions. He decided that if Pankov was going to pursue this route, then he was free to pursue a path of his own. For some time now, he felt that more pressure should be applied to stir up a greater response on the part of the G-7, OECD and other top oil consuming countries. Another contamination of a large oil property was what Axel had in mind, something Pankov had vetoed in the past. The United States was the venue Axel planned to strike.

"Very well, Gnady," Axel replied. You have your priorities, and I still have mine."

"What are you implying?"

"We can still do much more to apply pressure to the situation if we desire a lasting commitment to weaning the world off its reckless course of excessive oil consumption. It's time to make a final demonstration of the power of our bacteria against the world's oil supply. This time, I've chosen the Port of Jacksonville, Florida, which maintains a large oil and gas storage yard. I have an old friend, a climate activist there, living on nearby Amelia Island, who is waiting for me to tell him to proceed with a new insertion of my bacteria. And I have another friend, a former member of the Earth Liberation Front, stationed nearby a Houston refinery, and he is also set to transform the refinery's oil depot to harmless effluent."

"Are you mad?" Gnady fumed with his chin thrust forward. "Why would you take any further risks? We are well on our way to accomplishing everything we have set out to do."

"Our Manifesto said we would make another demonstration in the Western hemisphere, don't you recall? We need to follow through if the world's top energy users are going to take the reach of our project seriously. Our credibility is at stake. And besides, the Jacksonville facility is perfect, Gnady. It's just opposite of the Gulf Coast, the USA's most dense location of oil terminals and refineries. The U.S. government can't fail to understand the dagger I'm placing at its throat. So, you choose your risks, and I'll choose mine. An incident outside of Europe will magnify our cause, not to mention your profits. And far from creating more risk, it will lead the Port of Gothenburg's investigation away from our doorstep. A few more feathers yet require ruffling," Axel said. Then he added, "It appears our collaboration has come to an end," and he abruptly ended the call. Gnady's return call went immediately into Carlsson's voice mail. Pankov cursed Carlsson under his breath and poured himself a tumbler of Hennesey cognac from a Baccarat crystal decanter.

If only that stubborn scientist had as commendable a character as this drink, he thought.

Pankov sipped slowly as he walked over to his Bloomberg displays. The green lights glowing on the screens soothed him as he scanned the markets; but there was only so much aggravation he could stand in a day.

It was after midnight, and Carlsson used a burner phone to place a call from the comfort of his lab. The sun would soon be setting on Amelia Island, Florida. A soft eastward ocean breeze cooled the shoreline, and the songs of various frog species had struck up in the lush saw palmettos when Russ Lancaster answered his cell phone. He was sitting in the lanai of his home in a development called The Preserve, across from the Ritz Carlton hotel, munching boiled peanuts and enjoying a Bud from a can. His faithful black and tan coonhound, Loonie, rested beside him, with her front paws crossed and eyes bloodshot.

"Russ, how are you, my friend?"

"Axel you ol' dawg, I'm doin' juss fine! Ain't you up awful late? I sure do love that batch of salmon you sent here the other day. Almost as good as them sweet reds I catch in the marshes, right south of our Little Talbot Island."

"Only Sweden's finest for you."

Lancaster had made a fortune selling a solar panel installation company he started in the 1980s, just as Jacksonville's growth had started to take off, transforming it from a sleepy Southern town to the largest city in Florida. Lancaster and Carlsson had met each other at a conference focused on conserving the Everglades, the vast area of alligator-infested swamps and marshland in southern Florida. The two became close but were an unlikely pairing, a red-neck Southerner and an urbane, worldly Swede.

The common ground they shared was their alarm at the damage caused to the Everglades. Rampant land development, industry, and agriculture pressure had already destroyed more than half of its original, sensitive ecosystem. Lancaster was passionate about saving the remainder of the Everglades and, like Carlsson, radically decreasing the world's dependence on fossil fuels. With the wealth he gained from selling his company, he funded a variety of environmental causes and donated a substantial sum annually to Carlsson's Foundation.

One week earlier, a generous-sized box of frozen Swedish salmon filets had arrived at Lancaster's front door. Tons of the high-priced catch were shipped annually to the U.S. by various fish exporters. The insulated container of fish was cooled during shipment by packs of dry ice, one of which innocuously contained an icy syrup of oil and bacteria from the lab on Marstrand. Russ kept the entire box in a garage freezer and was eager to deploy the contents. Then he could get to grilling the filets.

"It's time for you to take that little adventure we talked about, Russ."

"Dang, I been lookin' forward to dis! Ol' Russ been chillin' here, waitin' on your call. Tonight alright?"

"The sooner, the better."

"Give you a ring when it's done wit. Ya'll take care."

Lancaster hung up and went to the garage where he removed the pouch of oil and bacteria from the salmon box in the freezer and tossed it on the back seat of his Volvo X-Country station wagon. He opened the door for Loonie who effortlessly hopped onto the front seat and looked up at his master for clues as to where they were going. Still munching his peanuts from a Rubbermaid bowl, Russ drove past the Ritz Hotel on a road covered by a lush maritime forest canopy until it dead-ended on Route A1A. Soon he was driving south toward Jacksonville on Hecksher Drive, a gorgeous motorway with a jungle-like landscape interspersed with marsh and deserted beach views. He eventually passed the Jacksonville Zoo entrance where a string of several school buses turning into the Zoo's drive slowed him down, an apparent field trip. A little later he pulled into a dirt side road leading to a boat launch used by the locals for fishing and pulled the car to the side and onto a patch of weeds. After placing the car in park, he cracked the windows open for Loonie who would remain patiently behind. Lancaster was big-boned and had a heavy frame. It took little effort for him to untie and take down a stand-up paddle board and paddle from the Volvo's rooftop. With the sack of oily fluid secure in the pocket of his bathing suit, he began to paddle along the north bank of the St. John's River, huffing and sweating as he went, as he was about 40 pounds overweight. After 10 minutes of vigorous paddling, he found himself near an oil and liquid natural gas storage facility. The entire area comprised about 300 acres, with just a chain link fence along the Zoo Parkway and no protection at all along the riverbank. Lancaster found a little beachhead there and landed his board. After a minute of walking, an open field of storage tanks loomed in front of him. Guided by the silvery rays of the moon, he easily found his way past the Marathon Oil tanks to the ones owned by the U.S. Navy. These tanks stored fuel oil for the Navy fleet stationed in Mayport, a couple of miles back north in the direction of Amelia Island. Russ had long resented that such a pristine environmental sanctuary was used for stationing warships and a fleet of over 100 fixed and rotating aircraft that disturbed the tranquility of the area at all hours. Today, he would exact revenge twice: first, against the world's petroleum producers, and second, grounding the Nation's third largest Navy station.

It took him a few minutes to ascend the stairs lining the exterior of the tank's shell. He stepped on the floating roof of the first tank where he opened the lid on its release vent and squeezed about one third of the sack's contents into it. Then he descended from the tank and repeated the same task on two more of them. Each time he had to stop to catch his breath on the way up and to prevent his replaced knee from buckling on the way down. When he was done, he retraced his steps to his paddle board and made it back to the car where Loonie greeted him with a wagging tail and grunts of affection. After reloading the car, he attended to Loonie with a pat on the head before taking the deserted road back to his home on Amelia Island. With a stretched T-shirt sleeve, he swatted at the sweat dripping down his forehead while keeping his eyes on the road to avoid inadvertently flattening any of the gopher turtles that sometimes errantly strayed onto the road from their holes in the dunes.

In the early morning on Marstrand, Carlsson heard his cell phone ring. Lancaster's 904 area code appeared on Carlsson's screen. Sipping on another Bud in the lanai and speaking in his Southern drawl, Lancaster simply told him, "Dropped the torpedoes, Axel. Full speed ahead! Ya'll take care now, hear?"

CH. 43

On Friday, the phone in the Murmansk prison office rang late in the day. A male secretary – there were no females working in the prison – answered. On the line was Mikhailov's secretary who announced the name and office of the caller before commanding a connection with the warden. Yanovich's office was spare and utilitarian, not unlike the 1200 cells he oversaw in his facility. On his tidy desk was a land phone, a pen holder, and a small stack of papers. As Yanovich picked up the handset, he returned a pair of nail clippers he was using to a desk drawer.

"Boris Yanovich, thank you for taking my call," Sergei said.

"*Dobriy den*, Comrade Mikhailov. I am honored to speak with you. Is there something I can help you with?" Yanovich knew there would be. Inside the prison, Yanovich reigned confident and supreme but calls from Moscow such as these always brought their share of tension and duty. He felt his nerves shiver and throat tighten a bit from not knowing exactly where the call could lead.

"Indeed, there is. We have a most unfortunate situation that must be rectified. It involves one of your new prisoners, Dima Mostov. Have you met him?"

"*Da*, he is in safe hands."

"Very good, Boris. We have learned the Americans have set him up. You know how they make baseless accusations and divert the world's attention from their misdeeds. Well, we have caught them red-handed once again. It is *they* who have somehow caused the oil in Gothenburg to be spoiled, surely you have heard about this. Apparently, the whole affair is a trial they concocted, using a bug from one of their labs in The Ukraine, though the details are still being investigated, along with their attempt to frame the Federation's oil exporters for this unfortunate incident. It's a pretext for more punishment under their illegal sanctions. We believe some elements within the American administration wished to accelerate their insane green initiatives, and that what happened in Sweden was one of their covert operations. Seaman Mostov was a pawn and dupe in this endeavor, but I need to question him now in Moscow and prepare him as a witness against the Americans. So, I'm sending a driver to pick him up this evening. Please ready the prisoner for his release to the NSD's fraud division."

Silence on the phone, and Yanovich finally spoke up, sounding a little unhappy.

"Your request is rather premature, is it not? The prisoner seemed resolute in blaming a *Bratva* boss for his actions, so I had planned to question him further on Monday. I am confident in his confessions thus far. Over the weekend, he will experience some, how should I say, untoward pressure from some of the less than savory elements within the prison's general population. This will improve his willingness to speak more freely when I interrogate him. He'll do anything for my protection when I question him on Monday. These methods rarely fail. I also plan to bring in his local *Bratva* handler for questioning to see what more information may be revealed. You will learn everything the minute I do," Boris promised, hoping to retain his hold on to Mostov. The more he could extract, the bigger his payday.

"Thank you, Boris, I do not doubt your productive interrogation techniques. However, the NSD also has experience in questioning persons of interest, and I feel very confident he will cooperate with us as well. There are good cops, and bad cops. I can always threaten to return him to you if he fails to appreciate my hospitality. Yes? Besides, national security is implicated, and your prison is not, frankly, appropriate for this prisoner. I need access to him *immediately*," Sergei pressed.

Boris listened carefully, trying to anticipate the shifting wind. At last, he realized he had no chance of keeping Mostov and relented. "A shame, as I had looked forward to my session on Monday," Boris sighed, sniffing a level of corruption and intrigue he could not begin to fathom.

"Do not worry, Boris. Your efforts will not be forgotten. You will find a generous reward posted to your trading account on the first day of next month for your troubles in this matter. I have access to the account, in my position as the Federation's chief securities auditor. Just prepare the prisoner as I have instructed and say not a word to anyone about this matter, do you understand? A car will be there for him in three hours, I trust that will be enough time."

"Let us say 20:00, for the transfer?"

"*Da, Boris, da,*" Yanovich replied, mustering false enthusiasm so as to remain in good graces with Mikhailov.

Precisely at 20:00, an armored van and with two burly-shaped men dressed in black SWAT uniforms and masks drove through the prison gates to retrieve seaman Mostov. They each wore a standard service MP-443 Grach pistol on their belts. Yanovich studied them closely from a one-way mirrored window as they walked through the guard station a short distance from the prison and waited to get buzzed through the jail's first of several interior steel doors. Meanwhile, Mostov's leg chains were removed in the corridor, and he was allowed to change into his street clothes as the guards looked on in silence. One of them handed him a bag with his cell phone, wallet, passport and belt. Mostov appeared to be in shock as he rubbed an ankle that had turned blistery and chaffed from the leg irons. A guard led him by the arm and handed him over to the waiting van driver and his partner after they signed standard release papers. They escorted Mostov back to their idling van and helped him into the vehicle's back seat, a metal partition separating it from the front. The back doors locked automatically, and they drove away from the prison grounds. The transfer was over almost as soon as it began.

"So, where is it that you wish to go?" the driver said after several minutes of driving in silence on the forested road leading north, past the airport, to the concrete city of Murmansk. We have instructions to release you within the city."

"What are you saying?" Mostov stammered, dumbfounded from the turn of events. He wondered what had just happened.

"You are being released without charges or bail, on the condition that you agree to wear an ankle bracelet that will allow the Ministry of Internal Affairs to monitor your movements and call you in for questioning, as required. If these terms are not agreeable to you, we have instructions to return you to prison. Do you agree or not?"

"Yes, yes! Dima said excitedly." There was never any doubt. "In that case, take me to my apartment."

"Off Ulitsa Khlobistova street?

"You know it?"

"We know much, Dima Mostov. For instance, you could use a change of curtains in your disgusting apartment," the driver's companion snickered. Dima sulked.

Another twenty minutes later, Dima, outfitted with a new silver ankle bracelet, was permitted to exit the vehicle in front of a concrete jungle of high-rise apartments. The brutalist monstrosities were erected after the city was rebuilt in the years following waves of German airstrikes. It was now his home.

"Do yourself a favor, do not stray very far after your release," the driver cautioned Dima as he walked slowly toward the dumpy housing project. "And don't cause trouble."

Dima did not look back at the van as he entered the building where he kept a studio flat. An old woman, sitting in the lobby and wearing a babushka and faded blue apron from her days working in a fish canning factory, looked up momentarily as Dima walked by. Apart from her cold stare with a narrowed eye and thin lips, neither acknowledged the other.

It had been nearly two months since he was last at home, and when he opened the door to his apartment, he sighed as he surveyed the main room. It was in disarray; someone, apparently the two guards, had turned the room upside down in a hasty search for anything of interest they could find. Fortunately, a box with six liters of Absolut vodka was undisturbed, old contraband from a different trip abroad. Disgusted by the mess, he went straight to the bathroom where he undressed and waited a few minutes for the water to warm up before stepping over the mildewed tile threshold. After showering, he found a clean pair of underwear and fell into bed, exhausted. He would not get up until the next morning, having consumed nearly half of one of the vodka bottles before drifting off.

CH. 44

On Sunday afternoon, Thor identified himself to the cheerful attendant at the SAS business lounge at Arlanda Airport, and he was waived in with Stig trailing close behind. A commercial flight to Kirkenes awaited them. While laying over in Kirkenes, they planned to meet with crewmen Annarino and Berman at the nearby Varanger garrison to learn what they could about the attempted arrest of seaman Mostov. From Kirkenes, the drive to Murmansk would only be about two hours.

Thor was cautiously optimistic about getting approval to interview Mostov, but there was no guarantee. The Russians were unpredictable, and any delay could jeopardize the investigation. He wanted to be ready to move the moment he got word, knowing that every hour mattered in unraveling the complex web of deception they were facing. The pressure was mounting, and the investigation desperately needed a breakthrough.

The bar at the SAS business lounge was dimly lit, the soft hum of air traffic filtering through the large windows overlooking the tarmac. Thor and Stig sat in a quiet corner with their minds focused on the mission ahead. In the lounge, the clink of glasses and the murmur of distant conversations provided a subtle backdrop to their thoughts as they picked at their cheese, crackers, and shrimp salad from the food buffet and thumbed through magazine and newspapers provided by the airline. The flight to Kirkenes took off on time and the officers checked into The Fjord Hotel after their arrival.

On Monday morning Thor and Stig drove their rental to the Varanger Air Base entry gate. They were greeted there by a pair of security guards who pointed them to the NATO Joint Warfare Center where they were ushered into a conference room. Pilots Annarino and Berman were waiting and rose to meet them.

Cordial handshakes followed the introductions, but there was an underlying tension in the air. Annarino's firm grip and tight-lipped smile hinted at lingering frustration, while Berman's easy demeanor masked the gravity of their failed mission. As they settled into their seats, Thor couldn't help but notice the weariness in their eyes—these men had been through a lot, and the weight of their doomed operation still hung heavily on their shoulders. They found seats opposite each other at the conference table. Thor and Stig passed out business cards.

"On behalf of the Swedish Government, I would like to thank you for risking your lives to arrest seaman Mostov. We learned some details of your mission and are very grateful to you," Bjornsson began.

"It's a damn shame we didn't pull it off," Annarino muttered, his frustration barely concealed. "The storm's intensity caught us off guard, and I misjudged the waves at their peak. No excuses— it was my call, and the mission went south."

Thor nodded, sensing the weight of responsibility that Annarino carried. "You did what you could. In a way, it's better it played out like this."

Annarino leaned back, his jaw clenched. "Maybe. But it doesn't make it easier."

Stig replied, "We really do not see it that way, John. Had you actually succeeded, the Russian Federation would have objected strenuously and possibly retaliated in ways we could not predict. They are crafty and ruthless about these things. So, it's all for the best. And after applying a little leverage, Thor received permission for us to interview Mostov at the Murmansk prison where he's being held. We're staying in town, waiting for the call to drive there. It's a much cleaner arrangement," Stig finished.

"Do either of you recall anything from that evening about the seaman? Did the ship's captain say anything that could be useful?" Thor asked.

"Not much, unfortunately," Annarino said. "We were listening to the conversation through an interpreter. The conversation was recorded at NATO Command in Stavanger, and I've read the transcript several times, hoping to learn from my mistake. The ship's comms were unsecure, so we were able to listen to them on their channel the entire time we were there. Their conversation is captured in the transcript, too. The captain mentioned Mostov met with a Swedish guy during shore leave in Gothenburg," Annarino recalled, his voice measured. "Seemed like a throwaway comment at the time, but now, it appears to mean a lot more."

Stig sat up straighter, the hint of a lead sparking his mind. "That meeting could be the link we've been missing. If we can get Mostov to talk about who he met, it could crack this wide open."

Thor nodded; his mind was already racing. "We need that transcript. If there's anything else in there, it could be the break we need."

Annarino said, "You are welcome to it so long as I get clearance to release it. I'll put in a request to Stavanger now and courier it to you later this afternoon if approved," and he broke away from the meeting to call NATO command.

Berman said, "Is there anything else we can help with?"

"No, we appreciate your time," and the meeting ended.

Back at the hotel, Thor and Stig took a table in the restaurant, but neither had much of an appetite. The weight of the investigation hung over them, and they knew everything depended on getting that call from the Russians. Thor's phone buzzed on the table, and both men froze, their eyes locked on the screen. When he saw the embassy's number flash across it, Thor's heart quickened. This was it. He answered with a steady voice, but his mind was already racing ahead to what the next steps would be.

"Officer Bjornsson, the Ministry of Justice has approved your interview with prisoner Mostov on Tuesday, at 14:00. Can you be there?"

"Yes, I'm near the border now, Kirkenes, so that won't be a problem. Recall I will have Investigator Stig Renell with me, too, from the Port of Gothenburg Police."

"We'll send two diplomatic passes to the border checkpoint. Collect them there, and you'll be allowed through," the officer instructed. "Always keep the passes with you. Drive straight to the prison, do not take any detours. We will inform the prison of your visit," the officer said.

Thor hung up; his face unreadable as he relayed the information to Stig. "It's set. We're going in tomorrow at 14:00."

Stig leaned back, a hint of relief washing over him. But the feeling was fleeting, he knew this was just the beginning. The real test would be in Murmansk, face-to-face with Mostov.

"Let's hope Mostov's ready to talk," Stig muttered.

"He'd better be," Thor replied, his voice low. "Because time is running out."

CH. 45

Saturday evening and feeling refreshed from a good night's sleep and a warm shower, Mostov applied a heavy slap of cologne to each of his acne-pocked, hollow cheeks and strolled out of his building into the dreary, wet streets of Murmansk. Earlier that afternoon, he straightened up the apartment and decided the curtains were indeed drab and too difficult to rehang, so he stuffed them into the garbage.

Winter was approaching, the skies were cloudy, and they obscured any evidence of the dancing ribbons of green light so often on display in the sky at this time of the year, close to the arctic circle. As he left the apartment house, Mostov turned up the collar of his insulated pea coat. He headed down Lenin Prospect Street toward the shopping mall, passing several Soviet era war memorials. Eventually, he came to the Rolling Rock bar where a grunge band was in the middle of a set. He knew the establishment well. The bar was crowded, with couples dancing slowly like illuminated zombies under the flashing strobe lights. He sat at the bar and ordered a liter of dark beer, sipping slowly as he surveyed the scene. Earlier he decided against calling his usual hooker, Nadia, for a night of ecstasy. With the money he earned on the voyage and after the grief he experienced in prison, he decided to reward himself with a better-quality prostitute to enjoy the night with. He waited patiently at the bar for the right lady to approach him. *Khoroshiy tovar sam sebya khvalit,* he thought. Quality goods advertise themselves.

When I see the right one, I'll know.

Some minutes passed until two young women came by, giggling, hand in hand, glancing around and trying to make eye contact with patrons of the bar as they made their pass. It was clear they were high-end party girls, a cut above the common sex worker, who for a the right price would accommodate their john either alone or in tandem, whatever the preference. They worked for themselves out of a salon they rented where they could practice their unforgiving enterprise and make their home. A little young, but he found he was curiously in the mood. Mostov raised a brow, and they practically surrounded him. A motion to the bartender, and he ordered Stoli Razberi cocktails for the girls; after all, a little wining and dining never hurt, and he was feeling both generous and bordering on manic after escaping from his unfortunate but brief brush with the law. Some pleasantries and introductions followed. The girls were named Elena and Mimi. Elena soon excused herself to go to the bathroom, and Mostov took Mimi, a blond with hair cut short and bright red lipstick, over to the dance floor where she warmed him up with a well-rehearsed, slow grinding motion, her hands moving up and down his sinewy thighs, squeezing here and there. He returned the favor, sampling the goods and enjoying what he found.

As they danced shamelessly to the music, a man wearing a dark knit hat and leather bomber jacket watched them with interest from a table near the front door. It was the driver of the van that picked Mostov up from the prison. He and his associate tracked Mostov to the bar by monitoring the GPS signals from the ankle bracelet they placed on him. The man typed something into his cell phone and then lit up a cigarette as he waited for a reply. A few moments later, he stubbed it out and walked to the bar where he ordered a shot of Jack. Then he turned back to the dance floor and saw Mostov and his new friend, still gyrating with the beat. He pulled his coat collar up to ensure he could not be seen by them.

Oh well, two will pay dearly tonight instead of one.

The assassin was not one to question instructions when it came to fulfilling targeted executions. With the bartender busy mixing cocktails for his patrons, the man stealthily removed a small bottle with an eye-dropper top and deftly squirted some of the liquid into Dima and Mimis' drinks. It was a mix of synthetic opioids and morphine that he prepared earlier in the day. The combination had worked in many other such killings, and he was confident it would work once again. Then he slipped the bottle back into his coat pocket and with one elbow on the bar, threw back the rest of his whisky and smoothly exited the bar.

A perfectly appropriate ending for these lowlifes, the police won't waste much of their time on these two.

He rejoined the other security agent in the waiting van, and they sped away.

After a while, Mostov was aroused and had had enough dancing. As the band finished a song, he and Mimi returned to the bar where she opened her small purse to refresh her lipstick. Mostov caressed her bum as she nodded her head to the beat of the next song, a pulsating technopop number, and sipped her drink from a straw. In between sips, she applied a thin coat of red lip gloss.

"What about your friend, Elena?"

Mimi smirked and winked, "She's busy, and can take care of herself."

"Come on then, let's go. Is your place nearby?"

"A short walk."

"Here's to short walks!" he said.

They each raised their glasses and clinked them together.

"*Payékhalee*," Mostov said as they gulped down the last of their drinks.

They put on their coats and walked out of the bar into a chilly sea wind with Mimi holding tightly onto his arm. Along the way, her tummy began to flutter a little, and she developed hot flashes while her legs stiffened.

Shit, was the cocktail's juice spoiled?

And possibly a little heavy on the vodka, she thought.

Really, of all times for an upset stomach!

When they arrived in front of Mimi's apartment, Mostov opened the door and felt the pace of his heart quicken and his chest tighten. The flat was on the second floor, and Mimi steadied herself with a hand against the wall as she climbed the stairs. She unlocked the door to the apartment and turned on the vestibule light, mumbling that she needed a moment in the bathroom as Mostov peered around the comfy looking apartment. There was a main room with a sofa with two club chairs and a small drinks cabinet. A floor lamp had a red silk shade with fringes that hung down. All in all, a bit gaudy, but good for the clientele. He took a seat on the sofa beside the lamp and waited for Mimi to return from the bathroom. At this point, he began to feel tingling in his hands and feet, an odd sensation he tried to stop by rubbing his hands together, and soon he felt his head start to buzz as well.

Must be from the cold temperature outside.

Some more minutes passed. Mostov's eyes were closed when he heard a muffled sound from the bathroom. He heard a voice cry out softly, "Dima, my legs are numb, come quick!" He stood up but fell back to the sofa, as the room began to spin, and he felt short of breath. Another push upward succeeded, and he stumbled through the hallway to where he heard the voice. When he opened the bathroom door, the first thing he saw was Mimi's purse lying open on the ground with a condom carrying case that had spilled out of it. She lay crumpled on the floor, her legs twisted, as she convulsed and retched and began to cough from the vomit. Mostov dropped to his knees to pick up her head so she would not choke, not knowing what else to do. Mimi suddenly appeared comatose and was breathing shallowly. Dima looked about helplessly and was in a full panic mode, feeling like he too had the urge to vomit. He fumbled in his pants pocket for his phone to call an ambulance, but it was in his pea coat that was hanging on a peg near the front door, and he dared not leave Mimi. He wasn't even sure if he could make it to his phone. He tried to pick Mimi up to revive her, but even with her slight frame, she felt like a deadweight, and they fell back onto the floor together, pinning him to the cold asbestos tiles. He grabbed at the sink top to gain some leverage, but his legs, now numb like hers, would not work to pull himself up. He fell back against the floor, sputtering for air, his lungs feeling as if they were about to explode from a lack of oxygen. He looked down at Mimi and saw that her lips were blue, not rouge as before. The sight made him clutch his stomach, and he vomited a vile mix of the beer and ramen noodles he had made himself for lunch. His eyeballs began to flutter rapidly, and the last thing he saw before losing consciousness was Mimi's lipstick tube as it rolled from her cold, white hand and clattered onto the floor.

CH. 46

The Jacksonville Zoo opened as usual on Sunday morning, and since the peak summer tourist season was over, the entry lines were short, and they moved fast. Even so, the tiger, jaguar and giraffe pens attracted hundreds of zoo guests every day. The zoo's bird collection was among the best in the nation, featuring a great variety of storks and herons that roosted in the live oaks above the warthog and cheetah exhibits. Everything from hummingbirds to bald eagles could be viewed, a one-stop-wonder for birders who flocked to the zoo in great numbers from far and wide.

Over the years, the zoo found itself in an improbable area due to the rapid commercialization of the natural habitat all around it. When the zoo opened in the early 1900s, the surrounding area was a pristine maritime forest, perfect for the exotic creatures who were put on display. In recent years, however, acres of warehouses, a large oil and natural gas facility and a cruise line terminal all encroached on the natural preserve.

A mom pushed a stroller with a toddler while keeping an eye on her five-year-old running ahead. The mom caught up, only to find her girl sobbing, with tear-streaked cheeks.

"What's wrong, my love?"

"They're dead, mummy. They're dead. I want to go home."

Kneeling to comfort her girl, she said, "Who is dead, dear?"

The little girl pointed a finger at an enclosure designed for small birds. Under the suet stands, the grass-and-straw-covered floor was littered with a tangle of about 40 dead birds, most of them resting on their back with their wings tucked, feet clenched and glassy eyes open.

The mom bit her lip. "Sweetie, they're not dead, it's just their nappy time. Let's not disturb them," she said as she took the wide-eyed girl by the hand and backed away slowly. "Shhhhh."

The little girl looked over her shoulder, not entirely convinced. On her way toward the African Safari section, the woman pulled a zoo attendant aside and whispered to him to get to the bird area *stat*; something was clearly wrong. When the docent arrived at the small, caged area, he promptly closed it off to visitors. One of the zoo's bird handlers and the day shift nurse were called in to assess the situation. When they entered the cage, they donned gloves and collected a few different bird specimens in separate bags, two of each species for split toxicology sampling and autopsies. Time was of the essence, since whatever had killed the birds could easily spread to the rest of the zoo's population. They needed to get to the bottom of what happened in the hours after the zoo's closing on Saturday. Perhaps it was a bird virus or another pathogen. In addition to the birds, all the suet, seed and water dishes were collected and sealed in bags, in case the feed was tainted by mold or some other contaminant. As nightfall approached, a team of volunteer toxicologists from the nearby branch of the University of Florida medical system finished up its tests on the birds. Far from any pathogen listed as the cause of death, they determined the birds had all died of carbon monoxide poisoning. The data was checked again, with the same conclusion. The chief zookeeper waited anxiously for the report, and upon receiving it, cursed the nearby oil and natural gas tank farm. He immediately suspected that a plume of carbon monoxide or some other noxious gas had belched up from the facility and wafted over to the zoo, causing the death of his cherished, sensitive birds— proverbial canaries in a coal mine.

At about the same time as the birds were being gassed, Elena returned to the apartment she shared with Mimi. She had already serviced one john in the bathroom of the bar, a young man who was treated to her charms by his friends for his 18th birthday. The bathroom was the best they could afford for their friend. After lingering in the bar and waiting for a more rewarding trick, she finally gave up when none materialized. When Elena arrived at her apartment, she found it strange that the door was unlocked and the living room lights were on, but no one was in the living room or Mimi's bedroom, after she called for her. She shrugged, perhaps Mimi and her lover were hungry after a session of sexual fulfillment and had gone out to find a bite to eat. It wouldn't be the first time. Elena filled the electric kettle with water from a plastic bottle, preparing to make a hot cup of tea before going to bed. Then, a trip to the bathroom to pee before the kettle boiled, but she froze in the hall when she saw Mimi and Dima's bodies intertwined on the bathroom floor. She could not believe her eyes, and then she let out a blood curdling scream.

The popular and sometimes entertaining local news channel, News 14 JAX, led its evening show with the breaking story of the exotic birds found dead at Jacksonville's beloved zoo. Standing in front of the zoo's entrance, a news anchor pointed out that behind her a scene of "fowl play" was discovered, possibly the result of a spill or release from the nearby oil and gas facility which she also pointed to, to her left. Her gesture looked more like an accusatory finger than an indication of direction. More information was expected by the 11 p.m. show, so stay tuned, she advised.

Lancaster turned up the volume on his widescreen TV to hear more about the unfortunate incident. He was genuinely upset upon hearing the news, and even less happy when a commercial for Chick-fil-A, a regional favorite, tastelessly appeared between show segments.

Damn, that weren't supposed to happen. Dem poor 'lil birds.

But, blood had been spilled for the greater good, he rationalized by the end of the show.

In addition to the goings on at the zoo, a flurry of activity was also in process at the normally tranquil oil and gas storage facility, because a pressure alarm sounded off early in the morning, alerting the security team that monitored the grounds from a control room nearby. They quietly called in the yard superintendent who took an engineer with him to inspect the tanks that tripped the alarm. Nothing seemed out of the ordinary to them, most likely a wire corroded by the salty ocean air was the culprit, until a spigot at the base of the last tank was turned to take a sample. A rotten-smelling slurry oozed out into a quart-sized glass beaker held by the engineer. He frowned as he held it up into the morning light, took a whiff and made a face. "This ain't oil, whatever it is. Pee-utrid, I say. We'd best call the Navy. It's their dang mess in these tanks," he said with a drawl.

Across the St. John's River, the Naval Air Station engineering office received the call. A team of environmental engineers and chemists assembled with their equipment to visit their oil storage tanks. It took then less than 15 minutes to prepare, based on the safety drills they routinely carried out as part of the disaster management function of the base. A patrol boat quickly ferried them across the river, and they landed not far from the spot where Russ had beached his board on the thin strip of sand that separated the river from the land. Fortunately for him, any of the heavy footprints he might have left were dissolved by the turn of the tide which ebbed and flowed every six hours due to the river's nearby outlet on the Atlantic Ocean.

The Navy chemists split into three teams to test the tanks, and they finished up their work in about 20 minutes. As a precaution they also tested the contents of the surrounding tanks. After huddling, the same picture emerged for each of the affected tanks. The sludge now held in the tanks was confirmed to be contaminated with micro-organisms, most of them dead, but some still alive. The oil was diluted and inert, and one of the chemists lit a butane torch and held its flame over one of the beakers to demonstrate that it would not ignite any more than the water from the nearby river.

The teams wrapped up their work and headed back to the base after radioing ahead. A security detail stayed on to keep the tank farm secure. The base's Command Master Chief was keen to be debriefed by the returning team and waited for them at the environmental support office. One of the scientists addressed the elephant in the room, namely, the apparent similarity between the tanks they just visited and the ones in Sweden that had gained so much of the world's attention over the past few days. A consensus in the room affirmed his hypothesis. The Chief thanked the team and classified their findings as confidential, though he knew word of the sabotage would soon spread. Then he called the base commander's office to bring him up to speed.

CH. 47

Thor and Stig rose early on Monday and enjoyed a quick visit to the breakfast room of their hotel. Local herring and salmon, four types of yogurts and a healthy variety of berries were featured on the buffet. Bread was freshly baked and hearty, with seeds big and small sitting atop the loaves, like a star-filled galaxy. After finishing, they checked out of the hotel and made coffee to go at a complimentary coffee station next to its entrance.

It was only a short drive to the Russian border. At the guard station, they presented their IDs and passports to the security officer who scanned their information and waited good-naturedly for their background checks to pop up on his screen along with a green signal approving their entry to the country. A minute or two later, one of his superior officers walked over to the checkpoint with a folio from which he removed two diplomatic passes and handed them to the guard, who handed them to the Swedish visitors, stamped their passports and waived them through with a polite smile. Stig pulled a container of *snus* out from his jacket pocket and placed a pinch beneath his upper lip.

A little over an hour later, they reached the outskirts of Murmansk and took the 4-lane further south toward the prison.

They announced themselves at the guardhouse which let them pass, and they parked their vehicle in the guest parking lot. The grounds of the prison were meticulously maintained, courtesy of prisoners who volunteered their work in exchange for extra fruits, vegetables and eggs they could get in return from a small jail store.

The men walked through the main entrance of the facility and spoke through a bullet-proof window to a pair of stern, athletic-looking guards seated behind it. A busy office hummed in the background.

"My name is Thor Bjornsson, and this is Investigator Stig Renell. We've traveled here from Sweden to meet with a prisoner named Dima Mostov, number 95183. The interview has been arranged through your Embassy in Stockholm. The Embassy also provided these diplomatic passes." Thor held them out to the nearest guard who looked at them through the thick glass with indifference. "We have an hour to meet with him, so your cooperation is appreciated."

"Please have a seat over there," the other guard said, nodding his head to the left.

The two men walked over to a guest area while the first guard placed a call to the warden's office.

The warden took the call and momentarily panicked. Something was wrong, and he could not figure out what to do. It was only on Friday that he was asked to release the prisoner.

If there is a problem, it won't be mine, he swore.

"Tell the Swedes to wait, I will be with them as soon as I can," he coolly told the guard who solemnly listened to the warden and confirmed the warden's instructions to Thor and Stig.

Yanovich clenched his hands together, patted his brow with a paper towel and collected his thoughts. Sergei Mikhailov had gotten him into this jam. Yanovich impulsively placed a phone call to Mikhailov's office in Moscow. Time to punt the ball.

Yanovich was put on hold for several minutes until finally he heard Sergei's unpleasant voice on the other end.

"My dear Boris, how are you today?"

"Please tell me how I should feel, Chief Inspector. There are two Swedish security officers in our lobby, requesting to interview that prisoner you told me to release on Friday. They presented papers from the Russian Embassy in Stockholm, authorizing their visit. They claim their interview of Mostov was approved by the Ministry of Internal Affairs."

"Interesting. That might very well be, however my office has jurisdiction over matters affecting the Federation's markets and securities. I am the one who determines who is eligible for bail or unconditional release, and based on good information I determined Mostov was wrongfully accused. As I explained, he is not guilty of crimes involving our securities laws and was entitled to his release. If he did anything wrong, it's no more serious than a charge of littering. He's a flyspeck. Do you understand?"

"Yes, Comrade."

"So just tell your Swedish visitors that there has been an obvious miscommunication. Let them know prisoner Mostov is no longer in custody. The Federation does not incarcerate anyone who is truly innocent. I'll contact the Ministry of Foreign Affairs in Moscow to update them in case of any blowback against our Embassy in Stockholm. Is there anything else you need?"

Damn that Gnady, he better have a plan to finish this razdolbay already.

"No Sir, ah, just one more thing.... Will my account still be updated next month?"

"Of course, Boris, of course. Be patient, you will be pleased."

Mikhailov hung up the line.

Yanovich smiled in satisfaction but still felt uneasy. He found it difficult to read the upper levels of criminal life, the links and loyalties, but he trusted that his connection with Mikhailov was well placed. He had done as he was instructed, after all.

Warden Yanovich called the front desk where the guards sat.

"Inform our visitors that the prisoner they wish to meet is not in custody here, he was released. Say no more, is that clear?"

"*Da, boss.*"

The reception guard motioned Thor and Stig to come to the window, where he informed them just as Yanovich said.

"That's impossible," Thor stammered.

"I have no further information," the guard said.

Thor and Stig looked at the guard in disbelief, but it was clear the guard would be of no further use to them.

"Let's go," Stig said, and the two left the facility. Stig drove.

Bjornsson shook his head and said, "Crazy Ivans. All this way for nothing."

"Maybe not, Thor. Look in Mostov's folio, you'll find a photocopy of his passport, taken from the entry visa from his recent visit to Gothenburg. Anna placed it in the file for identification purposes. It should have his home address in it; I bet it's current, we can still make a stop there on our way out of town. Maybe we can still have a word with him if we get lucky."

While Stig drove, Thor rifled through the file and found the passport with Mostov's address.

"Bingo, Stig, let's go."

The GPS system in the region around Murmansk was frequently jammed by the Russians, especially with NATO's Varanger airbase nearby. With no access to GPS, Stig had to stop at several gas stations and convenience stores to pinpoint the address. It took longer to find than they expected with the daylight fading in early afternoon. Eventually they reached the drab apartment block that Mostov called home. The dreary street was littered and full of potholes, and Stig drove carefully to avoid them. With the streets largely empty, they easily found a place to cut the engine and stake out the apartment house. They waited about 20 minutes before deciding to enter the grimy building. When they got to Mostov's apartment, they saw a ribbon of yellow crime tape sealing the door. They knocked on a neighboring apartment door, and a young woman in a bathrobe answered, holding a baby. She spoke no Swedish, but her English was passable. She said the police had been there all morning but had left after lunch. She overheard one of the police say the occupant of the apartment, who mostly kept to himself, had died of an apparent drug overdose. *Such a tragedy, and not uncommon.*

Bjornsson thanked the woman, and the two officers walked back to their car. A lamppost flickered outside the apartment building, but the weak light was of little help to the officers who had to step carefully to dodge the potholes in the road.

Stig turned the ignition on for the return trip to Kirkenes where they hoped to catch the last flight to Stockholm and Gothenburg.

"A dead end, after all." Thor said inside the vehicle.

"As dead as it gets."

CH. 48

Monday afternoon in Paris, the shoulder tourist season was winding down and employees were back at work after the August holidays, doing their best to remember their holiday by the seaside. The streets were quiet, yet a large group of mostly young people began to coalesce into the Tuileries gardens, near the entrance to the Place de la Concorde. Prompted by the mysterious Manifesto, social media websites run by climate activists urged their followers to meet at the Concorde's obelisk and then march onward to City Hall. Their orders were automatically echoed by fake websites operated by Russia, always on the watch and eager to fuel divisions within the West. By noon, a raucous throng of nearly 10,000 eco-warriors made its way toward the Louvre. They pelted the Pei pyramid with bricks and spray-painted many centuries-old statues along the way. The police were unprepared to control the crowd, and they mostly stood guard by the various entrances to the Louvre, a last-ditch but effective ground plan to protect the precious galleries from harm. Instead of marching to the City Hall, however, the protestors decided to remain camped out at the Louvre, ensuring greater attention from the world press for their cause. Their chants called on the G-7 to meet the Manifesto's demands. The mayor's office had no appetite for the riots and foreseeable strikes that could paralyze the city. Munching on a crispy-edged madelaine, the mayor called the Prime Minister's office to see what could be done to quell the mounting demonstrations.

Similar protests were underway in Brussels, where masked rioters and members of their left-wing alliance surrounded the Europa building, the seat of the European Council. And Gothenburg was being assailed once again by the same rabble that trashed the city during the first EU Summit that attracted violent public protests in 2001. Several other cities in Europe witnessed protests and shutdowns that morning, with no let-up in sight, fueled by the power of social media.

By afternoon, the G-7 leaders were poised to publish their press release in response to the Manifesto, hoping to limit any further escalation by the unruly marchers. In the end, they largely rehashed the press release prepared by the working group that had met at Vossared. The text focused on quicker implementation of decarbonization regulations and funding less developed countries' transition to clean energy. Their press release also included promises for funding battery technology research, subsidies for electric vehicles and renewables, and taxing carbon emissions, among several other measures. Finally, they adopted a goal of cutting carbon usage by 50% over the next 17 years, a last-minute change urged by the French Prime Minister who finally buckled from the pressure coming from the streets, not to mention Paris City Hall.

The press release was published and word of it began to appear in various online, TV, air and print outlets.

The G-7's meeting also included a briefing from a U.S. representative on early reports of the new tank farm sabotage just south of Amelia Island. The palpable tension at the meeting site increased after this update was over. The group further discussed enhancing security measures around the world for the key oil depots and refineries, but a feeling of unease pervaded the room based on one participant's candid assessment of the energy infrastructure's exposure to more such events. After the meeting ended, several participants expressed doubts over the sufficiency of their reply to the Manifesto. A check of the markets fueled their concern with the price of oil initially spiking six percent higher after the reply's release. The market's lack of conviction spoke volumes. By the end of the trading session in London, oil was up eight percent more on the day.

Before boarding his evening flight home, Stig called Eva Dahlquist to inform her of the fruitless day he and Thor had attempting to interview Mostov. They commiserated that his untimely demise was suspicious, a big blow to their investigation.

"I guess we'll never know who Mostov met when he was on shore leave. Anna will be disappointed," Dahlquist said.

"Uhhmm," Stig said.

"The flip side of the question now is who might Mostov have met with? If we can figure that out, we will be close to learning who is behind this conspiracy."

Stig thought for a moment. "How many sources of this new bacteria could there be, especially if they are from Sweden?"

"A tough question. There are so many life science firms these days in Gothenburg. And don't forget Stockholm, Oslo and Copenhagen. I'm not sure we could cover them all with the little time and resources we have."

"We'll have to think of something."

"Meanwhile, I'll let the others know about Mostov. Safe trip home, Stig. See you tomorrow."

After speaking with Anna and the rest of her team, Dahlquist texted Daniel to see if he was available. A few moments later her phone rang.

"Hi Eva, how are you?

"Could be better, Daniel. It's been a long and rather disappointing day. We've heard nothing official about the G-7's reply, have you?"

"Nothing on our side. Perhaps that's a good sign, maybe whoever wrote the Manifesto is at least considering it?"

"One can only hope. The protests in Gothenburg are a real pain. Our jails are full for now, the city decided the best defense is offense. We'll hold them as long as we can. And now a piece of bad news to tell you. I just hung up with Stig. He and Thor are flying home from Kirkenes as we speak. It turns out Mostov was released from prison sometime late last week, or maybe this weekend. He was found dead of an overdose, way too coincidental in our view. But we will never know the truth, I'm sure of that."

"Damn, that's too bad and very suspicious. We'll have to think who in Sweden is powerful enough to arrange his killing, if that's indeed what happened to him. On second thought, a Swede? That sounds unlikely, doesn't it? It's more likely someone in Russia arranged the hit. Maybe someone working with a Swede, right?"

"You make a fair point, Daniel."

"Do you recall Axel Carlsson, the biologist Anna and I met last week out at Marstrand? He gets financial support from a wealthy Russian oil trader. I met the guy once at a private event in Stockholm. Maybe he has the connections to do something like this. I'm not sure of a motive, however."

"I think you've just added another person of interest to the case," Eva said. The next time the Russian flies to Sweden, Border Control will ensure that we get a chance to speak with him."

"That could be some time," Daniel said.

"What we Swedes sometimes lack in humor, we make up for in patience. Let's keep in touch."

The wheels were turning in Daniel's head. More current information about Pankov was needed, and he knew of one source to find it.

CH. 49

It was another dark and gray Tuesday morning on the Kola peninsula, home to Murmansk. Snow clouds were gathering once again,
threatening another early storm like the one that suddenly appeared the week earlier and delivered seaman Mostov to Yanovich's
custody. This time, the snow might linger for a while and ice on the
roads could last into the morning hours. It was still too early in the
season for the municipality to send out the salt trucks.

A driver arrived at Yanovich's home in the northern wooded sub-
urbs at 8:00 a.m. as usual, driving a late model Toyota RAV with
4-wheel drive. Ever precautious, Yanovich strapped on his shoulder
holster and checked his revolver before turning up his coat collar
and walking to the waiting car. The driver, a chauffeur employed
by the prison, opened the car's back door. With Yanovich comfort-
ably settled in his seat, the driver got back in, and they sped off.

Traffic in Murmansk was light and soon they were out of the city,
heading south. There were several miles of isolated roadway between
the airport and the prison. In one of those stretches, the driver saw
the headlamps of the black van in his rear-view mirror flashing and
noticed it was closing in on them fast. There was no cause for concern as it entered the left lane, attempting to pass them.

Perhaps an urgent delivery to the prison, the driver thought? Not unusual, meds were frequently delivered this way for ill inmates.

But as soon as the van re-entered the right lane in front of the RAV, it slowed, forcing the chauffeur to brake along with it and close the distance between them. Suddenly, the van's back door swung open, as did the chauffer's mouth an instant later. He instinctively reached for his gun, but it was too late. A man suited in a black SWAT uniform fired a burst from his PP-19 Bizon into the chest of the RAV driver and then trained his rifle on the left front tire of the car, blowing it apart. The car veered to the left, crossed the road, flipped and rolled twice before coming to rest just off the road's berm. In the back seat, Yanovich lay stunned and nearly unconscious, the top of his head bleeding and his face lacerated from flying glass.

The van driver braked completely and turned his car back around in the direction of Murmansk. He stopped the van near the RAV. There wasn't a lot of time. The driver walked to the driver's side of the RAV and shot a *coup de grace* into the chauffer's head. His accomplice meanwhile assessed Yanovich through the broken window where he sat moaning, still buckled in. The agent held a pistol in one hand beneath the hip of the car so Yanovich could not see it.

"Who is behind this brazen attack, tell me," Yanovich demanded, slurring his speech.

"You have many enemies from your years as a warden, don't you, Boris? It's not like that, this time. This is from one of your friends."

Yanovich winced. His mind now raced as he tried to figure out the answer to the age-old question of who was in charge. Who had he aggrieved?

"Boris, tell me, who else knows what prisoner Mostov said during his interrogations?"

"Mostov?" *That little shit.* "No one knows anything," Yanovich replied, sobering up.

Could this simply be a warning?

"Were any recordings made of his interrogation?"

"No," Yanovich moaned, suddenly realizing his mortal danger.

"Very well, Boris".

The driver tapped his watch in the air impatiently. In the end, the assassin speaking with Yanovich could have easily pumped two rounds into his head, but instead the triggerman just as effectively shot him twice in each lung. It was a begrudging and deliberate final favor to Yanovich from Pankov for having released Mostov, in case there was to be an open-casket funeral.

Yanovich's eyes turned glassy, and he began to stare vacantly into the distance. His head slumped to his moist chest, and before his heart stopped beating, warden Yanovich had a final vision. It was his wife, dressed all in black at his funeral, saying "We all die sooner or later, but it was unfair that my husband's life should end this way. And Boris, where did you hide all our money?"

He was not the first, and not the last, to die trying to make a living from Russia's Darwinian gulag system.

The two contract killers returned to their van and drove in the dusky morning light until they reached the highway entrance for the return drive to Moscow where they were based. It would take them a day and a half to get home, and they would lay low until receiving their next assignment, sanctioned by their very rich and powerful boss in the *Bratva*. The team of two specialists was assigned to Pankov and instructed to work at his discretion, courtesy of his associates in the *Bratva*, to help tie up any loose ends he perceived. The senior-most bosses of the *Bratva* were keen to ensure their exponential paper gains held up until the expiration date of the options contracts that Pankovneft had purchased, less than two weeks away.

That morning, Pankov was pacing in his office, anxious to know how the Murmansk operation was going and pained that the Fabergé egg was still conspicuously missing from its stand. With that in mind, there was just one more loose end that needed to be carefully tied up.

On a bright note, oil futures were once again up, heading for their second week of gains.

Shortly before lunch, he placed a call to the driver of the van from his secure cell phone.

"Has everything gone according to plan?" Pankov asked.

"Perfectly, sir. We are *en route* to Moscow, and both accounts have been closed. We'll be home tomorrow."

"Well done. I have one more assignment for you. Will you be available to work when you are back?"

"We remain at your disposal, both day and night."

"Thank you. I'll call you with the information you will need tomorrow, remain on standby. Whatever the *Bratva* is paying, I will match it with pleasure as a bonus if you successfully complete your next assignment."

Pankov grinned as he hung up the phone. If they were indeed successful, the Fabergé egg he cherished would be resting once again in the amber stand where it belonged.

CH. 50

After the phone call from Lieutenant Dahlquist, Daniel's mind remained focused on the potential connection between Carlsson and Pankov. The whole thing seemed off to him. Why would a Russian oil oligarch be involved with an environmental foundation in the first place? A contribution from one of the supermajors like Shell Oil to the SBF made sense on one level, but what concern was climate change to a private Russian oil trader?

These sons of bitches are mercenary and don't have an altruistic bone in their body.

Frustrated, he picked up the phone, late as it was, and speed-dialed Karin. She had a way of helping make sense of things.

"*Hej* Daniel."

"Sorry I'm calling so late, but something is bugging me. You ok to talk?"

"Sure."

"First the big news. Do you remember the Russian seaman I told you about, suspected of involvement with the contaminated refinery tank and the oil storage cavern at Tor Harbor?"

"Yes, and the attempt to arrest him failed, right?"

"Spectacularly. He landed in a Murmansk prison cell, but then he was somehow released a few days ago. You're never going to believe what happened to him next."

"Don't keep me waiting, Daniel."

"He's *dead!* Supposedly an overdose, but that's unconfirmed. Eva hopes to get a copy of the autopsy report, even though it will likely be unreliable."

Russian autopsies were notoriously discretionary and routinely gave the wrong reason for the cause of death. In this case, Mostov and his pert escort were just as likely to have their cause of death listed as heart failure as a drug overdose. And no pathologist would waste a minute checking into whether these two were the victims of a homicide.

"That's just terrible. Poor man. What will happen to the investigation?"

"It's a setback, but the trail is still warm in Gothenburg. Anna and Stig still believe Axel Carlsson and Gnady Pankov are somehow involved or at minimum know more than they are willing to say. However, I doubt there is sufficient cause to arrest Axel, and Pankov obviously cannot be touched in Russia. Eva wanted to know how many biotech firms in the region have the capacity to engineer a bacterium like the one we found in the tanks. Based on my understanding of the biological and related research firms in the region, there are simply too many to consider."

"That doesn't sound good, with just Axel's Foundation as the only local suspect for now, and a distant one at that."

"Indeed. And it sure would be good to rule him out, if possible, but I'm not exactly sure how to do that," Daniel said.

"Well, perhaps I could have a word with him? My company is still the SBF's accounting firm. That leaves the door open."

"It would be very tricky to approach him directly, Karin. He's unbelievably sensitive about this, as we've seen," Daniel said.

"True, but I don't think he will have an unfriendly reaction to me. Let me think some more about it, I'll speak with my partners."

"Ok, thanks, but don't do anything that could jeopardize your firm's relationship with Carlsson. One way or the other, we will figure him out."

"How is everything else going?" Karin asked.

"A little better. As you probably saw on TV, the G-7 made a significant concession to whoever wrote the Manifesto. Protests are starting to subside in Paris and Belgium, a good sign."

"It's amazing to think that the G-7 countries are going to seriously make changes to their carbon consumption. It's a new era, Daniel."

"You're right. When you think about it, the perpetrators of this whole fiasco have outwitted the entire oil lobby in the span of two weeks. They've changed history."

"I miss you," Karin said.

"I miss you, too. How about dinner tomorrow evening? We can talk more about this then. Eventually all the meetings will die down, this will pass. I'm thinking we could plan a long weekend soon, a place where it's still warm. Are you up for that?"

"Yes, I'd love to get away. What about Marrakech? I've always wanted to go there; it sounds so romantic. We can find a little riad and stay in our hideaway, eating just figs and dates, and then go out for tagine dinners at night!"

"Great idea, will you check into it?"

"I'll let you know tomorrow at dinner what I've found. Why don't you come by, I'll make a simple main course of salmon and roast potatoes."

"Sounds delicious! Let's talk tomorrow afternoon, love you."

"Sweet dreams."

Wednesday morning and Gnady called the *Bratva* assassins to ask them to meet him in his home, where he knew the security was ironclad and they could safely converse. The pair arrived at lunchtime, just in from their overnight drive from Murmansk. A security guard met them at the door and wanded them for radio transmitters, just in case.

"Welcome, gentlemen. I have some refreshments here for you," pointing to a side room beyond the parlor where a table was filled with delicacies and samovars of tea and coffee. They helped themselves and Gnady motioned them to join him in a book-lined parlor off the main entrance hall. The room had bookended mahogany panels, a matching pair of Tiffany floor lamps and art nouveau panels painted with scenes by Czech artist, Alphonse Mucha.

"Please make yourself at home. You've had a long journey. Were there any issues that I should be aware of?

The driver spoke while his associate pushed a caviar-laden cracker into his mouth. "Not *per se*. The only side matter we can inform you of is that we had to eliminate a sex worker who Mostov was seeing. A shame, she was young, quite sweet. But we did so out of an abundance of caution in case he told her anything about his stay in Gothenburg. One can never be too cautious, I trust you agree?"

"I most certainly do. You are to be congratulated on your thoroughness," Gnady praised the killer. He reached into his sports coat pocket and removed two envelopes.

"For you," he said, passing them to his guests. "A bonus for your successful trip to a most unpleasant city. Let's forget about it now."

The two men accepted the thick envelopes, placing them beside them on the table as they continued to listen intently.

"On to new business, then," Gnady said with a raised brow. "I have another job for you. On Friday morning, Chief Auditor Sergei Mikhailov of the National Settlements Depository will follow his usual routine of taking the subway to his office at Spartakovskaya Street. The underground will be busy as usual, packed with commuters wishing to avoid the usual traffic jams. Follow him from his home to the Teatralnaya station, where he makes a final transfer. The station will be packed. You'll have an opportunity in all the commotion. Make it appear as an unfortunate accident. Such places are inherently dangerous, with tracks and speeding trains so close to the riders. Corpulent men lose their balance easily. I will leave the details with you. Are there any questions?"

The men looked at each other and back to Gnady before shaking their heads.

"Very good, we'll update you on Friday, Mr. Pankov," the driver said.

"Please do, I will be waiting."

The men stood to leave and Gnady patted them on the back on their way out, as if they were old friends.

Gnady returned to the parlor and dialed Mikhailov, who picked up promptly.

"Gnady, how are you, it is such a pleasure to hear from you."

Gnady winced. *With any luck, this will be the last time I speak with this impudent Cheshire Cat.*

"Fine, fine, Sergei. I just wanted to tell you a couple of things."

"Go on."

"Those two accounts in Murmansk. I just learned they have been closed."

"Any balance to be concerned with?"

"No, all clear."

"Say no more."

"And one more thing, about your daughter's account in Cyprus, the funds should have cleared this morning. After you have confirmed it yourself, just make sure you deliver that security item you removed from my office. I want it back no later than the close of business on Friday. Are we in agreement?"

"Most certainly, if what you say is correct," Mikhailov replied. "A deal is a deal."

Pankov terminated the call, thankful that it was mercifully short.

A small price to get rid of this parasite once and for all.

CH. 51

The winds howled into Gothenburg from the North Sea, carrying the weight of a storm that had battered the British Isles. Rain would soon start falling along a familiar band of geography that stretched across northern France, the low countries and southern Scandinavia. Dark clouds churned overhead, mirroring the uneasiness Karin felt as she watched them drift eastward. The arrival of Gothenburg's dreary fall weather felt like an omen, one that matched the uncertainty she was about to face with Axel.

Karin stared out her office window, the low-hanging haze a reflection of her swirling thoughts. She had been wrestling with doubts about Axel and the SBF for weeks, and now, the weight of responsibility pressed down harder. Axel had been a trusted client for years, but something about his recent behavior set off alarm bells. As much as she tried to push away her growing suspicions, she couldn't shake the feeling that this meeting would change everything.

Earlier that morning, she had spoken with one of the partners about Axel and the SBF. The partner expressed some concern about the account. Her accounting firm had clear rules when it came to client engagements. Transparency, concern for reputational risk and respect for the law were all top hallmarks of building solid relationships, and they came before anything else. On that basis, the partner suggested she meet with Axel to conduct some further diligence on the SBF's relationship with Pankov.

It was a slow day, and her appointment calendar was open for the rest of the afternoon. She was thinking ahead about dinner that evening and decided to leave work early, wanting to stop at her favorite specialty market where she could get all the items she needed, including fresh dill, for the romantic meal she planned to prepare. As she drove out of the underground garage, the idea of visiting Carlsson suddenly popped into her head. There was plenty of time to pick up food for dinner later, so why not peel back the band aid on this festering wound and clarify things once and for all? Her partners would be pleased, and so would Daniel, with any additional information she might glean from an informal talk with Carlsson.

Karin took the highway north and turned off the exit that led to Marstrand. At the road's terminus in the small harbor area, she found a place to park in the congested lot and waited to board the ferry. It was midafternoon, and the shops along the waterfront had begun to bring their goods inside due to the approaching storm. Karin walked quickly up the main walking path that led to the island's imposing fortress and soon found herself in front of the SBF's gate. As she approached the front door, she heard a crack of thunder roll in from the sea.

Karin's hand hovered over the doorbell for a moment, her mind racing. She took a deep breath and pressed it, hearing the distant chime echo through the building. Through the door's glass panes, she saw Axel approaching down the corridor, his expression warm and inviting—but something about his easy smile felt off. As he opened the door, his charm washed over her, but Karin couldn't help feeling a chill creep up her spine. What exactly am I walking into? she wondered.

"*Hej* Karin, please come in!"

"Thank you, Axel, it's so nice to see you," Karin replied as he led her to a seating area off the main lab room. She placed her coat on the seat next to her and her purse on the coffee table.

She must be here to make amends, Axel thought.

"Another surprise visit, I see." Axel's voice was smooth, but there was an unmistakable tension in his tone. "I suppose you've heard all about the unpleasant encounter I had with your friend Daniel and his so-called investigator. They certainly didn't waste any time pressing my buttons."

Karin forced a smile, trying to keep the conversation light. "Daniel did mention it, but he felt bad about how things ended. We all have our off days, don't we?"

Axel's eyes flickered with something darker for a moment before his grin returned. "Off days, indeed."

"I was sorry, too," she added, hoping to staunch his ire.

"Alright, apologies accepted. What brings you to the Foundation? Everyone left a couple of hours ago, there's an approaching storm, and I'm in the process of straightening up. Do you mind if we talk while I finish cleaning the lab?" Axel placed his phone on the coffee table and then walked over to the rows of countertops and ceiling-height glass shelving filled with beakers of oil samples and lab supplies. He went back to wiping down the counters.

"Go right ahead, I don't want to interrupt your work. But to answer your question, my firm is prepping for its annual review of client accounts. We're doing a little more diligence of some accounts where there is a potential for concern over the flow of funds coming here from Russia. You must be aware of the

UN and other sanctions on many of the transactions involving Russia. Of course, we understand there are exemptions, but we need to satisfy ourselves. Consequently, the donations you've received from Pankovneft are on the firm's radar screen, Axel. His company is the only Russian one we have on record of contributing funds to the SBF. Is that correct, do you have any other Russian donors, Axel?"

Christ, again with Gnady? He bristled inside but kept working, showing no emotion. "No, that's the only one", he said curtly.

"Great, that helps to keep things simple." Karin reached into her purse and took out a small pad and a pen to take notes. "And can you tell me where you first met Mr. Pankov?"

"I think it was around 2010 or 2011. We were introduced at a petroleum industry conference. I went there to learn about new spill management technology. The Foundation was beginning to get active in this area, too. Naturally, I made a pitch to Gnady about supporting the Foundation, and he took an interest."

"Since then, Mr. Pankov has become an important donor. Do you expect contributions of the same scale to be made next year?" Karin asked.

Carlsson paused his work and thought for a moment. He turned to look at Karin and said, "Funny you should ask. We recently concluded the main project Pankovneft was funding, and it is unlikely that firm will make the same level of contribution in the future. In fact, Gnady and I recently agreed to wind down our cooperation." Carlsson went back to aggressively wiping down the countertops. Karin watched him uncomfortably as he rubbed compulsively with his back still turned to her.

Damn if this bitch won't shut up already. Who does she think she is? Just then, Axel's phone lying on the coffee table made a beep and a message momentarily appeared at the top of the screen, close to Karin.

The message read, "Congrats on the JAX job, you were right, call me. Apologies, Gnady".

Karin read the message as it lingered on the screen for a few seconds. She looked up inquisitively to Axel as he walked over and picked up the phone to read the message, and after reading it, he looked down at Karin.

"I can explain," he said softly, setting down the phone.

"Please, go ahead," Karin said, her brow furrowed. Her mind was racing fast; "the JAX job", it could only mean one thing: the recent sabotage at the storage tank farm in Jacksonville. She inhaled deeply and held her breath for a moment. He saw that she made the connection when he looked into her eyes.

Axel sighed. It felt as if a great weight had just been lifted from his soul. Karin studied him intently and he seemed resigned as he walked over to sit down beside her on the sofa.

Axel's expression darkened, his voice lowering as he leaned closer. "Since the 1970s, the world has turned a blind eye to the destruction of our planet—oil spills, pollution, unchecked abuse of the environment. And for what? To satisfy their greed. I've watched the world decay, Karin. I've stood by, helpless as the powers that be ignore every warning sign." His eyes gleamed with a manic fervor now, and Karin could feel her heart racing.

"As we speak, Karin, there is a continent of plastic waste accumulating in our oceans, and the world continues to look the other way. Uncontrolled greenhouse gas emissions are causing the icecaps to melt, for heaven's sake! This pains me greatly, Karin. I'm tired of seeing this and feeling incapable of doing anything but watching from the sidelines as our precious environment spirals downward and we head back to the Stone Age.

"When Gnady approached me a few years ago, his firm was in the middle of a takeover by the Russian mob. He could no longer operate independently and knew the day would come when he would have a spectacular miss in the market with the mafia's money. He needed insurance, protection in case there was a misstep his partners could not forgive. You must give him credit; he has a keen sense for survival."

Karin's mind reeled as she listened, each word Axel spoke sending a wave of disbelief crashing over her. It was like watching a mask slip—this wasn't the Axel she thought she knew. The man sitting across from her, speaking so casually about sabotage and destruction, was a stranger. She tried to keep her composure, but her heart pounded in her chest. Is this really happening? she thought, her voice barely a whisper when she finally managed to say, "Go on."

"That's when he approached me with the idea of creating a new life form that he could use to radically transform the oil markets in the blink of an eye, if needed. The Foundation worked for nearly three years to perfect such an organism, and we have carefully cultivated and preserved it here in the lab, waiting for the time when it was needed. The time came two weeks ago, Karin, and so we released it."

"Incredible," Karin uttered. "But why are you telling me this now?"

"I'm tired of hiding it from you, Karin. You of all people can appreciate the revolutionary environmental solution I have created here. It's my hope you will see the tremendous potential for using my bacteria in a constructive way, not in the demonstrations you have recently read about in the news. Those were just to bail Gnady out of some bad market bets he made. Valuable to him, but a game-changer to me. You must understand there are hundreds of miraculous applications where we can use our bacterium; all are harmless to humankind and are good for the environment. We can literally eradicate poisonous exhaust from engines, clean up abandoned gas wells, eliminate methane from city landfills, stop gas flaring from the top of oil wells. And those are just a few examples!

"The next several years will be significant ones here, Karin. I'm telling you this because I want you to join me at the Foundation and help oversee the commercial exploitation of our discovery. You've been with my Foundation from the beginning, help me run it, now. You have the business acumen I need. We need to license the SBF's technology to industries all over the world. Just think of all the good we can do together! I'll figure out a way to get past what's happened at the port. The world will under-stand, you'll see," Axel said, suddenly smiling and putting his arm around Karin as he finished making his appeal.

A tense silence stretched between them, Axel's intense eyes nar-rowing as he realized Karin wasn't reacting the way he'd hoped. She sat frozen in utter disbelief, her mind racing, trying to piece together the madness she had just heard. When Axel's arm slipped around her shoulders, she flinched, repulsed by his disrespectful embrace and fantastical lecture.

Without thinking, she shoved his arm away, her voice trem-bling. "You're insane, Axel. I would *never* join you. You're talking about destroying everything!"

Axel's face twisted with anger, his pleasant facade cracking. "I'm trying to save the world!" he snapped, his voice rising. Axel in turn became incensed and realized it had been a mistake to take

Karin into his confidence. He felt foolish for having done so and instinctively shoved back at her. In an instant, the situation spiraled out of control. Karin grabbed her purse off the coffee table and struck him in the face with it. Its side pocket zipper slit a thin gash on his cheek while its contents fanned out across the floor. A moment later, she found Axel on top of her, his hands closing around her throat as she thrashed beneath his weight. As her vision blurred, panic flooded her senses, and her world began to close.

CH. 52

Daniel left the office and went home to shower and get changed for dinner and the relaxing evening ahead. Before leaving his apartment, he called Karin to tell her he was on his way. She didn't pick up, and his call went into voicemail. He assumed she was in the shower or perhaps on a quick errand, needing something from the store. Daniel caught one of the blue and white city trams near his apartment and rode it to the stop nearest Karin's place. Before boarding, he bought a bouquet of flowers from one of the florists near the top of the Avenue. He bound up the stairs and knocked, but there was no reply. That seemed odd, and he called her again on the phone. She didn't pick up. He waited in the hall another 20 minutes for her, until he decided to call Renell on his mobile phone.

"Stig, this is Daniel Lake. I'm sorry to call you like this, but I could really use your help right now."

"Sure Daniel, I'll do what I can for you. Please let me know what's happening."

It's my girlfriend, Karin Lofgren. I'm afraid she seems to have gone missing. We had a dinner-date at her apartment this evening at 7 pm. I arrived a few minutes early and knocked on her door, but she didn't answer, and I don't think she is at home. This is really unlike her, and I'm afraid something might have happened to her. I can't imagine any scenario that could explain why she's not answering the door at her apartment or her phone."

"I'm sorry to hear this, Daniel. If you stay put, I can send out a request to a locksmith to open the door and see if she is there. Sometimes people fall in the shower."

"That would be great, Stig, please send someone right away, I'll wait here."

Stig added, "I'll also put out a bulletin to the hospitals and clinics in the downtown area in case she was in an accident. Finally, I'll check her license plate from the City's vehicle database. Just text me her home address. The main roads have license plate readers on them, especially the highways, so we can almost instantly track her if she has gone somewhere by car. I'll place the request as soon as I get your text."

"Thank you so much, Stig, I have an uneasy feeling and really appreciate your help."

"No problem. If there is a license plate match, I'll let you know where she was last spotted. In the meanwhile, just sit tight and don't worry. I'm sure there's a good explanation, and help will be on the way soon."

Some minutes later, Daniel heard a siren wailing in the distance. A police cruiser escorting a locksmith van pulled up in front of the building and their occupants met Daniel in front of Karin's door. After a quick introduction, Daniel signed a release slip, and the locksmith used a tool that opened Karin's door within seconds. The police officer entered first and Daniel followed right behind him. They searched the apartment but soon saw that no one was in it. Furthermore, no dinner was being prepared in the spotless kitchen.

"I'm sorry, but I'm going to have to close up the apartment now," the officer said. You won't be able to stay inside."

Daniel nodded and thanked the officer and locksmith who packed up and left. A few minutes later, Daniel's phone rang, it was Stig, sounding upbeat.

"Guess what, we got a match on her vehicle, Daniel."

"Thank heavens. Where is she?"

"She took the E6 north, the last traffic photo of her license plate placed her at Kungalv at around 15:00. There are no more records of her plates being seen after that."

"Thank you, Stig, I'm pretty sure this solves the riddle."

"How so?"

"The next exit is where you get off to go to Marstrand," Daniel explained. "We spoke about her talking with Axel Carlsson to see if he had any further information on the different groups that could be involved with issuing the Manifesto and sabotaging the Port's oil facilities. I had no idea that she might go there this soon. If she drove there, she must have gotten delayed. Possibly the storm. I think I'll take a drive and see if she's been to the SBF. It's the only place she could be."

Stig replied, "Please let me know if you find her, you have my best wishes."

"Thanks Stig, I owe you," and they hung up.

Back at the lab, Carlsson stood up from Karin's motionless body. He paused to wipe his cheek and saw a small smear of blood on his hand. Irritated, he walked over to a nearby countertop, tore a paper towel from a dispenser and applied pressure to his cheek with it until the bleeding stopped.

Then he walked back to Karin and picked her up. He carried her to his study and placed her on a daybed where sometimes he rested in the afternoon. He gingerly propped her head up with a pillow and felt beneath her nose to see if she was breathing, and she was. He was not prepared to kill her there. He was extremely nervous and hoped she would remain unconscious for some time more to let him figure out what to do next. In the meanwhile, he bound her up with rope and gagged her mouth, just in case she reawakened. Then he walked back to the lab and straightened out the seating area. He collected all the contents of her purse from the floor. The last item of hers that he picked up was the candle lighter with the white Dala horse handle, which he tried. It worked nicely. Figuring she would have no further use for the lighter, he placed it on a countertop near a row of beakers. It would be useful at the lab's Bunsen burner stations.

Daniel took the tram back to his apartment and grabbed an apple and a bottle of Ramlösa for the drive to Marstrand. It was a lousy substitute for the dinner he hoped to have, but at this point he no longer had an appetite. The rain was streaming, and the wind was howling as he neared the coastline. His car's high beams reflected on the glistening road and silhouetted the smooth rocky outcroppings that dotted the shore as he approached Marstrand. The parking lot at the ferry stop was mostly empty at that time of the evening, especially since most people had left the island to ride out the storm on the mainland. As he entered the lot, he saw Karin's parked vehicle, one of a handful still there. His heart lifted. All he could think of was finding Karin safe and sound. He felt responsible for her decision to visit the SBF and feared he might have placed her in harm's way.

Luckily, the ferry was still operating even amid the billowy whitecaps, and Daniel paced in the snack shop at the jetty while he waited for the boat to dock. He finally boarded it, and when the bobbing ship got to Marstrand a few minutes later, Daniel noticed he was the only person to go on shore.

He jogged impatiently up the now familiar path to the SBF and rang the doorbell. Thankfully, he could see a light was on and he peered into the door window. Down the hall he could see Carlsson working in the open lab area, walking about, talking on the phone. Daniel looked on, unnoticed by Carlsson, hoping to catch a glimpse of Karin.

"Gnady, I'm really scared right now. I don't know what I should do," Carlsson spoke as he paced. "She saw your damned message on my phone screen and that triggered more questions from her. She put it all together. I had to come clean to her about our efforts, hoping to enlist her support. I felt sure she would understand, appreciate what I had accomplished," Carlsson said. "Then, suddenly, she snapped and wasn't going to have any of it."

"We have to be very careful now, Axel," Gnady advised, thinking fast. "There's just one way now. You will have to make it look like she slipped and fell off the quay, waiting for the ferry to take her back to her car. Can you do that?"

"I think I can, Gnady. There's a raging storm out here now, it's the perfect time. No one will be at the south end of the quay, it's a few hundred meters from where the ferry docks."

"Good, get this done as soon as you can. With any luck, they'll find her body and you will just need to say that she left your lab, and you never saw or heard from her again."

Daniel had had enough. He was desperate to find Karin and felt odd spying through the door window. He rapped on the door urgently. Carlsson looked down the hall toward the door and their eyes met. Carlsson looked back at his phone, said something and ended the call, then he walked toward the door and opened it.

"Hello Axel, I'm sorry to bother you on a night like this. But I'm very glad you are home. May I come in?"

Not wishing to appear surly or raise alarm, Axel invited Daniel in.

"Thanks, Axel". They walked over to the seating area in the lab. "It feels odd to tell you this, but I'm here, hoping to find Karin or see if you know where she might be. We had dinner plans for tonight, but she never showed up." Daniel tried to read Axel's face for any reaction, but Axel appeared unruffled. "I just noticed you have a small gash on your cheek, and it's starting to bleed. Let me get you a Kleenex," Daniel said.

"Please don't, it will be fine," Axel motioned him to keep still.

Daniel got up anyway. "No worries, Axel," and he walked over to the counter where he spied the paper towel roll. As he tore a piece from the roll, he noticed a white Dala horse lighter with the monogram initial "K" on the countertop next to a Bunsen burner. It made Daniel freeze for just a moment when he saw it.

What are the chances this bastard would have the same lighter as Karin?

In an instant, everything added up to him. Her car, her lighter, Axel's bleeding cheek. Suddenly he became even more concerned about Karin's safety. If she was there, she would have met him at the door. He decided to play it cool to see if he could learn more. He handed the paper towel to Axel and sat down again.

"Well, I'm sorry to say that I have not seen Karin since we were all together in Stockholm, at her firm's client event," Axel said with a cryptic look that betrayed his outward composure.

Daniel sensed he was being told a blatant lie and decided he had heard enough. "Well, that's odd. Because I just saw her car parked in the lot opposite Marstrand. And now, on the counter-top over there, I see the Dala horse candle lighter she bought with me. Frankly, Axel, I think you are full of shit. You better tell me what you know, while I take a little look around." Daniel rose and started to walk toward the area behind the lab where there were several offices.

Suddenly, Daniel felt his arm being pulled from behind, and a heavy blow punched him in the gut. Another blow pounded his face. Daniel staggered backward and fell on top of the glass coffee table, shattering it. He managed to get to his feet and saw Axel coming at him, red-faced and in a rage. The two were built similarly, but Daniel knew Axel was a lot more athletic than he was. He allowed Axel to charge him, and deftly sidestepped Axel's next attack. The move gave Daniel a chance to back away and brace himself against the counter with the shelves of oil-filled beakers above it.

"Where is she?!" Daniel thundered.

"You can forget about her, and you should never have come here. And now you're going to regret your meddling once and for all."

Axel charged a second time at Daniel, who deftly grabbed a large beaker of oil on the shelf behind him and hurled it with both hands at Axel. The glass container exploded when it hit Axel in the chest, covering him in oil. Startled, Axel swore and swiped at the pungent, sulfurous oil that soaked much of his shirt and pants. He stooped, red-faced, to pick up one of the larger shards of glass from the floor and resumed his charge. Daniel suddenly found himself trapped between the counter and Axel, and Axel's outstretched hand was about to thrust the glass fragment into his neck.

Daniel somehow caught Axel's right hand at the wrist and stopped Axel's advance. The two struggled against the counter. As

Axel's hand got closer to his neck, out of the corner of his eye Daniel saw the Dala horse lighter sitting on the counter. He slowly worked his free hand over to it and grasped it. Axel saw the butane lighter also and made a last, strong push to slice into Daniel's throat, but it only took Daniel a moment to use his thumb to depress the fuel lever and flick the striker wheel against it. He turned the little flaming torch to Axel's chest, where it erupted in a ball of flame which spread instantly down the length of his body. In that moment, Daniel wrested himself free from Axel's grip.

Axel looked down, stunned. It was as if his head had been decapitated by a guillotine, and he was looking up at his body from the basket. He released the large piece of glass and fell to the floor, flailing about and trying desperately to smother the flames. Daniel dropped to his knees as well, exhausted and mortified. He scrambled away from the conflagration but then tore his shirt off to try to snuff the flames out, a last-ditch effort to save Axel. But Daniel's shirt was not big enough to have much of an effect, and the flames from the highly combustible oil made it too hot for Daniel to get close. Axel continued to writhe and scream on the floor until he mercifully passed out. The inferno continued to burn for another minute, with Axel's skin charring as black as the beakers of oil in the lab, and Daniel looking on, holding his hand to his mouth in horror.

CH. 53

Sore and in shock, Daniel took a few seconds to process what had just occurred. There was nothing more he could do to help Axel. He stood up and went searching for Karin through the back offices of the Foundation. He finally found her, tied up and gagged on the daybed, her eyes looking frantic, but relieved to see Daniel as he entered the room. He quickly ungagged her, and in a few more moments she was free. They just held on to each other as she wept in his arms, and he kissed her and caressed her head.

"Oh Daniel, it was terrible. Axel told me some of the things he's been doing here. You won't believe it. He developed the bacterium that devours oil! And he's been working with Gnady Pankov to release it. They must be behind the Manifesto you've been working on with the G-7, Daniel. The last thing I can recall is Axel on top of me, choking me. I must have passed out. What happened, where is he?"

"He's dead, Karin."

She trembled and buried her head in his shoulder.

"I'm going to call the police now. At least it sounds like the mystery of what happened to the oil at the Port and the cavern at Tor Harbor has been solved. Jacksonville too, most likely."

Daniel reached into his pants for his phone and dialed Stig.

"Daniel, are you calling with good news, did you find Karin?"

"Mixed news, I'm afraid. I *have* found Karin here at the SBF, thank heavens. She's in good shape as far as I can see, just shook up. But Axel is dead. He attacked Karin, and then he tried to kill me. We struggled; you'll see when you get here. It's a God-awful mess, I'm afraid."

"I'll be there straight away, Daniel. Sit tight. I'll have a paramedic crew come to check you and Karin out, too. And please, don't touch the body."

Karin rubbed at her wrists. "What now?"

Daniel said, "We have a little time before all hell breaks loose here. Let's take a quick look around, it might be the only chance we get to find some evidence that could shed more light on what Axel and Gnady have been up to. Just don't go back to the lab, you won't want to see Axel looking the way he does."

The two went to Axel's desk and Daniel sat down behind it. Karin opened a drawer and began thumbing through the folders. Daniel opened the top desk drawer and found a file with some documents in Russian that he could not read, but some of the papers were in Swedish and others were in English. He leafed down some more and came across a typewritten page of the Manifesto, in English. At its top were dated, handwritten notes that read, "Reviewed with Gnady." Daniel leaned back and took a deep breath. He showed it to Karin.

"That was the time we saw them in Stockholm, at my firm's client event! They must have used that weekend to finalize their scheme."

Meanwhile, Karin was reading files from a cabinet that appeared to contain the history of how the genome of the *A. borkumensis* bacteria was genetically altered over several years to produce a new species. The new microbe's efficient, carbon-consuming capabilities were described in detail. The files were a virtual recipe book of what Axel had done to develop the rod-shaped strain.

"You found the Holy Grail there, Karin. We'll show all of this to Stig when he arrives. There's nothing further to do now but wait."

The two walked back to the lab, and Daniel shielded Karin's eyes as they walked past Axel's smoldering corpse. They waited in the vestibule by the front door, comforting each other.

A police boat idled on the other side of the waterfront, ready to take Stig and the paramedics out to Marstrand. Eva and Gunnar pulled up in her cruiser and joined them after being updated by Stig as to what had happened. After speeding across the short waterway, they rushed up to the SBF along with several other officers who had followed behind them in their patrol cars. Daniel and Karin were relieved to see the squad and let them in.

As they entered, Daniel cautioned them about the gruesome corpse on the lab floor. Stig was the first to enter the room and walked over to the body. He glanced from it up to the nearby shelves of oil beakers, whistled and said, "It's a miracle this whole fucking place didn't go up in flames!" His remark was a relief valve for some of the anxious energy felt by the several officers who had congregated the room.

Two paramedics soon were sitting down with Karin, checking her vital signs, and one of them eventually gave Daniel the thumbs up sign. Daniel assured the paramedics he was okay, even after the brawl. He suspected he might get a black eye, nothing more.

"Stig, Eva, there are some offices that way," Daniel said, pointing to the rear office area. "Go to the last one, it must be Axel's office. I found Karin tied up there. On the desk you'll find an edited copy of the environmental Manifesto. There's more than enough evidence to arrest Pankov, I would imagine. There's also a whole filing cabinet on the oil-eating bacteria created here. I'm sure Professor Gisslen will have a field day reviewing all the lab's information. Could you please give him a call and tell him what we found?"

"Of course, Daniel, we'll take things from here" Eva said. "But for now, you two go home and get some rest. You've had some night. I'll get some officers to take you back to Gothenburg, they can drive your cars. We can meet at my office tomorrow and get statements, go over everything. Get some rest, now."

The police boat took Daniel and Karin back to the parking lot. They decided it was more important to be together in one car, so they climbed into the back of one car and let each officer drive one of their cars. They told the drivers to take them to Karin's apartment. When they got there, the officers walked them upstairs and saw them safely inside the door. Then they left with another cruiser that was waiting out front.

The couple embraced when they entered the apartment, relieved and grateful to be there. Miraculously so.

"God, I'm famished," Karin said, "I've not had anything since lunch. You must be too. What a horrible day you've had. I'll make up a plate of cheese and crackers for us, hardly the dinner I planned to cook tonight, but I promise to make it up to you! Do you mind getting a bottle of wine from the fridge? Also, bring out a tray of ice, and I'll fix a compress for your swollen cheek."

Daniel could not believe the strength Karin exhibited. It was only hours earlier that she had nearly been murdered, and here she was, fussing over him, disregarding her own trauma. If anything good could have come of the day, it was that Daniel felt an even more intense and deep affection for this remarkable woman.

In a wistful moment, he marveled at how far they had come in such a short time.

Karin went to look for the Dala horse lighter in her purse to light a fresh candle for their table, and that's when Daniel told her that the lighter was the clue that tipped him off that she had been to Axel's Foundation. It was still there, probably on the countertop. She smiled when he promised to take her back to Drottningholm Palace, where they had their first date, to buy her a new one in the gift store. The first one was sure to wind up in an evidence locker. He noticed it was her first smile that evening, and it was then that he knew everything was going to be alright.

As late in the evening as it was in Gothenburg, Washington was still very much open for business.

As soon as they finished eating, Daniel placed a phone call to the State Department's Office of Legal Advisers. That office, he reasoned, would be able to quickly reach all the proper interests needed to convey what he learned about the SBF and Pankovneft. The office had ties to scientific, economic and military affairs. In a matter of hours, the State Department would inform the G-7 taskforce members of the evening's stunning developments. Daniel's recorded debriefing with one of the Office's Deputy Legal Advisers lasted a little over an hour.

In the meanwhile, Dahlquist had already spoken with Bjornsson. She apologized for the late call, but he assured her he was delighted she called, especially after the disappointing visit to Murmansk. A lucky break, at last. He asked Dahlquist to convey his appreciation to Daniel along with best wishes for a swift recovery from the traumatic confrontation. Bjornsson assured her his next step was to inform his colleagues in the Office of National Security. Not knowing exactly who might be collaborating with Carlsson and Pankov, he instructed Dahlquist to maintain tight security over the SBF's facility. She told him four guards would remain posted there around the clock. In addition, she would assign two roving patrols to the island. He informed her that eventually the investigation would be transferred from the municipality to the Ministry of Justice, but cooperation between the two offices would continue.

It was 1:00 a.m. when Daniel finished his call. Karin had already put away the dishes and wine glasses, and she had showered and changed into a silky robe. Underneath it was a sheer negligee. She flipped off the light switch and looked magnificent in the glow of the candlelight.

"What would have happened to me had you not rescued me?"

He cocked his head, "Well, a rather good chance you would not be about to kiss my aching jaw, if you really want to know!" She dabbed at it with the cold compress she prepared and then set it down on the counter.

Then she untied her robe and let it sink to the floor. She took Daniel by the hand and walked him into the bedroom, pulling him near and nuzzling his swollen cheek with her lips.

"Ooh, that really hurts," he said, rubbing his cheek, feigning agony.

"My hero."

CH. 54

Given the shocking developments of the evening before, Bjornsson knew that Thursday promised to be busy and unscripted, so he arrived at the office early, prepared for whatever the day would bring. He cleared his schedule, knowing there would be meetings with staff from the Prime Minister's office, though they had yet to be scheduled. Fortunately, the discovery of the authors of the Manifesto had not yet leaked to the press. The break in the story was a tightly kept secret for now and appeared to be holding. Forensic verification was usually required ahead of any announcements. And fortunately, none of the residents on Marstrand had noticed anything amiss that fateful night on Marstrand, given the storm which was still actively pummeling the area. Everything looked like business as usual on the island. Even so, Eva and her team were at work inside the lab, pouring over documents at what was designated a crime scene. They would soon be joined by national security personnel who were flying in from Stockholm. Axel's remains were bagged by the paramedics after photographs were snapped of the scene. The large shard of glass was found with a nice set of dried prints on it, undoubtedly matching Carlsson's. Given the obvious cause of death, there would be no need for an autopsy, nor a need to risk making a spectacle of shipping his body off the island. That would only prompt rumors and questions from the locals. For now, his corpse would remain laid out on ice in the SBF's convenient cryo-fridge, tucked in among numerous containers of undetermined lab material.

Bjornsson placed a phone call to the Federation's Stockholm embassy, asking to arrange a call with the Russian securities market auditor's office. He planned to report Sweden's concerns over the SBF's collaboration with Pankovneft, and more specifically, Pankov himself. The implications for the financial markets were potentially momentous. His call was routed from the Embassy to Mikhailov's office.

"This is Sergei Mikhailov, chief auditor of the National Settlement Depository. With whom am I speaking? Please note, we are on a recorded line."

"My name is Thor Bjornsson. I work for Sweden's Office of National Security. I'd like to speak with you about two firms, one Swedish, the other Russian. There is reason to believe they have been coordinating market activity in a potentially illicit way."

"I'm listening."

"The Swedish firm is named the Svenska Biomarina Forskningsinstitutet, or SBF. It has offices near Gothenburg. The name of the Russian firm is GP Pankovneft, it's based in Moscow."

"I am familiar with Pankovneft, it is one of our regulated firms." A free concession.

"Good. According to information we have developed, we believe the SBF and Pankovneft conspired to unlawfully manipulate the price of oil. They may have done so by publishing the environmental Manifesto which you have doubtless read," Bjornsson said.

"I am aware of it, naturally. Please, would you tell me more about the evidence you have to support this theory? Your charges are very grave. The Federation needs reliable substantiation before it can seriously consider claims against one of its companies or citizens."

Bjornsson sneered, *That's rich, coming from a place that constantly fabricates charges out of thin air, or worse.*

"We found a copy of the Manifesto at the SBF, with a notation documenting that it was discussed with Gnady Pankov, the owner of Pankovneft. His firm has been a contributor to the SBF for several years as well, according to our tax authority. So, there is a connection, it's clear as day. Our investigation will focus on their communications, but it could take some time to develop more evidence than that."

"And do you have a motive?" Sergei asked.

"That's undetermined at present. It's clear however that the SBF has long supported environmental initiatives. Although as you know, the Manifesto is very radical, we believe the founder of the SBF would likely subscribe to it, according to colleagues I've spoken with in Gothenburg. I'm not sure of Pankov's motives, but financial considerations doubtless come into play. Do you have any theories that could explain Pankov's relationship to the SBF?" Bjornsson inquired.

Mikhailov decided it was best to remain tight-lipped. He was safe for now. "I am not able to make any comments at this point, Mr. Bjornsson. I will accept your information, and we shall open an investigation. If you have any further developments, please share them with me. I will revert to you with any corroborating evidence we may uncover. Pankovneft will receive an impartial review under Federation procedures. We are a country of laws. And if you have nothing further, thank you for your interesting call."

"You are welcome," Bjornsson said, and then he ended the call. He had intentionally held back the fact that Carlsson was dead, not willing to disclose at this stage that the primary source of information in Sweden was resting in a cryo-freezer well south of zero degrees Celsius.

Mikhailov reflected on the call, trying to figure out its implications. It would only be a matter of time before the news broke about the origins of the Manifesto. In that case, he believed the markets would go haywire. Global oil prices would drop like a stone, with the knowledge that further oil disruptions had been neutralized. The market's wild ride would come to an abrupt end. He wavered between alerting Pankov to his suspicions or not. In the end, he decided to let fate play out. And since he disliked Pankov, he reasoned the man deserved whatever he had coming to him. Considering the pressure that would mount from Sweden's law enforcement if not INTERPOL, his office would soon be forced to initiate Pankov's arrest, so Mikhailov needed to be extra careful. He'd stay as far away from the proceedings as possible, fearing Pankov might implicate him in a plea deal of some type. Being sold out by Pankov was a painful possibility. If he got a call from Pankov, Mikhailov would see what he could do to save his own skin, if it came to that.

By Thursday afternoon, members of the G-7 were insisting on issuing another press release, to provide an update on who was behind the Manifesto and the sabotage of oil in Sweden and Florida. Restoring calm to the markets and quelling the continuing environmentalist demonstrations were deemed to have priority over maintaining the confidentiality of the ongoing criminal investigation. Eventually a consensus was reached, and the G-7 issued a statement naming the SBF as the prime suspect, along with foreign co-conspirators whose identities remained confidential. The global oil market absorbed the news, and the price of oil instantaneously dropped 18% in a brutal session of panicked trading. By the close of the day, oil had dropped 31% in the U.S., and futures for Friday morning turned further negative after hours. Conversely, the regular stock markets finished up in full relief-rally mode. All the recent buyers of oil shares were seriously underwater and would be desperate to cut any further losses. Their frenzied selling made the price of oil see-saw further and further downward. Meanwhile, on the sleepy island of Marstrand, life went on much as before.

On Thursday evening, a summit meeting was convened in an ornate *dacha* in the wooded countryside safely beyond the outskirts of Moscow. The residence that accommodated the meeting was built in the classic style of the imperialist period, featuring timbered walls, lyrical architectural trim and a pair of matching onion domes. Until the Revolution, it had been a very happy home, a summer folly of a long-dead industrialist. The scene of summer feasts and flowing wine. But ever since those troubled times, it was either sadly neglected or a place where evil men conspired.

Today the refurbished dwelling was owned by the powerful Moscow boss of the *Bratva*. He and most of the brotherhood meeting there behind closed doors wore tattoos, some on their chests indicating their high rank, while others had them on their knees suggesting an unwillingness to submit to the authorities.

A glossy-tiled stove in the corner of the room crackled from smoldering birch branches. Bottles of fine vodka and filigreed silver cups sat on the elongated dining table where the men sat. A methodical conversation proceeded about the apparent, sudden loss of their organization's *obshchak*, the capital the mob had invested in GP Pankovneft several years earlier. At its core, the *Bratva* was about one thing, money, and a red line had just been crossed. But as powerful as the mob was, it was not powerful enough to fully control the price of oil, at least not yet. The market was simply too huge. By the following Friday, the gangsters understood that Pankovneft would be wiped out, along with their very substantial investment, and just like any other option trader facing an out-of-the-money trade, there was nothing they could do but accept their losses.

They didn't have to like it, however.

Pankov decided against going to the office on Friday and was working from his town home. He was in full damage control, trying to figure out if he could ditch his firm's now worthless options contracts at any price. He'd take whatever he could get, but there simply were not enough buyers for the volume of contracts he had to sell in markets ranging from Moscow to London to New York. A few pence to the pound were the best he could find. Pride would not allow him to book such a loss, at least not yet. He somberly kept watch of his portfolio's losses on the Bloomberg terminal as the minutes slowly ticked by.

There was blood in the streets, and the trail led to his door. While glumly partaking in a mid-morning respite of tea and red currant *pain au chocolat*, Pankov's guard informed him that the two security agents had arrived and were waiting for him in the parlor. Pankov set aside his teacup. Two fresh envelopes lay on his desk, and he picked them up on the way to meeting his guests.

Finally, some good news today.

"Welcome back, gentlemen. The last few days have gone by quickly. Tell me, did you find your target this morning in the subway?" Pankov asked.

The driver glanced at his associate and then replied, "Not exactly, sir. There were some....... complications."

"I see," Gnady replied, looking disappointed. "I had hopes that your efforts would succeed. What do you intend to do now?"

"We received some intervening instructions, from our *other* boss."

Pankov paused when he heard this information, unsure of its meaning.

The driver and his colleague glanced at each other and then calmly reached in tandem into their jackets and removed matching PSS silent pistols from their shoulder holsters. Their eyes revealed no feeling. Gnady froze, unable to process the situation. It seemed surreal to him, given the assassins' phlegmatic behavior. Why? How? The two professional hitmen pointed their pistols at Gnady's handsome brow and fired off two rounds each in quick succession, blasting a moonroof in the back of Pankov's skull. He never felt a thing, not even the sting of the bullets as they entered his uncreased forehead and sent him into oblivion. A few minutes after the killers had exited the house, the security guard returned to find his boss sprawled out on an antique Persian carpet. The guard, an ex-KGB agent and a cultured admirer of the art nouveau style, sighed when he noticed that one of the room's splendid panels of a languorous summer maiden, painted by Alphonse Mucha, was now lamentably spattered with brains and blood.

CH. 55

Three weeks passed. The investigation of the SBF, managed by Sweden's Office of National Security, was nearly wrapped up. The SBF had no choice but to file for bankruptcy protection, and a temporary receiver was appointed to conserve its assets. The case would drag on for a while, but after the firm's creditors were paid off, any remaining assets including intellectual property rights and trade secrets would be forfeited to the Swedish State which was keen to reorganize its operations. In Moscow, meanwhile, Mikhailov oversaw the investigation of Pankovneft's misfortunes from the shadows, steering its direction far away from him at every turn. In the end, he was relieved to sign off on a final report concluding Pankov had acted alone with Carlsson. Once again, unfettered capitalist impulses were to blame for the fiasco, according to the official script. Pankov's elimination was characterized as a likely execution by one of his revengeful, wiped-out clients. There was no mention of the *Bratva,* no mention of seaman Mostov, and the case was considered tied with a neat bow and closed.

Mikhailov never had a clue that he had been less than twenty-four hours away from meeting his fate on the fetid rails of the Moscow subway system.

Daniel's heroism in saving Karin, and their relentless pursuit of the truth behind the sabotage of oil at the Port of Gothenburg, had earned them not just the admiration and thanks of the nation, but a place in Swedish history. They had faced danger together and came out stronger, their bond solidified by the trust they had built amidst the chaos. The honors they were soon to receive felt like a symbol of that shared journey.

On a sunny, late November morning, the honor guard of the Royal Palace paraded out into the cobblestoned courtyard and assembled in formation. They were there to meet the newest member of the Royal Order of Knights. The festive ceremony was held to also honor Karin, who was set to receive the Order of Vasa, Sweden's highest award for service to the State and society. Precisely at noon, a series of canon shots were fired, the echo of their blasts rolling over the entire harbor area. The streets were lined with applauding admirers as Daniel and Karin arrived on a royal stagecoach. It was a true hero's welcome. Upon stepping down from the carriage, the crowd cheered, admiring Karin in her white, pearl-studded gown. Daniel made a fine appearance in a black and white tux. The couple was escorted to the courtyard by a quartet of grenadier guards. Waiting for them were Eva, Anna, Stig and Thor, who were also dressed in formal attire. The air felt thick with anticipation; the crowd's eyes fixed on them as they walked toward the stately, baroque palace. The entourage followed a robin's egg blue carpet into the palace where they ascended its center staircase to the ballroom. His Majesty, the King of Sweden and Her Majesty, the Queen, welcomed them, and to the applause of the guests including officials representing the G-7, the Monarch bestowed them with their honors. The formal award ceremony was held in the Queen's Guardroom, and their achievements were celebrated with a State lunch in one of the mirror-lined palace halls.

When the ceremony was over, the couple dressed back into casual clothing, quietly took their leave and boarded the night train back to Gothenburg. They were thankful that no one recognized them on board and enjoyed the relaxing trip together. For the first time in a long while, they allowed themselves to breathe, to take in what they had achieved. Karin placed her head on Daniel's shoulder. "I didn't realize how much we've been through until now," she said quietly. "We're different people than we were at the start of all this."

"Better," Daniel said, his voice full of certainty. "Stronger."

Karin and Daniel took the next day off from work. Their lives were upended by the events of the past weeks, and important decisions needed to be made. They chose to enjoy a quiet dinner at Smakling where they could talk things over.

Klaus was at his usual post behind the bar, and he made a deep bow when they entered the restaurant.

"Welcome! It's not every day we have two knights of the realm visiting us," he said with a wink. "Dinner is on the house."

Karin and Daniel exchanged a glance, the tension that had once gripped their lives now gave way to laughter. Klaus joined them in laughter too, stepping proudly as he escorted them over to their regular table.

"So, this is how it's going to be from now on?" Daniel asked.

"Oh no, after tonight, it's back to business as usual. You order, I serve, you eat. But please clarify for me, must I call you 'Sir' and 'Lady' from now on?" Klaus jested.

"We won't stand on ceremony, Klaus, so long as you keep serving us your delicious meatballs. Should you fail, though, remember who you are dealing with. As knights, we are capable of slaying dragons!"

Karin nudged him.

"And also winning hearts," she added.

More laughter followed.

Over an appetizer of Swedish *toast Skagen*, Karin elaborated on a call she had received earlier in the day from the Swedish Ministry of Commerce and Industry. Karin couldn't hide the excitement in her voice as she explained the offer from the Ministry. "It's everything I've ever wanted—a chance to lead, to be at the helm of something revolutionary. But it's daunting, Daniel. The weight of it… the potential is enormous, but so is the risk."

Daniel took her hand, his thumb brushing lightly over her knuckles. "You were born for this, Karin. You know the stakes better than anyone. And you're not doing it alone. I'll be with you every step of the way."

Her heart swelled, the uncertainty that had been gnawing at her fading in the warmth of his encouragement.

The Ministry had offered her the position of Managing Director of what would be a newly constituted SBF, after it exited its bankruptcy procedure. It turned out that Axel had already prepared a business plan for commercially exploiting the carbon-eating bacteria he developed. Experts at the Ministry had reviewed it and found the plan had tremendous commercial potential. It included several product lines that used varying concentrations of the bacteria. An experienced person from the private sector was needed to oversee the company and the licensing of the technology. A proforma income statement they showed her projected a global royalty income stream of billions of kronor over a five-year timeframe. That period matched the term of the employment contract they promised to send her as soon as she gave them the green light. They told her to send them any specific requirements she wanted. It sounded as if they were offering her *carte blanche* and wanted her badly to lead up the new business concern. As an incentive, the job included a huge bonus for when the company would be taken public by the Swedish State at the end of five years of operation. After that, she'd have a shot at remaining with the company if she and the company's new board agreed on the terms. But if all went well, and she wanted to step down, there was a very nice exit package whose terms were such that she would not have to work another day of her life.

"You know, you really are the ideal candidate for this job," Daniel commented. "Who is more familiar with the SBF's finances than you? You also have a great network of people throughout Scandinavia to build your organization and ramp up operations fast. And obviously, the business know-how. The world is waiting for this technology, Karin. Think of the impact you will have, what you can accomplish. I don't see how you can turn this down."

"It's nice of you to say so," Karin said. "And it's true, I have wanted to go from the consulting side to the client side for some time. It's an amazing opportunity for sure; I'm going to think hard about it, and I'm leaning toward accepting it," she said with a smile. Daniel noticed she was glowing with happiness.

Then he shared some career developments of his own. A long-hoped-for promotion was on the table in recognition of his brilliant role in bringing together the varying political and economic positions of the G-7 members. Saving the day at the SBF was another factor. Daniel was told he would soon be nominated to be the next US Ambassador to Sweden, as the position was open and had been for some time. Moreover, he was told he had earned it.

"You're the first person to know, Karin, I've kept it totally confidential since getting a call yesterday from the Chief of Staff's office. They'll do some further background investigations, and then I go through the nomination process, assuming everything checks out."

Karin was stunned. "Oh my, that's so amazing, Daniel! she said excitedly. "You are so qualified, and I am so happy for you!"

"It came as a total surprise. I had hoped to get an Undersecretary position, if I was lucky, but this is truly a dream come true. I feel we did it together, Karin, didn't we?"

"I wouldn't overstate it, Danial, you earned this all on your own, a cap to a terrific career. Hmmm…. "Ambassador Lake", I kind of like the sound of that! I guess this means you'll be sticking around for a while, then, Mr. Ambassador?" she grinned.

"I wouldn't leave for all the meatballs in Sweden!" he said.

She laughed, "I guess we'll be spending a lot of time on the train between Gothenburg to Stockholm."

"That's fine, but what if you were able to negotiate relocating the SBF to Stockholm? You could set up shop there, the Foundation needs to be rebuilt from scratch anyway."

"Wow, that's a great idea! There are tons of resources in Stockholm, and I love the city every bit as much as Gothenburg. We'd be there together," she said with a hopeful look in her eyes.

"That's it, then, a wonderful plan for the two of us. And we are both perfect for our new jobs."

"And our new jobs are perfect for us."

Taking her hand, he said, "And you, my dear, are perfection for me, the one I've been waiting to fall in love with."

Karin beamed in the candlelight, and Daniel ordered a bottle of champagne to celebrate. The two took their time finishing their meal, chatting about the following week's trip to Marrakech and

how life might be at Villa Åkerlund, the US Ambassador's residence in Stockholm. Eventually, it was time to leave, and with
Klaus waiving farewell, the couple strolled away from Smakling,
arm in arm, into a starry Swedish night.

EPILOGUE

It was a soft and breezy summer's day, and the young girl, about age twelve with flowing blond hair, stooped down into the sand to pick up one of the many shells she had seen as she walked along the brightly lit beach.

"Do you know why I picked this one, Papa?" She eagerly held it up to him and watched him as he turned it over carefully, judging it from every angle.

"Is it the shape?"

"No."

"Is it the color?"

"No."

"Is it the size?"

"No."

"Maybe its fine details?"

"No," she laughed.

"Then why did you choose it?"

"I'll tell you when we get inside, when we are together with Mama."

She slipped the shell carefully into her pocket.

The two left the beach and trudged up a sandy trail that finally connected them to a boardwalk. At a service kiosk he bought her a strawberry ice cream cone and for himself, he got a bag of colorful loukoumi, jelly-like delights that made him happy.

"Don't tell Mama we had these treats," he said, reflexively pursing his lips before popping one of them into his mouth.

"I know, Papa, she won't be happy if we spoil our lunch."

They strolled along for some time until it led them to an exclusive development where he pressed the gate code into a keypad. The steel security door swung open, and eventually they reached a newly built, modernist villa, a gleaming white gem overlooking the aqua colored water of Fig Tree Bay. The closest town to them was Paralimni, a traditional settlement on the southeast coast of Cyprus. The house was a bit off the beaten track, where one could live a life in obscurity and simplicity, if not luxury. The father and daughter hosed their feet off before entering their home and put on a pair of *tapochki*, Russian slippers that waited for them by the door.

The girl ran upstairs to join her mother, working in the kitchen.

"You are just in time, come sit," she said as she brought a plate of grilled artichoke and fried octopus out to the table. They were dining *alfresco* on a balustraded patio overlooking the lazy sea that glimmered below. The air was filled with the piquant smell of garlic, bay leaf and thyme.

"How was the beach today?" the girl's mother inquired.

"Wonderful, Mama. I'm so happy here, let's never leave."

"We won't, darling, her mother said. "It' our home now."

The man nodded with his plump arms folded on his chest.

"Now, tell me about that shell you found," her papa said. "I almost forgot."

"One moment, Papa." She got up from the table and walked back into the living room where she carefully lifted a plexiglass box and came back to the table with it. The girl rested the box on the table next to her father, and his eyes lit up, as they never failed to do.

She held the shell next to the plexiglass. "See, my shell is perfect. That's why I chose it! Just like the perfect Russian easter egg you keep in this box."

Viktoria carefully opened the box and held the wondrous Fabergé treasure aloft. It gleamed in the sunlight. She carefully depressed the cap on the bottom and the classic melody, "Dances of the Swans" began playing as she hummed along with her father who had recently taught her the tune.

"No, my little swan. We'll never leave, I promise," Sergei purred. "Not for all the oil in the world."

ACKNOWLEDGEMENTS

This book would not be what it is without the tremendous editorial assistance provided by family and friends including my sister, Miriam Sterling, who took the project on with her customary skill and thoughtfulness. Also, Craig Impink, an editor's editor, and a co-conspirator in travel, art, food, literature, and of course, our love for dogs. Plus, fellow authors Jerry Berman and Motti Sharir provided critical advice while CAPT. James W. Morgan USN (Ret.) was of tremendous assistance with the sea rescue chapters. Finally, Angela Smith graciously dug into the manuscript and caught a bunch of blunders. Heartfelt thanks to one and all.

Sweden will always possess a unique and fond place in my heart. I made over 150 trips there during my 29-year career as an in-house lawyer for the Volvo Group, and I came to appreciate its people, values, aesthetics, and customs like no other.